BLOODSTAINS

By Andrew Puckett
BLOODSTAINS

BLOODSTAINS

ANDREW PUCKETT

A CRIME CLUB BOOK
Doubleday
NEW YORK   LONDON   TORONTO   SYDNEY   AUCKLAND

This is a work of imagination. The Tamar Blood Transfusion Service
does not exist and all the characters are entirely fictitious and bear
no resemblance to any living person.
I should like to thank my mother, Mrs. Pamela Puckett, for typing and
encouragement; Mrs. Trude Dub, for professional advice and encouragement;
Mrs. Joy Smith, for typing.

A Crime Club Book
Published by Doubleday, a division of
Bantam Doubleday Dell Publishing Group, Inc.
666 Fifth Avenue, New York, New York 10103

Doubleday and the portrayal of a man
with a gun are trademarks of
Doubleday, a division of Bantam Doubleday Dell
Publishing Group, Inc.

Library of Congress Cataloging-in-Publication Data

Puckett, Andrew.
Bloodstains / Andrew Puckett.—1st ed.
p.   cm.
"A Crime Club Book."
I. Title.
PR6066.U35B55   1989   88-21929
823'.914—dc19   CIP

ISBN 0-385-24620-X

For my wife, Carol

CHAPTER 1

Ten Red Bottles/Hanging on the Wall—the jingle of the stupid advertisement was going round my head all night—*Nine Red Bottles* . . .

I hadn't realized in time to turn it off, hadn't quite realized until it was too late, and by then the image was so firmly implanted that even though the television was dead, the jingle and the images went on. All night . . .

It must have been an omen. Marcus's call came after I had been brooding for a couple of hours in my office over some indigestible files, the images of those red bottles marching across them like a firing squad.

"Tom, are you busy?" He knew that I wasn't.

"No."

"I've got something interesting here. Can you come up?"

You can taste excitement over a telephone, and his infected me to the extent of taking the stairs two at a time rather than waiting for the lift.

"Come on in, Tom," he called as I knocked, "take a seat." He indicated the chair in front of his desk and leaned back in his own. "I think this is what we've been waiting for."

"Oh?"

He grinned and sat up. "D'you remember all the fuss a year or so back when those three men were jailed for pinching blood from the Transfusion Service?"

I went cold. "No."

"You must do, it was in all the papers."

"No."

"Oh. Well, these three blokes, a doctor, a laboratory manager and an industrial link man, managed to half-inch a hundred and fifty grand's worth of blood from the West Thames Transfusion Centre. I never knew it was worth so much . . ." The words blurred into a faraway scream as my face prickled in the prelude to a schoolboy faint. I can't do it . . .

His voice came back into focus. "Anyway, Sir Edward quietly had a computer check run on all the other transfusion centres in the country to see whether we had any more public servants with entrepreneurial ideas, and one in particular looks rather promising. We want you to go and have a look at it."

My throat had stuck.

"Tom?"

"I'm sorry, Marcus, I can't do it."

His eyebrows twitched. "Why ever not?"

"I—I'm scared of blood!"

He gave a grunt. "Well, it's not my favourite—"

"You don't understand, I'm terrified of it. I faint when I see it."

"You're having me on?"

"No."

He stared at me, genuinely incredulous.

At last: "But you must have seen plenty of it in the police."

"Not really." I searched for the right words. "It's got worse since then. I—I could force myself at first, then I was transferred to the Fraud Squad where it didn't matter."

After another pause, he asked quietly, "Have you seen anyone about this?"

"A shrink, you mean," I said angrily. "Oh yeah, they told me it was a phobia, like people who are scared of snakes or spiders, great help! Mine's even got a name, Haemophobia." I stopped abruptly.

"Is there no treatment?"

"Only to learn to come to terms with it, or learn how to avoid it."

"And you've tried coming to terms with it?"

"Yeah," I lied.

He tapped the desk with the end of his pencil. "Tom, we've got a problem."

"The problem's mine," I snapped.

"No, it's mine too."

"I appreciate your fatherly interest, but—"

"Don't be so bloody rude!" He pointed the pencil at me. "If you turn this job down after the trouble I've had setting it up, then I'm afraid you're out."

"Then I'm out."

He raised his eyes helplessly at the ceiling. "All right, all right. Tell me, I'm not just being nosy, do you always faint when you see it?"

"Sometimes not, if I have warning."

"Doesn't the fact that you're full of the stuff bother you?"

"Not so long as I can't see it."

"In that case, don't you think there's a difference between seeing it leak out of a body and seeing it in a bottle or something?"

I swallowed. "I suppose there might be."

"Well, there you are, then. If it's not so bad through glass or plastic, and the psychiatrist said to come to terms with it, this is your chance."

I shook my head. "Sorry."

A pause.

"Any idea why you have this . . . haemophobia?"

"No," I lied again.

He returned to the attack. "Tom, you must do this job, for both our sakes. Can't you see how important it is?"

I stared silently back at him and he almost shouted in his exasperation.

"Look, you'll be too busy working out who's stealing the blood to be worrying about blood itself."

"No."

"Very well." He looked up at the wall clock. "I'll accept that answer, and your resignation, at three o'clock this afternoon."

Jolly old sport to the last, I sneered inwardly—give the condemned man every chance . . .

Then he did something unexpected. He extracted a bunch of keys from his pocket and unlocked a drawer in the side of his desk. I heard him finger through some files until, with a grunt, he pulled one out and handed it to me.

"Read that in the pub over lunch, and don't let anyone else see it."

I looked down at the slim manilla folder that bore my name.

"If your answer's still the same at three, you'll get no more arguments."

I stood up. "It will be," I said ungraciously.

He shrugged. "Let me know at three," he said, and paid no further attention to me as I walked out.

It was a very slim folder. I took the top off my beer and stood the glass on the copper-topped table before settling back in the corner to read.

Thomas Alfred Jones, I read. Born London 1953. Height, five feet nine, slim build, brown eyes, brown hair, no distinguishing marks. Divorced, no children.

Well, I couldn't argue so far.

Had my parents known what they were doing when they named me Tom Jones? I wondered for the umpteenth time. It must have seemed a good joke in the halcyon days of early marriage, a chip off the old block and all that. Well, they couldn't have been "wronger" and the smiles must have faded quickly enough.

Education: Paddington Primary School followed by Paddington Grammar until age 17, when ran away from home to join the Army just before taking A-levels. (How the hell did they know that?)

Joined Police Force at age 20, promoted to Detective-Sergeant before resigning at age 30. Variety of jobs since, punctuated by unemployment, until present position with DHSS, Hannibal House.

Well, well, my life summed up in a few monochromatic paragraphs, no hint of the colours that lay between.

I flipped over the flimsy sheet to find a letter in familiar blue ink, my old chief, Superintendent Foxwell.

. . . I should say he is just the person you are looking for, his experience with the Fraud Squad, both in the field and with computers, make him ideally suited for the post you have in mind. I must add that I was personally very disappointed when he left the Force and did my best to dissuade him . . .

I quickly turned the page.

Another flimsy, a copy of a report written by Marcus the year before, setting out his reasons for wanting to establish the post.

The DHSS has a budget exceeding £30 billion per annum. A calculated loss of 0.33%, or £100 million per annum, due to fraud and corruption could well be an underestimate. If we could save some of this by a combination of prevention and detection, it would provide the money to pay enough doctors and nurses to enable the Government to answer some of its critics . . .

Clever Marcus, beating the political drum as hard as the humanitarian one.

There were copies of administrative letters and then a last sheet which I read with growing surprise.

It was a transcript of the interview board's discussion and it seemed that Marcus was almost alone in wanting to appoint me.

. . . what you refer to as a chequered career, I see as evidence of a survivor, the sort of character we are looking for . . . excellent reference, police training, experience with computers, with fraud and undercover work, a unique qualification . . . yes, I would be prepared to accept full responsibility if he were appointed . . .

I remembered that interview.

"Why did you leave the police force, Mr. Jones?"

"It was an attempt to salvage my marriage. My wife couldn't stand the unsocial hours."

"But it didn't work?"

"No."

Well, I couldn't really say: My wife then discovered it was me she couldn't stand.

"You seem to have had a variety of jobs since then."

"None of them really suited me."

I couldn't say: It was the drink; it lost me more than just my driving licence.

"But you think that this job would suit you?"

"Oh yes."

And amazingly, I'd got it, because of Marcus. It was all that stood between me and the pit.

And now I knew that Marcus needed me as well. To walk out now would expose him to a chorus of humiliation. We needed each other, and perhaps he was right, perhaps it was my chance to kill the past . . . No! No, I couldn't do it.

A shadow made me look up—it was him, Marcus.

"D'you want a refill?" he said, indicating my empty glass.

I nodded.

When he'd bought the drinks, he sat opposite me and we drank for a moment in silence. Then he said, "Not so many people in here as usual."

"No."

A pause. "Did you finish the file?"

"Yes." As I handed it back to him, I met his eyes. They were pleading with me.

"Well?"

Brown eyes they were, like mine, but there the resemblance ended, for he was one of the baldest men I have ever met. I think he was in his late forties, yet the semi-circle of hair that circled his head like an old-fashioned collar was black, no grey, like the thick moustache that hung from his heavy nose. His skin was London pale, like mine, yet held the clarity of health, and I realized as I looked at him that he was one of the very few people I actually liked.

"Well?" he repeated.

"All right, I'll do it," I heard myself say.

His face lit up from within. "Good," he said softly. Then: "Let's drink up and get back to the office."

For a moment I was filled with the purest elation: If I can do this, I can do anything . . .

Then the chatter of the people in the bar faded until they were like children in a far-off playground.

What have I done?

Marcus touched my shoulder and I followed him out.

I can't do it.

My legs were like wheels.

But you must, you've just told him you will.

The traffic became muted, there was just me and the lonely shrilling of the sparrows—and Marcus. I think he was saying something. And the scratchy wingbeat of a pigeon pushing its way through the plane trees in the bright summer afternoon.

By the time we got back to Hannibal House, I had myself under control. You've done it before, I said silently, you just force yourself, a matter of willpower.

We reached Marcus's office, he waved me to a seat, seized a box file and shuffled through its contents.

"The West Thames incident," he said, opening a file and passing a newspaper cutting to me.

The article was from the *Guardian* of July 1984, and was peppered with headings such as "Artery of Conspiracy" and "Vein Glory." The up-shot was that the three men, the laboratory manager from the Transfusion Centre, a consultant haemotologist from the Heart Hospital and a contact man had stolen something like 100,000 donations and sold them to a Scandinavian drugs firm for an estimated £158,000 profit. The consultant got three years, and the others two each.

"The amazing thing is," Marcus said as I handed it back, "that most of the blood was time-expired, that is, too old to be used as actual blood. They extracted the plasma from it, in the consultant's garage of all places, and sold that."

I fought to keep my voice steady. "If it was out of date, how come there was anything of value in it?"

"Oh, apparently some of the components last indefinitely if you can get them out in time. However, as our three friends found to their cost, you have to be careful. Some of the plasma got infected with bacteria and spoilt, the drugs firm complained, and the whole thing came out."

"Unfortunate for them."

"Very. Well, as you can imagine," he continued, "this was all extremely embarrassing for the blood barons. Donor recruitment's difficult enough as it is, and when they heard that the people who've been setting themselves up as saints are really crooks, they say 'Bugger that for a laugh' and stop donating."

"Yes, I can see that," I muttered, for something to say.

"Well, our masters reacted quickly for once, starting with this."

He handed me a DHSS circular which said that in future all blood donations should be traceable from when they are taken from the donor until they are given to the patient.

"Fair enough," I commented, handing it back.

"Easier said than done, so next, the computerization of the Transfusion Service was speeded up, while Sir surreptitiously ordered a statistical study on all Centres in the country."

"What were the parameters?"

"Basically, he compared blood usage per unit population. You can study detail later. As I mentioned before, one Centre looked suspicious, Tamar in Devon.

"Then, last week, this arrived on Sir's desk." Like a rabbit out of a hat, he produced an opened brown envelope.

The letter inside was headed "Tamar Blood Transfusion Centre."

Dear Sir [it read], We think you should know that there are people here who are stealing blood, same as they did in London. We don't work for the money we get for this to happen; we think you should do something about it. Yours truly, a Wellwisher.

I glanced at the envelope. First-class stamp, postmarked Tamar, Devon.

"What do you think?" said Marcus, as I handed it back.

"Rather determinedly working-class," I said.

"True, but are the contents real, or just spite?"

"I'd say both," I said after a pause. "Somebody's trying to drop someone else in it."

"What makes you think that?"

"The virtuous overtones; I've seen them before. 'We think you should know . . .' and so on."

Marcus nodded slowly. "I agree. So now all we have to decide is when you go."

So this was it.

"What about cover?" I asked.

"That's been taken care of. The Centre was about to have a work study done on it—"

I let out a groan.

"What's the matter?"

"I take it you want me to go as a work study officer?"

"That's right."

"Well, after tax inspectors they're the most hated—"

"Good cover, my boy, they'll be so busy hating you, they'll never suspect why you're really there. Now listen, I've fixed for you to go to the North London Poly and learn something about work study under a Miss Heather—"

"Marcus," I interrupted, "you said that these centres are being computerized."

"Well?"

"Well, wouldn't it be better if I went as a computer officer, to see how they're getting on?"

He shrugged. "You could be right. Unfortunately, they're expecting a work study officer."

"It'd be a pleasant surprise for them."

He grunted. "You'd better sort that out with Miss Heather. Meanwhile, I think you ought to study this lot—" The telephone on his desk rang; he said "Excuse me" and stretched out his hand.

"Sir Edward!" As he uttered the name, he seemed to grow by two inches as though he were sitting to attention. I rose to leave, but he waved me back to my chair.

"No, I haven't heard anything." There was a pause, and his eyes opened almost comically.

"My *God!* Do the police have any . . . ? Disappeared? . . . Well, it sounds open and shut . . . yes, he's here now . . . Yes, Sir Edward."

Like a man in a dream, he replaced the receiver and turned to me.

"The most extraordinary development. One of the lab staff was found dead this morning in the Tamar Centre."

"Accident?"

"No, the traditional blunt instrument, by all appearances."

"Who's disappeared?"

"The night orderly. The cleaners found the place deserted this morning, lights on, but nobody there."

"Do you think it's connected?"

"Got to be, hasn't it?"

I nodded slowly. "Well, it certainly changes things. I can't go now."
"Why not?"
"The police won't tolerate an outsider snooping around the scene of a murder."
"Leave that to me," he said. "They'll have to tolerate it."
I met his eyes for a moment, and not for the first time wondered about the power he wielded; it always seemed to be more than his position warranted.

That got me thinking about the power he had over me, the way he had maneuvered me into taking the job, and something inside woke up and began gnawing again. I settled into a hidden misery and tried to listen to what he had to say.

The bar was already crowded as I eased my way to the front.
"Evenin', Tom, a pint?"
"Please." I drank it and went on thinking about the job. There was no one I could talk to, the few close friends I had lived out of London now—refugees or exiles, depending on your point of view.

Another pint. Would the sight of blood really still have the power to terrify me? Oh yes. Was there anything in what Marcus had said; was this my chance to break loose?

Easy for Marcus to talk, he didn't know the story . . .
"Evenin' Tom, long time no see."
I looked up to see one of the pub regulars. "Oh, hullo, Mike."
"What's yours then, a pint?"
"No, I won't, thanks. Just going."
I turned and left, regretting the refusal of simple friendship, but my thoughts had taken hold of me.

Another pub, another drink, and the story, the one Marcus didn't know. Perhaps I should have told him.

My brother Francis was born when I was four. Memory is a strange thing, so much of it is imagination, so much of it hearsay, but I do remember the euphoria when he arrived, euphoria that I shared.

"This is your little brother, Tommy, touch him, give him a kiss. Would you like to hold him, Tommy?"
I loved him with all my heart.
"You must look after him, Tommy, always. He's your brother; he's special."
I loved him and tried to share my toys with him.
"Don't do that, Tom, be careful, you must be careful with him." The anxiety had crept in now.

I tried to show him my favourite games.

"Don't do that, Tom, don't!" Mum screaming and snatching him away.

I couldn't understand. Why couldn't I play with him like the other kids played with their brothers? And why did he get all the attention?

I began to resent him and looked for opportunities to play roughly with him when Mum and Dad weren't looking.

"Tom!" That frenzied scream again. "Dad, stop him!"

"How many times do we have to tell you, Tom?" Dad, his voice scarred with fear and anger, his hand reaching for his belt.

And then came the day when I hit him, my darling brother; I punched him on the nose when he was trying to take my best toy. He knew that he could get away with it, knew that he was the favourite and that I had to obey his every whim. The look in his eyes as he snatched told me that he knew, knew ultimately I would have to give in.

And so I hit him on the nose with my fist. It bled and he screamed.

It bled and bled and wouldn't stop although I pressed my handkerchief to it, then Mum came and screamed too, and Frank was taken to hospital.

Dad thrashed me, but later said he was sorry. That was when the doctor was with him, coaxing him to explain to me.

That was how the new word was added to my vocabulary.

Haemophilia.

CHAPTER 2

With barely a lurch or squeal, the 125 slid aseptically out of Paddington and gathered speed through the grass-strewn yards and factories that lined the track. There isn't much to look at between London and Reading, so I settled with a paper and tried not to think about the job waiting for me.

After Reading, the cotton belt becomes a bit more interesting, so I let my attention graze on it. Why, I asked myself again, didn't I follow my friends into the green hills and photosynthesize with them; they suggested it often enough . . .

But they'd been happy cabbages anyway; no, my place was in London, I'd hide awhile yet in the shadows.

Without my realizing it, the velvet train lulled me into sleep; I was dimly aware as we stopped at stations and didn't begin to re-emerge until we were skirting the sea and the spearheads of light from the wave-tops pricked me into consciousness. Then a strident loudspeaker was calling Tamar! Tamar! and we had arrived.

I stepped from darkened train to dim station corridors, had my ticket punched by a flinty-eyed collector, then, without warning, stumbled into brilliant sunshine that blazed from car windows and splashed from every street corner like a lighted stage.

I stopped for a moment while my eyes adjusted, then looked at my watch. Not quite midday, good, time to find a taxi, drop my bags at the hotel and visit the local nick before reporting for duty at the Transfusion Centre.

The familiar blue lamp over the arched doorway of the police station grinned wryly back at me, then, true to form, I was kept waiting for about fifteen minutes among the posters of wanted men and missing children before a uniformed constable beckoned and led me to a bare cramped office. Behind a crudely veneered desk sat a small man with wiry hair and a thin, lined face. Not a tired face, though; the eyes were bright and fast-moving like a weasel's.

"Bennett," he said, leaning over and perfunctorily shaking my hand. "Sergeant Bennett."

The weasel analogy wasn't far wrong; he went for my jugular the moment we were alone.

"This whole business stinks." He fixed me with his eyes. "Last week I could've sent you packing, but now someone's been pulling strings, haven't they?"

My sympathies were with him, but I couldn't let him see that yet. "Is that the view of your superintendent, or just your own?"

"We all feel the same way."

"So far as you're concerned, I'm just a member of the public with whom you've been asked to cooperate because our jobs overlap, you don't even—"

"It doesn't overlap; it interferes."

I said mildly, "Whether it interferes or not is up to you."

There was a moment of silence, a sort of armed neutrality while we appraised each other afresh.

I said, "I was in the Met for over ten years myself, so I know how you feel."

"Do you?"

"Yes. The strings have got me tied as well; I had no choice about taking this job."

"Are you saying you don't like it?"

"Not much."

He grunted. "Well, perhaps I was a bit hasty, but imagine how you'd've felt in my place."

"I know." Now that he had calmed down, I could hear the pleasant West of England burr in his voice. "But perhaps we could help each other."

"How?" he demanded bluntly.

"Haven't you considered that the two cases might be connected?"

"Sure we've considered it, but just now we've got to catch the killer; we can look at the whys and wherefores after."

"You'll need a motive; this could be it."

"It'll all come out when we catch him."

We were getting nowhere. I said, "D'you think I could see the reports on what you've found so far?"

He stood up and unlocked a grey filing cabinet and extracted a folder, then, to my relief, read from a brief and succinct report.

"The emergency call was received from the Transfusion Centre at 0826 hours Monday 10th June and the nearest Panda car was on the scene in five minutes. I arrived ten minutes later.

"In the Blood Bank we found the body of Michael Edward Leigh, a senior scientific officer at the Centre. The body was lying outstretched on the floor and had bled considerably from a head wound. A large spanner lay beside it."

I closed my mind to this image.

"The pathologist has told us that he was hit from behind very hard, probably just outside the Blood Bank and then dragged into it. The spanner matched the head wound."

"Time of death?"

"I was just coming to that," he said testily, and after a pause continued: "The temperature of the body had been lowered to 4°C, the temperature of the Blood Bank, and this had the effect of slowing down *rigor mortis*, not increasing it as you might think. The best estimate is some time between 2300 and 0200 hours."

"That's a hell of a leeway!"

"Just so, but it's the best we can do."

"What about the night orderly who's gone missing?"

"Why don't you just let me tell this in my own way?"

"Sorry, my mind was jumping ahead."

He looked down at the file and deliberately turned a page before continuing.

"There are three orderlies working three shifts. I say shifts, but our man, John Hill, was permanently on from midnight to 0800, although the other two swap around.

"Anyway, the bloke on the previous shift says that Hill took over at midnight as usual, and that's the last anyone's seen of him. The place was empty when the next bloke came in at 0800."

"Except for the body."

"Just so. He was having a look-round for Hill and didn't try the Blood Bank until 0810 or thereabouts."

"But you didn't get the call until—what? 0826."

"No. He called the Director of the Centre, Dr. Falkenham, first."

"Why did he do that?"

"Apparently, Dr. Falkenham is held in great respect," said Bennett drily. "As you will find out."

"And you've heard nothing of Hill since?"

"Not a whisper. We've searched his digs, questioned his landlady and everyone who knows him—nothing. He's just vanished."

"No leads at all?"

"His bike's missing, if you can call that a lead. He always used it to go to work."

I thought for a moment.

"Supposing my boss is right, and blood has been pinched from the Centre; Hill would have been in a good position to do the pinching, wouldn't he? And then suppose he was caught by this senior scientific bloke . . . what was his name?"

"Leigh, and we worked that one out as soon as your guv'nor phoned, which is why we told him that we didn't need you down here—"

"So you think Hill is still alive," I said quickly to change the subject.

"Oh, he's alive all right, and we'll catch him in a day or two. It's one thing to lie low for a few days, but then you begin to need food and clothes and so on. We'll find him."

"What would Leigh have been doing in the Centre so late?"

"He was on call."

"I see. So what do you think happened?"

He leaned forward eagerly, a weasel on the scent now. "It all fell into place when your boss phoned. Hill walks out of the Bank with blood he's got no business with and bumps into Leigh. Leigh asks him what he's playing at, and instead of saying, "Ha ha! Silly me! like you and me would have done, he comes out with a load of balls. Leigh says he's going to report it, and walks away; Hill picks up the spanner and belts him. Silly bugger, if he'd kept his nerve, he could've bluffed it out, 'stead of which, he's facing a murder charge. Still, that's the way most murders happen."

I nodded in agreement. "That's one way it could have happened—"

"What d'you mean, one way?"

"Well, Hill could have found Leigh already dead—"

"And then run away? Anyway" —he leaned forward— "why was the murder weapon covered in his fingerprints?"

"You hadn't told me that."

"No. Well, it doesn't have much bearing on your job, does it?"

"Perhaps not." It was time to stop while I was ahead. "Well, I'd better be off to the Centre. I'll be in touch if I find anything useful."

"Fine," he said unenthusiastically, the moment of camaraderie gone now. I thanked him for his help and went to look for a taxi.

My heart was beating in earnest now with a steady thump-thump-thump so that I didn't notice anything about the town as the taxi slid through it. I remember only the white fortress-like block of the hospital, approached by a raw new road that wound up towards it through rows of tied saplings, and grass that was too neat.

The Transfusion Centre lay behind the main block, in the ground floor of a similar but smaller satellite connected by a double-decker corridor of darkened glass, metal and concrete.

I waited among the profusion of plants in the bright reception area, my misery increased by the apparition of Noel Edmonds beaming down, assuring me that it didn't hurt and might save a life. Garish booklets entitled *Eleven good things that come out of blood* grinned at me from every available space, and I'd had enough when at last a secretary came and guided me through furlongs of corridor to the Director's office.

He stood up as I walked in and held a hand out over his desk, but made no attempt to smile.

"Good afternoon, Mr. Jones, please sit down."

He was the first man I remember seeing who was even balder than Marcus; there wasn't a single hair on the shining dome of his head. But looking more closely you could see that this was intentional, the top of his skull with its brown spots of age contrasted with the pale velvet of the sides where he shaved them. His face was smooth and pale grey eyes swept over me from above a predatory nose.

"I'm Dr. Falkenham, Director of this Centre, as I'm sure you already know." His voice was harsh, almost gravelly. "And this is Dr. Chalgrove, who is Deputy Director, and also runs our Plasma Fractionation Laboratory."

The other, whom I hadn't noticed, smiled as he leaned forward to offer his hand, but gave no more feeling of warmth than had Falkenham. It wasn't that he didn't use his eyes; you simply couldn't tell, for the irises were so dark a brown as to be indistinguishable from the pupils behind the tinted lenses of his spectacles. The sallow face and greying hair might have belonged to a man of forty, or of any age for that matter—he was hidden behind his features.

"Dr. Chalgrove is here," continued the Director, "because I wish him to be a party to this discussion and to be involved in your assignment." I started to speak but he overrode me. "I have already given him all the details, so that he can start from the same point as ourselves."

This couldn't have been worse. I took a breath.

"Dr. Falkenham, with respect, I was told that you had been asked to keep the nature of my job a secret—"

"I was asked, yes, and after reflection decided not to comply with the request. Not only would it have been discourteous to Dr. Chalgrove; it would have made working arrangements more difficult."

"It is a matter of courtesy that my Department requests rather than instructs," I said, aping his manner. "It would have helped if you—"

"Young man, you listen to me." He didn't even raise his voice as he reached into his pocket and brought out a packet of cigarettes, placed one between his lips, and lit it with a gold lighter. It wouldn't have occurred to me to interrupt him.

"I have been a Director of Blood Transfusion for more than thirty years, and never have I had such an imposition placed on me." He blew out a long cloud of smoke, and from the edge of my eye I saw an expression of intense disgust pass over Chalgrove's face. "I accepted it under duress, and was astonished when your Department decided to persist with it after the killing of one of my staff. Again, I have been forced to accept, but I will not be dictated to, to the extent of withholding my confidence from my Deputy Director. Is that understood?"

"I understand your reasons, yes. Have you told anyone else?"

"I have not."

"Good. Perhaps we could proceed; the sooner I can get on, the sooner can the imposition be removed." His face remained expressionless. "Now I believe that the real work study officer was going to look at the whole Centre. It would save time if I pretend that my brief is with the computer aspects of work study only and stick to the relevant areas."

"That has already been arranged; you've been assigned to the laboratories and the blood banking and issue departments. Can you tell us how long you expect to be here?"

"No idea, I'm afraid," I said maliciously.

"Well, perhaps you'll keep me informed daily of your progress. And now," he continued briskly, "I think it would be best if Dr. Chalgrove introduced you to the people with whom you'll be working." He leaned back as a sign that the interview was over, and Chalgrove began to get to his feet.

"If you could give me a few more moments, Dr. Falkenham," I said, not moving, "I'd like to ask a couple of questions."

"Very well," he said tonelessly and Chalgrove sat down again.

"What kind of people were Leigh and Hill?"

"That question would be better put to the laboratory manager, to whom Dr. Chalgrove was about to introduce you."

"But I can't ask him those sorts of questions without arousing his suspicion."

Falkenham compressed his lips. "Very well," he said again. He thought for a moment. "Mike Leigh was a good technologist, conscientious and respected by his colleagues. Would you agree with that, Don?" he asked Chalgrove.

"I should say so, although I didn't have much to do with him." Chalgrove's voice had a light, pleasant flavour.

"Was he liked by his colleagues?"

"I believe so, yes."

"I see. How about Hill?"

"Different character altogether. Not very intelligent and with a chip on his shoulder."

"You didn't like him?"

Falkenham drew himself up. "In my position, one has to show impartiality, but I must confess that I didn't. He was a born trouble-maker, which is why I had him put permanently on the night shift."

"To prevent him making trouble."

"Correct." The irony had escaped him.

"How long ago would that have been?"

He drew in a breath. "Oh, about six months."

Chalgrove leaned forward. "Nearer twelve, I think, Robert."

"Really?" Falkenham regarded him frostily. "Well, we can always check later." He stubbed out his cigarette and turned to me. "Do you have any more questions?"

I shook my head. "I can't think of any more now. But we'll be meeting every day so that I can keep you up to date."

"Indeed we will." As our eyes met, the imperiousness was replaced for an instant by a look of utter desolation; he seemed to be on the point of saying something, but before he could, there was a noise from outside like an earthquake and the room trembled.

I jumped up and stared out of the window at the cloud of dust rising from the base of the scaffolding against the main hospital block.

Chalgrove gave a gentle chuckle. "No, it's not falling down. There's building work on the roof, and they're chucking the rubble down that chute. Nobody likes the row, but the builders say it saves time, and time is money."

As he spoke, there was more activity round the platform at the top and the long flexible tube of the chute trembled down its length as more rubble crashed into the skip below.

Falkenham said heavily, "I'll hand you over to Dr. Chalgrove now."

"That's my lab." Chalgrove indicated a door opposite his own office. "We won't go in now. I'll show you some other time if you're interested. I'd better take you along to Trefor Wickham, he's the Lab Manager." He held a door open for me and lowered his voice almost conspiratorially. "But it might not be a bad idea first if I showed you where poor Mike was found. I expect you'd appreciate a glimpse of the scene of the crime."

Without waiting for an answer, he strode up the brightly lit corridor with a rangy, slightly shambling gait, and I had a job to keep up with him. His demeanour had been transformed from the moment we left Falkenham's office. To our left was a series of laboratories, and as we sped past, I saw faces above white coats peering out at us.

Chalgrove pulled open a door to our right and we found ourselves in another, smaller corridor, not so bright and with a massive door covered with a shiny crinkled aluminum.

My heart hammered painfully in my throat as a detached part of me thought: Well, this is it.

"Well, this is it," echoed Chalgrove's voice as he grasped the handle. The heavy door swung open and cold air washed around us. "The famous Blood Bank," he said with a flourish, "although in reality it's nothing more than a large fridge."

On stilts, I followed him in.

I should have realized that nothing in life is ever quite so bad as you think it's going to be, just as it's never quite so good.

Certainly, I was surrounded by blood, or at least by plastic packs that I knew contained it, but the emasculated, almost milky redness belied the knowledge and was somehow an anti-climax.

"This, I suppose, is what our job's all about." Chalgrove indicated the rows of packs with a sweep of his arm. "There must be nearly four thousand donations here."

I swallowed. "H—how long would that last you?"

He peered at me. "If our sources dried up, you mean? About a month, I suppose, longer but for the fact that most of it would be out of date by then."

He reached out and, seizing a pack, thrust it into my hands before I could refuse. I held it without moving.

"Feel it," he said. "It's hard to believe that it's what all this fuss is about, isn't it? It could be anything in there, oil or molasses, but because it's blood, because the ignorant think of it as a life-force, it holds an aura of power. Go on, feel it, squeeze the pack."

I gaped at him. It was as if he knew of my phobia and was playing a tune on it . . .

I clenched my teeth and looked down at the cold object in my hands. It was like a tailored pouch, about six inches by four, with tubing coming from the end and a blue label stuck to the surface which read "O Rhesus Positive" and was followed by a computer bar code. I willed my fingers to move. It was like a cold sluggish cushion.

I handed it back to him, looked him in the eye and said, "I see what you mean, it does have a sort of aura." My voice was almost normal.

He peered at me again. "Are you all right?"

"Fine, thanks, why?"

He shrugged. "Thought you looked a bit pale." He returned the pack to the shelf and pointed down at the floor. "This is where poor Leigh was found. If you look closely you can still see one or two of the chalk marks the police made." He was right, the floor had been cleaned, but chalk still adhered in crevices in the concrete.

"It's bizarre, isn't it?" he continued. "Have the police told you what they think?"

I shook my head. "They share Falkenham's opinion of my presence."

He laughed. "Poor you. You've been handed something of a lemon, haven't you?"

I looked at him. "Something, yes."

"Well, I suppose I'd better take you along to Uncle Trefor." He strode out as though he'd suddenly lost interest in me.

I stopped him in the corridor. "Dr. Chalgrove. What did Mike Leigh look like?"

He gave me a puzzled smile. "What ever d'you want to know that for?"

I shrugged. "Background."

He thought for a moment. "Well, he was average height—a bit taller than you. Dark hair, almost black, moustache, rather rugged face. Is that enough?"

"Thanks."

"Be my guest." He opened the door into the main corridor.

CHAPTER 3

Trefor Wickham was somewhere in his fifties, tubby and short with thinning grey hair over a friendly, earnest face, at the moment reddened by the effort of explaining in an excitable Welsh accent why I wasn't needed at the Centre.

I let him go until he had nearly run out of steam, then slipped in "I don't want to interfere with established work practise, Mr. Wickham—"

"Trefor—we're very informal here."

"OK, Trefor, I just want to see how you're getting on with your new computer system."

"That bloody computer!" His face became red again. "When I think of the promises about all the time we would save. Ha!"

We were sitting in his office, he beside a desk that was more like the top of a huge waste-paper basket.

He let his hands fall. "A job creation scheme, that's all it is."

"That's very interesting. You're not the first person I've heard say that."

He looked at me hopefully. "Is that so? D'you think you could help us get rid of it, then?"

"I'm afraid that wouldn't be up to me." His face fell. "But if you could explain to me how it works, what its faults are, I could include that in my report."

He coughed. "Oh well, I don't know that I'd be the best person for that. No, I think one of the others, Holly Jordan perhaps. Yes, let's go for a cuppa and you can meet the senior staff." He jumped up and pulled off his white coat, hanging it behind the door. I walked with him down the corridor, wondering whether he really knew nothing about the computer, whether he could really be as ignorant as he seemed.

He ushered me into a small square room where four faces left off talking to stare at us.

"No Holly yet?" said Wickham.

"Oh, come off it" drawled an educated voice from somewhere inside a bushy pepper-and-salt beard, the lean body of its owner sprawled in an easy chair. "You know she never comes in until we've been here at least ten minutes."

A big healthy-looking man beside him of about thirty looked up. "Well, *someone's* got to get the blood labelled and banked," he mimicked in a falsetto, effeminately preening his shock of fair hair. There was an uneasy chuckle.

"Lay off, Steve." This came from a stocky, swarthy character who hadn't joined the laughter. "Just because she cares about her job."

"Oh, Sir Galahad," murmured Steve, and the swarthy one turned on him in fury.

"All right, boys, all right," interjected Wickham. "She'll be along in a minute," he said to me.

"Aren't you going to introduce us, then, Trefor?" said the bearded man.

"Oh yes, thank you, Pete. This is Tom Jones, the work study officer from—"

"Tom who?"

"Jones," I said to him, "and I'm not related."

"Not related to whom? The pop-singer or the eighteenth-century cocksman?"

"Neither," I said shortly, taking a dislike to Pete.

"Tom will be with us . . . a week, isn't it, Tom?"

"It might be longer. It depends . . ."

"On what?" demanded Pete.

"On how I get on."

"Well," began Wickham, "I'm sure you'll all cooperate—"

"Naturally," said Pete drily. "After all, we have so little work to do."

"He's only trying to do his job like the rest of us," said the harassed Wickham, and then paused as though expecting further interruption. None came, however. "I'm going to let Holly look after him—"

"She'll love that," Pete interrupted now.

"Well, I expect Tom has already formed an idea of the people he's landed among," said Wickham resignedly, "but I'd better go through the formalities. This is Steve Buck, who makes the reagents we use." The big fair-haired man flashed me a white-toothed grin. "Pete Coleton, who's already shown you the kind of person he is." Pete blew me a kiss. "His job is cross-matching our blood. Adrian Hodges"—he indicated the swarthy man—"is in charge of the storage and issue of blood. And David Brown"—he nodded at a slight figure with auburn hair and a baby face—"tests all our blood for diseases like hepatitis. Now let's have some tea. Do you take sugar?"

I sat with my cup in the silence that followed and glanced covertly at Adrian: so here was the person in charge of storage and issue . . .

"D'you have any ideas yet about how you're going to make us more efficient, Tom?" This was Pete. "I may call you Tom, mayn't I?"

"Of course, Pete. I think it would be premature to say anything until I've thoroughly examined your present system."

"But I thought you work study people had set formulae for everything?"

"Being a professional is not the same as having set formulae."

"Tom has been telling me that we are not the only Centre to be less than happy with computerization," said Wickham.

"Speak for yourself," said Pete. "I'm all for it."

"That's because you don't have to use it," said Steve. "At the moment, it's a pain, wouldn't you agree, Adrian?"

"I'm not sure that I do," said Adrian slowly.

"You moaned enough when it was put in."

"I can see its good points now," persisted Adrian. "At least it'll stop labelling errors."

Steve, who knew that Adrian disagreed for the sake of it, pounced.

"No need for labelling errors," he said smoothly, "if the people concerned did their job properly."

"Come on, Steve," cut in Wickham, "occasional human error is a fact of life."

"Well, it shouldn't be, not when human life is at stake," said Steve virtuously, with a broad wink at Pete.

"You're just getting at Holly again!" flared Adrian, who had intercepted the wink. "Just what have you got against her?"

As he spoke, the door opened and a girl of about twenty-five in a light summer dress, with an attractive square face and bobbed hair, came in.

"Who's got what against whom?" she asked lightly.

"Just the boys needling each other again," said Wickham tiredly.

"Nothing new, then." She poured herself some tea.

"Aren't you going to introduce her?" drawled Pete. "After all, she's got a vested interest, hasn't she?"

"Who's 'she,' the cat's mother?" demanded the girl, turning round. "What vested interest?"

"Oh, Holly, let me introduce Tom Jones," began Wickham. She suppressed a giggle. "Tom's the work study officer from London," he continued, "and since he has a special interest in computers, I thought I'd let you look after him for a few days—"

"Why me?" she demanded. "I've got more than enough to do as it is; why not one of the others who don't have so much to do?"

"That would be fairer," mumbled Adrian.

"Perhaps you'd like to take care of Tom, then," suggested Steve innocently.

"Impossible!" snapped Adrian. "I can't possibly with what I've got on at the moment."

Instructive though this display of camaraderie was, I felt it was becoming counter-productive.

"I'd like to spend time with all of you, if we could manage it," I said, looking round. "There seems to be some misconception about my function here. Perhaps I could explain."

I glanced at Wickham, who nodded with alacrity.

"I thought we'd agreed not to have shop-talk in here," said Pete.

"If you could bear to make an exception, just this once," I said, "I want to assure you that I'm not going to interfere with any of your established practices. I just want to see how you've incorporated the computer into your routine. Nearly all Centres either have a computer system or are thinking about it—"

"That's what I wish we were doing," said Wickham. "Just thinking about it. Sorry."

"Well, my job is to look at all the Centres, to pool the best ideas—"

"I thought this was to be a purely local exercise," said Pete. "I haven't heard of any national study."

"It was. We decided to start here with the national study," I said, making a mental note to tell Marcus, in case clever Pete decided to check. "I'm sure we could arrange to have the local work study done as well if you're worried about it," I added maliciously.

Groans. Then David, speaking for the first time, said, "Whose idea was all this anyway, checking our computer processes?" His strong Devon accent was tinged with petulance.

"Probably tied up with the row about the blood stolen in London," said Steve gloomily.

"That wouldn't concern my Department," I said quickly. I tried to retrieve something by watching each person's reaction as I spoke. Pete looked thoughtful and Steve a little smug. "It's the responsibility of each individual Centre." Adrian stared down at his hands. "Anyway, now that you've been computerized"—David stared at me, mouth slightly open and cheeks flushed—"there's no problem." Wickham's expressionless face looked down, while Holly's stared at me almost defiantly. "That's one of the advantages of a computer." Adrian still studied his knuckles.

"Anyway, as I was saying, I just want to spend a few hours in each Department so that I can build up a picture of the overall system."

Wickham had replaced his cup on the table. "Well, thank you, Tom, I think that's set everyone's mind at rest—"

"I'm still a bit puzzled—" began Pete, but Wickham overrode him.

"I think it would be a good time to show you round the Centre now, Tom. You can start first thing in the morning in Holly's laboratory." He deftly ushered me out into the main corridor before there were any more questions.

As soon as we were outside, he said, "I must apologize for their behaviour, Tom, they're not themselves, they're not usually like that." He walked on a few paces, then stopped and turned to me. "You must know about the tragedy we suffered here last week. Unbelievable." He shook his head. "It's affected them, all of us, deeply. I'm sorry. It's the main reason why I didn't want you here at this time." He took a few more paces, then stopped and turned to me again and I was certain that he was going to ask me about Pete's suspicions, then he changed his mind and walked on.

For the first part of the tour I made polite noises, not really paying much attention; I was trying to file in my memory the reactions of the

people in the tea-room. Then it occurred to me that it might be useful
to know the lay-out of the Centre and I became more attentive.

It was built on a square, and as Wickham took me round the perimeter, I began to realize just how many staff there were. Drivers, nurses,
donor attendants, all in their various uniforms. Porters, cleaners,
storemen and office workers.

I asked Wickham how many there were.

"A hundred and twenty-six," he replied promptly.

Washer-uppers, receptionists, registry clerks, and then back to the
laboratories, and inevitably, the Blood Bank.

He wasn't as eloquent as Chalgrove, but I was in no mood to notice.
It just didn't affect me so much and I was filled with the incredible
possibility of coming to terms . . .

It didn't occur to me until afterwards that all the time we were in
there Wickham stood in just one place. With his feet planted firmly
over the chalk marks on the floor.

At five o'clock it was over and we stood in the main corridor watching as staff streamed from the laboratories, and then as though by a
conjuring trick streamed back past us, ordinary people now, without
their white coats. The empty laboratories already looked forlorn and
sterile, the massive piece of machinery opposite us like a robot waiting
for someone to bring it to life.

Trefor stepped back hastily as two avidly talking girls swept past us,
shoulder-bags swinging.

"Depressing," he murmured as though to himself, then glanced up
apologetically. "It's a bit of an Exodus here at five o'clock. I wish they
wouldn't make their desire to be gone quite so obvious. In my day
. . ." He trailed off. "How are you getting back, Tom? Car, I suppose?"

I shook my head. "I'll find a bus."

His eyebrows lifted. "Oh. Where is it you're staying?"

"The Metropole—in the town centre."

"I know. Now who goes that way . . . ?"

His eyes fell on Holly, who was walking busily towards us with the air
of hoping not to be noticed.

"Holly." She looked up and stopped beside us. "You go through the
town centre on your way home, don't you?"

"Well, no, not really."

"Oh, I thought you did. Only Tom here was wondering if you'd give
him a lift."

I shot him a look of annoyance as Holly said, "Oh well, I suppose I could."

"Please don't bother if it's out of your way. I want to learn the bus routes anyway."

"It's no bother."

"Well, that's all right, then," said Wickham.

"I'd rather catch a bus," I said.

"Don't be silly," she said. "I insist."

"Well, thanks," I said awkwardly.

"Well, if we're going, can we go now, please?"

"Good night," called Wickham benignly, as we walked up the corridor.

As we turned the corner, a figure materialized from the room next to Wickham's. Adrian.

"Holly," he began, then saw me and stopped.

"Yes?"

"I wanted a word with you . . ."

"Well, make it quick. Sorry, but I want to get through town before the traffic builds up."

"Why are you going that way?"

"I'm giving Tom a lift."

"Don't let me stop you, then," he gusted. "I'll have to wait, won't I?"

She hesitated. "I'll speak to you tomorrow," she said gently. "See you then."

As she walked on, I met Adrian's eyes; a narrow hatred glowed for an instant as he turned away.

I followed Holly through the darkened glass doors of the lobby into the still hot sunlight. Her sandals slapped wetly on the tarmac of the road.

She stopped beside the silver Metro and unlocked it, flung her bag in the back and undid the passenger door.

The heat stuck in my throat and she wound down the window. "The Metropole, wasn't it?"

"Yes. I hope it's really not much out of your way."

"A bit. Not that much." She pulled out the choke and started the engine.

"Holly," I said firmly, "I'm sorry about this, but we neither of us had much choice, did we?"

"It doesn't matter." Her tone belied her words. "Put your seat-belt on, please."

"Oh. Yes." I reached behind and snapped it into place.

The car hummed and popped as it fell down the steep road that led away from the hospital. Painted iron lampstands alternated with the young trees held in place by wooden stakes. The car popped again loudly, and she irritably pushed in the choke. We drew up behind a line of traffic waiting at a roundabout, nudging forward as each car found a way out.

Above us, to the left, the white tiles and glass windows of the hospital suddenly caught the sun and blazed with light that seemed to come from within. Sweat pricked my brow and I was about to undo the seat-belt to take my jacket off when she found a gap in the roundabout and joined the traffic in the busy main road. A queue waited at a bus stop.

"Holly, drop me off here."

She hesitated. "Don't be silly. I said I'd take you to the Metropole and I will."

"Holly"—a nice name, I thought irrelevantly—"if it's really such an imposition, I'd much rather catch a bus." I deliberately unhitched the seat-belt.

"Put it back on at once," she snapped pettishly, and then, as though hearing her own voice, flashed me a chagrined smile.

"I'm sorry, I know it's not your fault. Please put your belt back on."

I grinned and did as I was told. We continued in silence, but a more comfortable silence.

I looked around as we approached the city centre. It must have been badly bombed, for nearly all the buildings were sixtyish style, composed of pastel limestone, their hard lines softened now by the growth of the trees planted at the time. Unlike the giant hospital, they seemed to absorb the light and fizzle like sherbet under the sky.

I stole a glance at Holly. Her suntanned squarish face might have been hard, but the feminine mouth was made softer by the dimple between it and her chin; her cheeks glowed a delicate pink and her eyelashes were long and curved—she turned suddenly and caught me.

She smiled impishly, then changed down as the car in front braked at a pedestrian crossing. We came to a halt.

"I wonder what you must think of us," she said, still staring ahead. "You must think we're a pretty unfriendly lot." She shot me a questioning glance.

"I've met worse," I said at last.

Her leg moved as she let in the clutch. "Well, that's something." Her accent puzzled me; was she an American? What was an American doing here? "We're not always like this, you know."

"No."

"I don't know whether anyone's said anything to you, but one of our colleagues was"—she hesitated—"was killed last week. It's left a very bad taste."

"Yes, I was told. I didn't want to come here in the circumstances," I said smoothly, truth and lies in one, "but my masters insisted."

"They should've had more sense," she said hotly. "More sensitivity."

"I agree."

"The worst of it is," she said haltingly, "it's looking at the people you work with, and wondering . . ." She trailed off. I said nothing, hoping for more, but all she said was, "Well, here we are, then," and deftly pulled into the space in front of my hotel.

I undid the belt for the last time and opened the door.

"Thanks very much, Holly. I won't pester you again, I promise."

"Don't be silly," she said, and smiled with her eyes. "See you in the morning."

"Oh yes. Promise broken already."

I smiled back, then slipped out and shut the door. She waved and pulled out into the traffic.

It was after I had eaten and spoken to Marcus from my room that the first of the telephone calls came.

"Hello."

"Mr. Jones?"

"Yes."

"I know about you. I know why you're here."

"Yes?" I waited for him to go on.

"I—I want to talk about it. I—" There was a click as he hung up.

I sat and thought for a while before going down to the bar. How had he known about me? The letter-writer?

The voice had been muffled, probably a handkerchief over the mouthpiece. An accomplice with cold feet? The killer himself? There was no way of knowing, but I had a feeling, a certainty almost, that they would be calling again.

CHAPTER 4

"Oh, hi, come on in." I followed Holly into her laboratory where about half a dozen people were busy at their benches with tubes and racks. No sign of any blood packs.

She leaned back against a bench beneath the window and faced me, folding her arms. "I'm still not really sure what it is you want to know."

"Tell me what you do here, how it fits in with the computer. It's the computer system I really need to understand."

"You don't want much, do you?" She looked down for a moment, thumbnail touching lower lip, face and fine hair silhouetted against the morning sky.

"What we do here," she said, looking up, "is find the blood groups of all the donations, then label and bank them. That's about four hundred a day, a lot, so we get that monster to group them for us." She pointed to a machine the size of a small pool table covered in wires and tubes, the one that had reminded me of a robot.

"It looks like a robot," I said.

She laughed. "You're not that far out. Its trade name is the "Super-Grouper," which is rather silly, since all the girls call him the Groper, and the men, the Groupie."

"What do you call him?"

"I prefer Groper. When he's going, he fusses and frets and tends to grunt. Just like a man—excuse me a moment."

She crossed to where a youth lounged half in and half out of the door as he chatted with two girls. A moment later she was on her way back, the boy gone. The tongue of one of the girls appeared momentarily and disrespectfully.

"What's so funny?" said Holly. I shook my head. "Where was I? Oh yes, Groper here tests all the samples, works out their blood groups on his own private computer, then feeds them into the main system—"

"Holly, before you say any more, I don't think that anything is going to make any sense until I understand the main system."

"I suppose not." She looked thoughtful again. "I'm just wondering who the best person would be to show you—what's so funny now?"

"Nothing. I'm beginning to feel a bit like a parcel, that's all." She looked blank, so I said, "Well, Falkenham passed me to Chalgrove, who passed me to Trefor, who passed—"

"All right, I get the message. I suppose I'd better show you myself; it's probably what Trefor intended anyway. Hold on a minute while I tell the others where I'm going."

She was back after a few moments. "It might be best if I showed you each process where it takes place. Is that all right?"

"Fine." It couldn't be better.

"Okay, let's go to donor registry, where the system starts."

"Lead on, Macduff."

She started for the door, then half-turned back to me. "I wonder why people always say that, when what Macbeth actually said was 'lay on'?"

"I didn't think I knew you well enough yet."

She smiled a tight little smile and walked on.

She was as much of a puzzle as ever, especially her accent, which seemed to be Transatlantic and English at the same time, East Coast perhaps. Maybe her parents had moved over when she was a kid—yes, that would explain it, the aura of clean-cut American health she carried with her, almost to the point of sexlessness. But not quite. Her bare brown ankles twinkled as she walked down the corridor, and the rhythm of her body beneath the white coat betrayed its shape as she moved.

Nice, but not my type.

Most of the computer systems I'd worked with before were for information storage. You keyed in your clearance code, then the name of your villain and out came his form. Or you could add to it if you wanted to. The other system commonly used is for stock control, such as in the big supermarkets.

This system was complex because it was a mixture of both, the records of the donors on an information storage system, and of their donations, separate on a stock control system. That was bad enough, but it was made worse because they were linked together at various points.

I concentrated on the donation system; after all, it was stock that was going missing. In essence, a record was created when a donation was taken, and then had information added to it at various stages (such as Holly's Groper), until the pack had a group label attached (through the computer), and was issued to a hospital (also through the computer). It was the last stage I most wanted to see, and needless to say, the one I didn't get to see.

Holly spent over an hour explaining it all to me, then we went back to the laboratory where she showed me the now operational Groper. I hung back, anxious to quit while I was ahead, although the blood, imprisoned in little glass tubes, didn't have quite so much effect on me.

"You're right about one thing," I said.

"What's that?"

"He does grunt when he's on the job."

We went for a relaxed coffee, relaxed because the others had gone.

"How well do your colleagues understand the system?" I asked.

"Pretty well, I think. We had lectures when it was installed."

"D'you know what language it uses?"

"MUMPS," she replied promptly. "Although what it stands for I can't remember. I can only think of the disease."

"Massachusetts University Medical Programs System," I said, "although I sometimes think you're nearer the mark with 'Disease.' "

She looked at me curiously. "What do you mean?"

"Well, those girls we saw in donor registry, tapping in information all day—haven't you noticed how much they're being conditioned by it? Oh, it's still the servant all right, none of that futuristic stuff—yet. But doesn't it occur to you how dependent you've become already? Is that healthy?"

She gave an uneasy laugh. "I hadn't thought about it like that. It's a funny view for a computer man to have."

Perhaps I'd gone too far. "What I mean is . . ." I paused. What did I mean? "People seem to have absolute faith in what comes out of a computer, because they've been told that computers don't make mistakes. *Computers* don't, not often, but the information they give you is only as good as the person who put it there in the first place. D'you follow?"

"Yes, I think so. It's like when you query your overdraft and you're told that it must be right because the computer says so."

"Exactly." I grinned. "And that's all I want people here to understand."

"I see. But you're still not like any work study or computer man I've ever met before."

"Well, I'm the first of a new model, see. Trying to improve the image."

She laughed. "That's what I mean—you've got a sense of humour."

"How long have you had the system now?" I asked to get her off the subject.

"Oh, about nine months, I think."

I turned this over in my mind, wondering whether it had any bearing on Leigh's killing.

The rest of the morning was not so successful. After talking a while longer, we went to David Brown's laboratory to see how he fed his results into the system. Not that there was much to see, they simply keyed them in on a VDU, but David's refusal even to be visibly polite infuriated Holly.

"Suit yourself" was about the best we got out of him; that was when Holly asked if she could show me his system. With shaking hands and two red spots on her cheeks, she called up his program through the keyboard and showed me how it worked.

"What's the matter with him?" I asked as we left.

"Just don't talk to me about him," she said between her teeth.

A thought occurred to me. "I noticed you put in your own password to get through to his program. Are all the staff's passwords as versatile as that?"

"Senior staff, yes, and a few of the others. Not many."

Could be important. I made a note to find out whose password did what.

She showed me how a blood pack was labelled and banked ready for use (scarcely a tremor), then took me to the Issue Room.

Adrian Hodges didn't even look up. "I'm far too busy this morning," he said.

Holly asked if she could show me.

No, he'd rather she didn't. Perhaps if we came back tomorrow?

"What about this afternoon?" said Holly. No, he was having a half day.

"I'm sorry," she said as we came out. "It's a bad time. People just aren't themselves at the moment."

No, they weren't, but why was she so much more forgiving with Adrian?

It was nearly twelve, so I persuaded her to show me the hospital canteen. She led me up some stairs and through the door into—a space-ship.

Yes—it was a passage, the double-decker tendril of concrete, aluminum and green-tinted glass I had noticed when first approaching the hospital. Walking along it gave the impression that you were suspended somewhere above the Earth, regarding as a Martian might the glittering city below and the sombre bulk of the moors beyond.

"Is that Dartmoor?" I asked.

"Mmm."

"It looks so close."

"It's only about five miles away."

The passage was alive: dangling stethoscopes and white coats stained green; nurses' uniforms rendered pastel by the muted sunlight, all hurrying somewhere in the living hospital.

A canteen is a canteen. We found an empty table and sat down.

"I'll never find room for all this," she said, looking down at her plate.

"It's good for you. Nourishing."

"Fattening."

"That's not something you need worry about; anyway, it's mostly salad."

She tried a mouthful. "If I ate like this every day, I'd blow up like a balloon."

"Don't you have lunch?"

"An apple. Perhaps a banana."

"Then I'm honoured."

A couple of noisy housemen sat at an adjacent table and began discussing patients.

Holly said, "How long do you think you'll be here?"

"A week. Two at the most."

"Then what?"

"I write a report. Make suggestions, although they'll be pretty tentative until I've seen a few more Centres."

She took a sip of water. "Doesn't all the travelling get you down?"

"No, I enjoy it."

"I think I'd get bored in the evenings. Doesn't that bother you?"

"Sometimes. I usually find something to do." An idea had been forming in my mind and I found myself putting it into action before I intended. "I usually find someone to go out with for a drink. Someone like you, for instance." I smiled. "Would you like to come out for a drink with me?"

I half-expected a flippant rejection, but to my surprise she flushed faintly.

"Oh no. You must think I'd been hinting; it wasn't that at all." She half-heartedly took another mouthful.

"I don't think that. I'd like to take you out. Would you like to come? Tonight?"

"I can't, not tonight."

"Tomorrow, then."

She hesitated, put down her knife and fork. "I can't eat any more of this." She looked up. "All right, then, tomorrow."

I was surprised by the pleasure I felt.

She said, "I'd better explain where I live," and it should have been my turn to blush, but I didn't.

"Er, Holly—I'm afraid I don't have a car. No, I'm sorry, tell me where you live and I'll get a taxi."

"Of course! I was wondering why you needed a lift yesterday. No, I'll pick you up. What time?"

"No, it was very rude of me. I'll get a taxi."

"Don't be silly, I insist," she said, and we both laughed loud enough for the housemen to stop and stare at us for a moment.

She leaned forward. "What time?" she said quietly.

"Eight. No, make it eight-thirty. I'll buy the drinks."

She smiled at me, then looked at her watch. "I must be getting back. No, you stay and finish your meal," she said, and something told me she'd rather be alone.

"OK. See you later."

She walked out quickly without looking back.

Not my type, although I might get some useful information out of her. I felt slightly cheap as I thought this.

The computer centre was within walking distance of the hospital and I strolled over, savouring the light breeze and washed-out blue of a summer's afternoon. The purple bulk of Dartmoor beckoned, and I wondered whether I could get Holly to take me there.

The computer staff were the usual cheerful, self-confident breed, and I enjoyed an afternoon of familiar jargon with them.

"Those Transfusion staff are just a bunch of amateurs, children," the manager told me. "It's still a new toy at the moment, but they'll learn."

"Doesn't it give them any product control?"

He compressed his lips as he shook his head. "It prevents them from sticking the wrong label on the wrong bag, but that's about all."

So much for Marcus's theory that the computer would make things more difficult for the villains.

But it was good to be back in the middle of a main-frame computer and feel it stretch its tentacles. They explained the system to me and gave me a password with access to all the Centre's programs. I would put it to use tomorrow.

"Mr. Jones, telephone for Mr. Jones at reception, please." The tinny voice overlayed for a moment the Muzak in the plush bar, plucked me from my reverie.

Marcus, I thought, typical—he's just remembered something else. We'd had a long talk after dinner.

"I'll transfer it to your room if you like, sir," said the eager-to-please clerk.

"No, that's all right, thanks. Hello," I said into the receiver.

"Mr. Jones?" Not Marcus.

"Speaking."

"I won't mess about, Mr. Jones, I know who you are."

"Good for you." The voice from last night, still muffled. "Why should you be interested?"

"I know who you are," it repeated. "I can help you."

"Why should I need any help?" I hedged, wishing I had taken the call in my room. Too late now.

"You'll never get to the bottom of it without my help."

"Are you sure you've got the right person?"

"Don't give me that crap. I sussed you as soon as I saw you. About the assets that have been bleeding away, get me? You interested or not?"

"I might be."

"Yes or no, now, or I hang up." A brittle panic in his voice told me he meant it.

"Yes."

"That's better. Listen, I can give you the lot, now. How much is it worth?"

"I haven't the authority to offer—"

"Bullshit."

"All right, a hundred."

"You're joking, this must be worth a thousand."

"Two hundred, and that's it."

A long pause. "How about immunity from prosecution?"

"Okay." I lied without hesitation.

"I want the money tonight."

"Fine."

"Get it and meet me in half an hour."

"No, you come here."

"No bloody way." Panic again. "You come here, you want to see how it worked, don't you?" So he was calling from the Centre.

"All right, but no money until you've shown me."

"You be here in the Centre half an hour from now. Any funny business an' I'll deny everything."

"Whereabouts in the—" But he had already rung off.

As we left the cash dispenser, I leaned forward to tell the taxi-driver to turn back. But I hesitated; ridiculous or not, I had no real choice.

The interior of the taxi flushed intermittently with yellow light as we sped through the city centre, and I went over again what I knew.

He must have seen me, perhaps even spoken to me at the Centre.

He wanted immunity. I was sure the money was just a front; it would have been too easy to cheat him out of it. So he must be an accomplice, scared by Leigh's killing.

Or could he be just someone who knew, perhaps someone who'd wanted to be part of it and was shopping them out of spite?

Well, I'd soon know. Maybe.

Or—the melodramatic slipped in unwanted—could it be a set-up, for me? I thrust away the image of Leigh's body.

The noisy rumble of the taxi faded, leaving a near silence; the traffic-roar of the city was muted as though it were leagues away. Soft night air rustled the saplings as my shadow merged with theirs in the moonlight. As I drew nearer, a nurse holding a tray passed one of the few lighted windows of the icing-sugar hospital.

I reached the Centre. The night orderly sat slumped in the Issue Room in front of a portable television set. Should I tell him I was here?

Yes, tell him I'd lost my wallet or something. No, he'd only want to come with me.

The glass door gave silently beneath my palm and I slid into the gloom of the lobby. I waited.

No movement, no sound save the ticking of the chart recorders of the Blood Bank, their round faces ghostly beneath the row of green warning lights.

What should I do, wait for him, for something to happen? Perhaps he'd seen me already.

A minute went by. Nothing. I made a decision.

I would walk once around the perimeter, check the tea-room, then wait in the lobby again. If nothing happened after five minutes, go.

I turned left in the corridor with the laboratories, tiptoed past the orderly's door. Low grumble of TV. The light from outside shone through the windows and open doors, stippling the corridor like a zebra crossing.

I slipped through, a shadow among shadows; the equipment assumed bizarre shapes, the Groper more than ever like a robot, a spherical flask became a spaceman's head—

As I reached the far door and pulled it open, another door banged faintly, somewhere ahead of me. Or was it my imagination?

This corridor was almost completely black, just the faintest glow from reception at the end. I became aware of the soft squeaking of my shoes, and other noises; the tick of a hot-water pipe, the whisper of a ventilator, noises that are everywhere in silence—a door knocked again, closer this time.

I hurried down the corridor, reception, a glimpse of the outside, a release from claustrophobia.

Another door, left again, the last leg of the perimeter. Darkness, tiny noises and a close, somehow stale warmth.

Ahead lay the turning that led back to the lobby.

This time it was unmistakable; the door to my left banged and footsteps receded stealthily away from the other side.

I pushed it open and slid through. Silence. It was the wash-up area Trefor had shown me yesterday, next to the central courtyard. Moonlight reflected from the white-tiled walls outside, diffused into the middle of the room in a great patch of light surrounded by looming shadows.

I made out a washing-machine and beside it, stacked crates of bottles glinting like jewels beneath the sea.

I stood absolutely motionless.

Nothing.

Then the faintest metallic tinkle that must be, had to be, another person.

I stepped into the moonlight.

"It's Jones here," I called softly, "come on out. I want to talk. I've got the money."

Nothing.

Another step forward, towards the shining bottles, where I heard the noise.

"It's all right, it's Jones—"

A shadow, then the bottles danced before my eyes as something crashed into the back of my head and I pitched forward.

I groaned, I think I must have stirred, then the blows began thudding systematically into my body. No voice, just the breaths of the shadow above kicking me repeatedly. Then a scratch, a creak, and then a thousand glass bottles shredding into a brilliant sound around me.

CHAPTER 5

Doesn't the fact that you're full of the stuff bother you? said a voice. *Not as long as I can't see it . . .*

I could see it now in the moonlight, staining my hands and cuffs.

A crate fell away from my back as I struggled to my feet. Hadn't the night orderly heard the racket? Broken glass crunched and I stopped, petrified by the thought that a shard of it would penetrate my thin shoes.

No good. Had to wash the blood from my hands, staggered to the sink, regardless of the thought that my attacker might still be there. Pulled out a handkerchief and wrapped it round the worst cut before limping to the Issue Office.

The grizzled orderly nearly fell from his seat. " 'Ere, who are you?"

I told him who I was and that I'd lost my way and had an accident looking for my wallet.

"I should say you did," he said, peering at me. "What happened?"

"Knocked over some bottles. Have you got a first-aid box or anything?"

"I wouldn't know about that, I think we ought to get Doc Chalgrove."

"Is he here?"

"On call. Lives just over the way." He peered at me again. "You don't look too special."

"I don't feel it."

"You better siddown while I phone him."

I let my head sink gratefully onto my arms, and the orderly's voice became a faraway echo.

A hand on my shoulder and a familiar voice. "So you've lost your wallet, your way, and now some of the red stuff." Chalgrove's face swam into focus as I sat up.

"Can't understand why 'e didn't come an' ask me," grumbled the orderly.

"Didn't want to disturb you, I expect, Bill," said Chalgrove. "Now, let's have a look at you, old chap." His words weren't in the least patronizing. "H'mm, that one's a bit deep, should get away without stitching, though. Can you walk? We ought to go to the donor ward."

"Sure—feel a bit dizzy, that's all."

"Not surprising. Come on, I'll help you."

"Need a hand, Dr. Chalgrove?"

"You could unlock the donor ward for me, please, Bill. And then perhaps you could clear up the broken glass you told me about."

Bill grunted.

Ten minutes later, Chalgrove was finishing off a very neat job of dressing my hands.

"Try not to get them wet, that one particularly." He indicated the left, which had the deep cut. "I know it's awkward, but they'll heal better if you don't. Come and ask the nurse here to change them tomorrow. So you lost your wallet," he continued as though it were the same subject. "It must contain some important things for you to come back tonight."

I looked at his impassive face, wondering whether to tell him.

"Considerate of you not to disturb Bill. Foolish, though. So easy to get lost . . ."

"Okay, so you know I didn't come back for my wallet."

"What did you come back for?"

When I told him what had happened, his first reaction was to examine my head.

"Skin not broken—I don't think you'll be concussed." He sat down and regarded me. "Dangerous game you're playing. What do you think, did they know something, or was it a hoax?"

"Some hoax!"

"H'mm. What next? The police, I suppose."

I tried to gather my wits. "No, I don't think so. What happened tonight proves that something is going on. I want to watch people for their reactions . . ." I trailed off, looking at him.

"A glance tells all, eh?" He chuckled. "Well, rather you than me."

"I didn't realize you lived so close, you were here in no time."

"Always have. Useful for being on call, useful for all-night experiments."

"All-night experiments! You must be dedicated."

"I take time off in lieu, I assure you." He smiled. "There's a look of inquiry on your face, which I suppose I'd better satisfy. My interest, my field if you like, is plasma fractionation, the manufacture of substances like Factor VIII, which is a substance haemophiliacs lack." I knew about Factor VIII, of course, but why did Chalgrove always seem to touch on my sensitive areas?

"Up until a year ago I did a lot of night work; now I don't do so much. In answer to your unasked question, no, there was no experiment on the night that Leigh was killed."

"Haven't you ever seen or heard anything odd when you've been here at night?"

"No, but then it's unlikely that I would. My laboratory is self-contained and virtually sound-proof, since some of the equipment is noisy."

"I'd have thought your presence would have been a deterrent, though."

He shrugged. "As I said, I haven't been doing so much recently. Anyway, to be perfectly honest, if I saw Hill or any of the orderlies with a crate of blood, I wouldn't know whether they were up to no good, or not. I'm assuming that poor Hill is one of your chief suspects."

"Why *poor* Hill?"

Chalgrove snorted. "Well, I wouldn't like to be in his shoes, would you?" He stood up. "With all due respect to your detective abilities, Tom, I suggest that you get to bed. Come and see me tomorrow, just to make sure there's no concussion."

He led the way out, switching off lights and locking up. He waited while I telephoned for a taxi, then walked swiftly away on his long shambling legs.

I phoned Marcus out of a sense of duty to tell him what had happened, only to be told I was a bloody fool for walking into so obvious a trap. I thanked him, had a strong whisky from my bottle, and went to bed.

When I woke up, it was after nine and I ached all over. With deep groans, I pushed aside the anaesthetic of sleep and stood up. The aches got worse and a livid bruise stained my thigh.

I was too late for breakfast, of course—the posher the hotel the more punctilious—so I ordered a taxi and went straight to the Centre.

The first stop was the donor ward, where a pleasant nurse clucked as she re-dressed my left hand. A plaster would do for the right, she said. Then I walked round to the laboratories.

It was an eerie sensation, knowing that any of the faces I saw could belong to the one who hit me. Perhaps he was watching me now, knowing but unknown.

Neither Holly nor Trefor were in their rooms, so I went to the tea-room, steeling myself to meet their eyes.

The talking stopped and heads turned as I walked in.

"Hello, Tom," greeted Trefor. "We'd nearly given you up."

"I was delayed." I forced myself to smile and held up my left hand. "Had an accident with some broken glass."

Now! My eyes quickly searched each face as Holly said, "It must have been nasty to need a bandage like that."

Her face showed concern, as did Trefor's. Pete's was expressionless, so was Adrian's, save for a glint of malice. David stared red-faced at his own hands, while Steve stared with a slight frown at mine.

"The handiwork looks familiar," he said.

"I got one of the nurses to dress it properly when I came in."

"Sit down and have a coffee," said Trefor. "You look as though you need it."

"Thanks."

There was silence while Trefor made it for me, then Adrian got up and put his cup on the tray.

"Don't forget you're going to show Tom the Issue programs this morning," Holly said to him.

"Was I?" He paused. "All right, bring him round in about ten minutes and I'll see."

As he stalked out, David got up and followed him.

"Trefor," said Steve as the door closed, "you're going to have to do something about that boy. The results from his lab are getting later and later."

"Oh? I haven't heard anyone else complaining. Surely it would affect Holly more than you."

"It is getting worse, Trefor," she said quietly. "I don't know what's got into him lately."

"We all had to start once," said Trefor. "Give him a chance to find his feet."

"He shouldn't have got the job in the first place," Steve said irritably. "It should have been advertised."

"It was his last chance, I had to promote him. What with the baby coming—"

"We're here to provide blood, not jobs for the boys," interrupted Steve, "especially neurotic ones. What's it going to be like when he starts testing for AIDS?"

"I don't think this is the place to discuss it," said Trefor primly as he stood up. "And I don't think you're being fair." He swept out.

"I don't think he liked that," said Pete from the depths of his beard. "Not in front of Tom, anyway."

"It's true, though, isn't it?"

Pete shrugged and turned to me. "Think you've got us sussed out yet, Tom?"

"I'm getting some ideas, yes."

"Don't make the mistake of placing too much weight on superficial knowledge."

"I'll try not to."

"I suppose you'll be wanting to come and see what I do soon."

"I don't think so. Your work obviously isn't in the mainstream of the Centre, so I don't think I need trouble you."

Steve chuckled. "I think that's his way of saying 'Up yours,' Pete."

Pete grinned unwillingly. "I took him to mean that he knew my work is out of his depth, and accordingly decided to leave it alone." He rose and carefully placed his cup on the tray before facing me again. "Actually, I hope you can find the time. My job is about saving lives. I'd like to demonstrate that point to you." He turned and left.

"And then there were three," murmured Steve. "You must think we're like a Tom and Jerry cartoon, forgive the pun, with Uncle Tref trying to pour the soothing syrup over us."

"At least he tries, Steve, which is more than you do," said Holly.

"I suppose so. He gets up my nose, though. I liked the way you handled Pete, Tom."

"Pete's easily the cleverest of us," began Holly.

"Maybe, but he has been getting at Tom."

"So have we all," she flashed. "You not least."

"Ah, but I did it decently, behind his back. There is a difference, you know."

I said, "I wonder who 'he' is? The cat's father this time, I suppose."

They both looked at me in surprise, then I grinned to show them they could take it as a joke and they both laughed.

A couple of minutes later Holly and I were walking to the Issue Room. She stopped suddenly in the middle of the corridor.

"You know, there is one thing we've forgotten."

"What's that?" Having prepared myself for this meeting, I didn't want to put it off.

"We really must arrange for one of the nurses to bleed you so that we can group—"

"No!" My back touched the wall.

She looked at me oddly. "You really mean that, don't you? What's the matter, are you needle-shy?"

I guessed what that meant and said yes.

"Well, you're not the only one," she said, and walked on.

The Issue Office contained three people, two bored-looking girls and Adrian. He was poring over the calculator on his desk trying to add some figures, the stubby fingers of his other hand thrust through his coarse black hair. He appeared not to notice us.

"Hello," said Holly. He looked up at her, not at me.

"Right, you want to see how blood is issued." His eyes seemed to come to rest between us. "We're about to issue some to Wyleford Hospital, so I'll show you myself."

"Perhaps I could leave you to it," said Holly.

"No!" His negative was almost as strong as mine had been. "No, it won't take long, and anyway, I might be called away . . ."

She didn't like it, but didn't say anything. I was glad; her presence might be an advantage.

"This is an order." Adrian held up a form. "It was taken, as you see, over the phone by Kathy"—he nodded at one of the two girls—"at ten o'clock. The non-urgent box is ticked, so it can go on the ordinary run. And here's what they want, twelve O pos., three O neg. and so on, about average for a small hospital." He sat down at a VDU. "What I do first is check with the computer that we have enough blood in stock. I know damn well we have, but still." His fingers rattled over the keyboard even faster than Holly's, and a list slid into view on the screen. "There, blood availability, and a recommendation of how we should fill the order. Since we've plenty in stock at the moment, it says that we can give them what they want, which is what I said in the first place."

"Is that normally the case?" I asked.

"Usually," he said tonelessly.

He logged off the computer with unnecessary force and stood up. "So now we go and get it." We followed him into the smaller passage where the bank was. He picked up a crate from a stack and pulled a heavy door open. We followed him through the wash of cool air, my heart giving no more than a protesting flutter at the muted signal of the packs.

As Adrian began sorting some of them into his crate, my eyes stole down to where the remnants of the chalk still clung.

Was I with the killer at this moment? I didn't think so, the case against Hill was too strong, but I could well be with his accomplice.

The flapping noise as the packs fell together stopped; I looked up to find them both staring at me, Holly curiously and Adrian with a leaden intensity. I smiled back at them and after a moment Adrian continued.

My eyes were drawn to the black hair on the backs of his hands. Was it he who had telephoned me? It hadn't sounded like him. Or had it?

"This'll do," he said, hefting the crate up with one knee. "Let's get back to the office."

We dutifully followed.

If it was him, then it had been a trap. Adrian wasn't the sort to squeal and then change his mind. But why? To scare me?

I could still feel the bruises as I walked, and my hand throbbed. A knot of anger tightened in my stomach as we arrived back at the Issue Room.

He dumped the crate with a bang beside the VDU.

"Next, I select the Issue Program." The keys rattled and the words "Blood Issue" appeared on the screen.

"I enter the date, the destination of the blood, and now, light-pen in each pack."

He did so, and as the light-pen slid across each bar code, its number flashed on to the screen.

"And that's all there is to it," he announced as he finished. "The computer now knows that this blood has gone to Wyleford Hospital."

"Is that the last that the computer hears of it?"

"Yes, unless it comes back unused."

"So the computer doesn't know its fate, what patient it goes into, or anything?"

"Oh, come off it," he rasped. "That's ridiculous. It would be impossible—"

"That information is recorded at each hospital," Holly said quickly.

"But the records don't come here?"

"No," said Adrian flatly.

"What happens if the blood isn't used at the hospital?"

He drew a breath and swallowed. "It comes back here when it's out of date, it's light-penned back into the computer, and if it's still got plasma, that's harvested and made into other products."

"What happens to the rest?"

"It gets chucked."

"Oh really? I thought every donation was supposed to be used."

Holly jumped in. "So it is," she said hotly. "At least some of every donation is used. There has to be a slight excess to cover emergencies."

"OK, I accept that. How many come back with plasma still on them?"

"What's this got to do with work study?" said Adrian between his teeth.

I smiled at him. "Just trying to get the picture."

Holly said quietly, "At least half our blood has the plasma taken off immediately and frozen, to be sent away to make Factor VIII."

"We get very little plasma back, as it happens." Adrian's voice was back under control. "Not that much blood is returned anyway, the local hospitals are better with their housekeeping now."

"So you only light-pen back into the computer the very little returned blood that still does have any plasma?" He nodded. "So in effect there's no real record of what has actually happened to the blood—"

"And I don't see how it concerns—"

"As I've said," I cut in sharply, "my brief is to see how your work patterns fit in with the computer, so I want to know everything about—"

"Well, now you do, so that finishes your business here, doesn't it?" A fleck of spray from his lips touched my cheek.

"Not quite. What about records, written records of donations before you had the computer?"

"Oh, sure, sure!" He sprang to a cupboard and yanked open the door to reveal a row of black ledgers.

"There!" He pulled one out and flung it down on the desk in front of me. "You can go through every bloody one for all I care."

"Stop this, you two!" shouted Holly. The mouths of the office girls hung open in disbelief. "Tom, we're going back to my lab, now."

I shrugged and followed her as she click-clacked furiously down the corridor. Just outside her door, she turned to me.

"I know Adrian is difficult," she said in a low intense voice, "but you were deliberately provoking him. Why?"

"I was simply trying to get the information—"

"You were being deliberately provocative. Why?"

"He gets on my tits, that's why."

"Well, you get on mine." This was a time when I should have kept a straight face. Unfortunately I didn't. "And if you think I'm seeing you tonight after this," she hissed, "you can think again." She turned and marched into her laboratory.

I stood in the corridor for a moment, naked and foolish. My heart was still beating violently and my head began to ache. Then I remembered Chalgrove's instruction to see him.

He was in his office. He looked up from his desk and grinned when he saw me, prodded my head a few times and asked a few questions.

"Well, I think you can come off the critical list now," he said in the mocking way I was becoming used to. "Any idea yet who did it?"

"Not yet."

"What, no guilty looks, no eyes unable to meet yours?"

"Give it time," I said, grinning back.

Then I went to find Trefor, and arranged with him to show me the plasma laboratory that afternoon.

I felt sorry about the quarrel with Holly. She was right. I had deliberately provoked Adrian. But it was worth it; the Issue system was full of loopholes that he might have been able to cover up otherwise.

The canteen was already crowded. I looked round for somewhere to sit amid the busy chatter and my eyes fell on Steve's blond head. He and Pete were avidly discussing something. Join them? No, I wanted to think—but Steve had seen me and was beckoning.

"So you've decided to try a culinary adventure," he said, as I sat down.

"Culinary misadventure," grunted Pete. "I'd put you down as a pub man," he said to me.

"I am, but the nearest is miles away."

"A quarter of a mile, to be exact. And there's always the bar here."

"Didn't know there was one."

"How's the job coming along?" asked Steve.

"Pretty well, thanks." I gave up fumbling with the cutlery and transferred the fork to my right hand.

"Painful?"

"A bit. Just awkward, really."

I took a mouthful of food and looked up to find Pete regarding me intently. His eyes were grey and bright with an intelligence emphasized by his high forehead.

"Holly was telling me about your—er—equivocal views on computers."

"It's not so much computers, more the attitudes of the people who use them. Computers are potentially man's most useful tool."

"But vulnerable to human error."

"Error and abuse, yes." I met the clear grey eyes. "That's why I'm here."

He smiled faintly. "Interesting. You know, you should consider calling yourself a 'Computer Study Officer'—might gain you a little more sympathy."

"Unfortunately, it's out of my hands."

"Ah." He placed his knife and fork together neatly on his plate and finished his glass of water. "Well, must be off." He glanced at Steve as he stood up, obviously expecting to be accompanied, but Steve, who had also finished, smiled and said, "See you later, then.

"Pete's a good bloke," he continued as soon as he was out of earshot.

"I never doubted it."

"Didn't you?" He looked at me sharply. His eyes were a piercing blue.

"It doesn't really matter. You're the level I must work with."

"How'd you mean?"

"Well, the Director spoke to me from a great height before passing me to the Deputy Director who spoke from a slightly lesser height and passed me to Trefor who was almost right, and—"

"And now you've sunk to the right level." He grinned.

"Something like that."

"What did you make of the Director?"

"One of the Old School?"

"You could say that."

"He must be pushing seventy—how come he's still working?"

"Good question. He did actually retire, from one of the northern Centres. Then to everyone's surprise, he turned up here."

"How long ago was that?"

"Oh, must be nearly four years ago. We couldn't understand why he wanted to go on working, assumed he wanted to eat his cake and have it. You know, live in a nice part of the country without having to give up his authority. They hate not being in charge of something, medical directors."

"So it wasn't a popular decision down here?"

"Not really, no." He hesitated. "It was the *wrong* decision. We already had a superbly qualified younger man on the spot."

"Chalgrove?"

"Precisely. A proven administrator as well as having done brilliant work in the haemophilia field."

I stiffened imperceptibly. "Perhaps he was too young."

Steve shrugged. "He was the right man. Still is."

"Won't he get it when Falkenham retires?"

"Not if Falkenham can help it. Besides, sometimes I think the old vulture's going to be here forever."

I chuckled. "Good description, but he did strike me as being dedicated to his work."

"Perhaps he was, once. Now, he's just dedicated to himself, his ego. He can't bear the idea of not being in charge."

"Those are rather hard words."

Steve thought for a moment. "Perhaps I'm being bitter. I'm dedicated, believe it or not, at least I was. When the last Director retired, I really hoped that the Centre would take off, and Chalgrove was the man who could have done it. We didn't need a caretaker."

"Where does he come from—Chalgrove? He's not local, is he?"

"London, I think. I know he spent some time at St. Mary's, Paddington."

"What did you mean just now when you said that he wouldn't get the job if Falkenham could help it?"

"They can't stand the sight of each other." I waited for him to continue. "It was bad enough being passed over, but Falkenham won't leave him in peace." He leaned forward. "Chalgrove was doing some brilliant original work in Factor VIII production; that's—"

"I know what it is."

"Well, Falkenham more or less ordered him to drop it and work on one of his own pet theories instead."

"Irritating."

"Humiliating. Anyway, I've said more than enough. Let's go back." He rose abruptly and took his tray to one of the waiting racks. I had finished some minutes before, but had remained sitting, hoping to hear more. I decided to risk pumping him.

"It's amazing how the attitudes at the top filter down through the levels," I said as I caught up to him. "I've seen it so many times before. How did Trefor take Falkenham's coming here?"

"Oh, he just accepted it, like he accepts everything."

"Not much else he could do, I suppose."

"Not about the appointment, no, but between them, they're a blob of inertia covering the place, strangling it." We were in the space-tunnel now, and his strong mobile face moved impatiently in the weird green light. "Let me give you an example. A few months ago, the senior position in the Hepatitis Lab became vacant. An area that's gaining importance, especially with AIDS testing coming, it needs someone who knows what they're doing. So what does Trefor do?" He held out his palm. "He hands it on a plate to David, because he feels sorry for him. Poor David, he says, one kid already and another on the way, we must help him. So he gives it to David, and Falkenham let him do it. Don Chalgrove would never have allowed that; he'd have held interviews and picked the best person for the job."

We stopped by the door that led down to the Centre.

"Is AIDS going to be that much of a problem?" I asked.

"You bet, it's the worst thing that's ever happened to the Service. Sure, other diseases are transmitted by transfusion, hepatitis for instance, but none of them are so resistant to treatment or so uniformly fatal as AIDS."

I looked up at him curiously. "It's not that common, though, is it?"

"Not yet, no, but it will be. In Uganda it's called Slim Disease and they're dying like flies. Something like a quarter of them carry the virus, that's men *and* women, so it's not just gays and junkies spreading it among themselves. If that starts happening here, then we're in real trouble. We're due to start testing every donation this autumn, but it needs someone good to be doing it—not David."

"What's wrong with him?"

"You've seen him; he's a tosser. He was no damn good as Mike Leigh's deputy; he's even worse now." He paused reflectively. "The trouble is, he thinks the rest of us owe him a living, thinks we're being unfair for drawing attention to his shortcomings—" He broke off. "But you're not interested in all our tittle-tattle, surely?"

"Yes, I am. I've found before that apparent faults in a computer system are really due to the tension between its operatives."

He nodded slowly, so I risked going a little further.

"Adrian, for instance, is perhaps the main user of the system, and he seems filled with resentment about something."

Steve grinned. "You've noticed, then. He's resentful all right. He couldn't pass his exams, and his only way up was to take the Blood Issue job. He feels inferior because his job's clerical rather than scientific—" He stopped. "Look, I must be getting back."

He told me how to find the library, then clattered down the stairs.

The only sounds were the turning of a page or the scratch of a pencil. People sprawled over the books on pine desks desperately trying to imbibe knowledge; one had fallen asleep, head resting on the open pages, perhaps in the hope that the contents would leach into his brain.

I found a place, sat down and made a plan of the computer system. Sat back and considered it.

The Issue side was full of loopholes.

For instance, there was nothing to stop Adrian telling the computer that he had issued twenty units to XYZ, when he in fact only sent ten. The computer would assume that they had all been used when in fact they had been put aside for Hill to sort out and despatch during the night. Yes! Hill would have been the perfect accomplice, until he turned killer.

Or perhaps Adrian could actually issue the blood to an accomplice in a hospital, who could then send it back. Possibly, but I preferred the first idea, although both illustrated the futility of relying on the computer for information, when it received no feedback from the hospitals served.

Was I prejudiced against Adrian? Yes, but he was still the most likely suspect; no one else had the same opportunity.

What about all the other problems and tensions—were they relevant?

I wrote them down. Why had Trefor promoted the obviously incompetent David? Why did Holly detest him and not Adrian? Why had Chalgrove not moved, if his position was so untenable? And why had Falkenham wanted to remain working long after most people retired? Perhaps none of them was relevant. Perhaps time would show that they were.

CHAPTER 6

Trefor's door was open, so I walked in, casually tapping the glass panel. He looked up. "Tom, I was wondering where you were." Not smiling for once. "Could you close the door, please."

Oho, whence the ominous tone? I thought as he waved me to a chair.

"Where shall I begin?" He stared at the ceiling for a moment, fingertips together. "You were aware when you came here of the—er—

difficult circumstances and the need to—er—handle people gently."
Adrian, it had to be.

"Well, I've received a complaint from Adrian that you harassed him
in his work this morning, deliberately antagonized him."

I started to speak, but he held up an imperious hand.

"Now I know that he can be a little difficult at times, but I think you
should remember that he works here, and you don't. I think you could
have been more tactful."

He stopped and waited for me and I realized that it was he who
needed the tactful handling now.

"I'm sorry about this, Trefor, but as you said, he can be difficult. He
was this morning. I have a job to do here as well, and a key part of it
concerns his work. I intended neither to harass him nor antagonize
him, only to find out about his job."

Not tactful enough. "Well, I must tell you that what he repeated to
me sounded rather like antagonism. Perhaps you have a different defi-
nition of the word in London."

Calm down. "Well, I'm sorry it happened."

"Perhaps you should tell him that."

Too much. "I'll try and keep out of his way in future."

"Well, that's up to you," he said shortly. "I was going to show you
the Plasma Lab, wasn't I? Let's do that now." He stood up abruptly and
made for the door. "The sooner we get it done, the sooner you'll be
finished here." This last was muttered into a non-existent beard, as
though he couldn't quite find the courage to say it aloud.

I would never have believed it was so easy. The two girls worked like
automata, each picking up a bag, placing it into a spring-loaded
squeezer and allowing the straw-yellow liquid at the top to flow over
into the satellite pack. When most of it had been tansferred, the thin
tubing was heat-sealed and cut. And that was the extraction of plasma!
No wonder the villains in West London had been able to steal it so
easily.

"The red cells are heavy, see, and gravity pulls them to the bottom of
the pack," explained Trefor, "either by being left overnight, or being
spun for a few minutes in a centrifuge." His voice had lost its tightness
now that he was talking about something he understood. "So it's easy
just to push the plasma over, see?"

"What happens to it now?"

"The bags are packed into these aluminum boxes and quick-frozen
in liquid nitrogen. Here, let me show you."

He picked up a full container and clamped it into a box-like device by the window. Then he pulled a lever; there was a roaring hiss and a white cloud of gas floated down to the floor. He pulled on a heavy pair of gloves and took the aluminum container out.

"There," he said proudly. "Frozen solid."

"Why?" I asked. "I mean, why freeze it?"

"To preserve the Factor VIII, of course. Goes off very quickly, does Factor VIII. You know what that is?"

"Yes, I do," I said quickly. "But won't it melt?"

He answered with great patience. "We keep it in a freezer so that it won't."

"Must be a big freezer."

"It is."

"Can I see it?"

He hesitated, then said, "I suppose so."

He picked up the aluminum box, and I followed him to a door in the side of the room which led into the corridor of the Blood Bank, but was separated from it by another door. A pair of very thick green suits hung on the wall and I asked what they were.

"Insulation," he replied. "This room is held at −40°C; if you have to stay more than a minute or two, you wear one of those."

He reached out and twisted a knob on the wall and a red bulb beside it glowed. "Lights," said Trefor. He pulled the lever-like handle on the heavy door. There was a snap as a catch was released and a dull kiss as the door parted from its frame and swung slowly open.

The brilliantly lit interior seemed to sparkle, but before I could make out any detail, a mist formed in the doorway like a sheet of frosted glass and the hairs of my ankles prickled in the rush of intensely cold air.

Trefor stepped inside. "We won't stay more than a moment; it's probably colder in here than anywhere else in the world, except perhaps Siberia or the Arctic."

I followed him through the curtain of mist where cold and warm air met. It was crystal clear inside.

We were in a room about eight feet by sixteen, the sides and middle of which were taken up by slatted wooden shelving, leaving space to walk around the perimeter. The brilliance I had glimpsed from outside was from the frost that thickly coated parts of the walls and ceiling, and in one or two places hung like snow on the eaves of a house.

For a moment as I breathed in, a familiar smell tantalized, then quickly faded as the moisture in my nostrils froze hard and stiffened round the hairs. As I moved, the freezing air pulled at my face like a strong after-shave, nipped at the lobes of my ears and nibbled at arms and shoulders through my thin summer jacket.

The shelves were stacked with metal boxes like the one Trefor held, the rack with tubes and crates of glass bottles, half-filled with what looked like Cornish ice-cream. Ice-cream, that was the smell! The smell as you bent over the freezer in the shop to pick one out.

"What's in the bottles?" I asked as he placed his box with the others.

"Eh? Oh, serum. Probably here because it contains a rare antibody."

"What happens to the boxes?"

"We send them off fortnightly to CPPL, Central Plasma Processing Laboratory, in London." His breath solidified like the steam from an old railway locomotive.

"I'll take you round once, and then out," he said. I followed obediently.

He pointed up at a heavy radiator-like object hanging from the shorter wall. "Refrigerator unit. There's another one on the opposite wall. They have to run almost constantly to keep the temperature this low."

I could see the static fan-blades behind the metal grille. "Why aren't they running now?"

"They stop automatically when the door's open."

He walked on. A row of spindly icicles hung from the bottom of the unit and I shivered. The cold bit through my shoes; my fingers ached and my jaw started to tremble.

"Has anyone ever been trapped in here?" I asked.

"Not that I can remember. Anyway, there are two safety devices in case that should happen."

We arrived back at the door. "If this should shut," he said, "this handle opens the catch from outside."

He pulled the door shut, and there was an angry buzz as the refrigerator units came to life. The movement of the air made it much colder.

Trefor pushed the knob on the end of the handle and the door swung open.

"And if that doesn't work, you pull this." He indicated a cord hanging from the ceiling. "It sets off a siren in the main corridor that would wake the dead. I won't show you, because it also has a pretty dramatic effect on the living." He chuckled at his own joke, the first I could remember him making. "Anyway, I think we've had long enough in here."

I nodded vigorously, my whole body was trembling now with a deep aching shiver as the heat was sucked from my flesh.

We stepped out and he slammed the door. "You'll feel like you're in a sauna for a few minutes, but don't worry, it soon wears off."

He was right. As I followed him back to the plasma room, my cheeks burned as though I had just entered a centrally heated building in midwinter.

I asked, "How long would someone last in there, if they were just dressed normally?"

"I don't know." He chuckled, then thought for a moment. "It would depend on the person. Twenty minutes? Certainly no more than half an hour."

Showing me the freezing room seemed to have put him in a better humour, so I asked him how the computer was involved with plasma separation.

He shook his head. "I'm the wrong person to ask, I've only been filling in here since poor Mike . . . Well, I'll do my best."

We went back to where the two girls were working.

"This blood has come back from a morning session, has to be fresh, see. Most of it comes back in the evening and is separated by the night shift.

"Well, when they've taken the plasma off, they put one of these stickers on." He showed me a tiny label with a bar code and the words "Plasma reduced." "Then, when the bag is labelled properly, this tells the computer that the plasma has been taken."

"Why does the computer need to know?"

"Because they're two different products; anyway, we have to keep the records of what's been separated." He held up a sheet of donation numbers. "This is what the girls write out to tell CPPL what we're sending them, and the computer counts them up as well."

"Oh, I see, so you can total by two different systems. D'you compare them to check that they tally?"

"Adrian does that."

"D'you check them yourself?"

"No," he said crossly. "Why should I?"

I changed the subject. "What about the whole blood that goes out, then comes back unused?"

"Oh, Time-expired blood. Er—that's light-penned into the computer, which then tells you to take off the plasma, as if you didn't know already. Very useful material, Time-expired plasma, you can make a lot of things from it."

"D'you see much of it?"

"A fair amount. Not that we'll be seeing it much longer, mind."

"Why's that?"

"Well, all blood will have the plasma taken off soon, won't it." Statement, not question. "Plasma's coming to be the most important part of it."

"Oh?"

"Well, it's obvious, isn't it? We've got nearly six thousand haemophiliacs in this country, most of them needing Factor VIII at some time. CPPL makes over six million pounds' worth every year, but that's still less than half our needs, so we spend millions buying the rest from the States. People don't realize just how much haemophiliacs cost this country," he continued artlessly. "Anyway, our Government have decided in their wisdom that we must become self-sufficient in the near future, thus the need for more plasma. Apart from the cost, our haemophiliacs keep catching diseases like hepatitis from the American stuff, so . . ."

I didn't know whether to feel sick or angry, but he didn't notice as he showed me how the plasma was packed, given batch numbers and stored ready for delivery to CPPL. Then, fatigued by his labours, he suggested the inevitable "cuppa."

I said I needed the gents'. Not true. I wanted to make notes of what he had been telling me before I forgot. He didn't know it, but he'd given me an idea.

The usual mutter of voices faded for a moment as I entered the tea-room. Holly wasn't there.

Then Pete said, "So you've been doing some real work this afternoon, then, Trefor?" This had to be for my benefit.

"I've been showing Tom the Plasma Lab, yes."

"Nice change from bum-polishing," observed Steve.

Trefor turned to me as I sat down with a mug of tea. "They have to pretend they despise my position—"

"No pretence," said Steve.

Trefor ignored him. "The truth is, if I were to win the pools and retire, I'd never live to enjoy it. I'd be killed in the undignified scramble for my seat."

"It's not the position we want," said Pete. "It's the money."

"An extra crust or two for the wife and kiddies," sighed Steve.

Pete looked at him in amazement. "You can afford *crusts?*"

"It's all right for you two," put in Adrian. "At least you could afford to get married."

"I shouldn't let it worry you," said Steve. "There's nobody who'd have you."

"Well, I had to manage with a wife and two kids," piped David's plaintive voice, *"and* before I was promoted."

"I don't know how you survived," said Pete, shaking his head. "I wouldn't have liked to have been in his shoes, would you, Steve?"

"I'd never have lived to tell the tale—"

"Oh, shut up, you don't know what it's like."

"Oh but we do!" Pete again. "You keep telling us."

"Lay off, Pete," said Adrian. He then caught my eye. "And what are you grinning at?" he snarled, "What's so funny, eh?"

I caught Trefor's narrowed eyes on me as Pete said, "Why don't *you* lay off, Adrian?"

"It's all right," I said, getting up. "Trefor, d'you mind if I use the terminal in your office?"

"Be my guest."

The VDU hummed as I switched it on; the screen flickered and glowed, resolved into a message inviting me to "log-on." The keys rattled musically as I fed in my password and settled gratefully into the union between man and machine.

Pressed M for Menu and a long list of options slid up from the bottom of the screen.

Selected "Display Donation Record."

"Donation number?" demanded the screen. I made one up and keyed it in.

"This donation number does not exist," the screen patiently informed me. "Donation number?"

I glanced around the room. The list would be in the Issue Office, and I wasn't going there.

My eye fell on a written list atop the pile of paper on Trefor's desk. I slid off my seat and picked it up. Donation numbers, consecutive, like the Plasma Lab list.

I keyed in the first and the information slid up the screen.

Donor's name . . . date bled . . . date labelled . . . Group . . . Hepatitis . . . other hieroglyphics . . . and yes! As Trefor had said, "Plasma Reduced."

I sat back and thought.

How does the computer know that? Because of the little bar code label Trefor had shown me. Because it had been told by somebody.

I pressed "Return" for the next screen, more information. Issue

Record: Date of issue . . . issued by . . . place of issue . . . date of return.

But there was no point in returning this blood, the cells were of no use, and there was no plasma to harvest. Or so the computer said.

I tried another number. The same.

There was a step in the doorway and I looked round. Holly!

Our eyes met and then hers slid away. "Do you know where Trefor is?"

"Probably still in the tea-room."

"Thanks." She turned away.

"Holly."

She turned back, her face impassive.

"I'm sorry about this morning."

She shrugged. "It wasn't all your fault."

"Some of it was, and I apologize."

She gave the ghost of a smile. "OK. Apology accepted."

"I still want to take you out tonight."

The smile vanished. "I don't know . . ."

"Please, Holly."

"It would be better not."

"Why not?"

Her eyes glided past me to the window. "Oh, all right."

"Are you still going to pick me up?"

She smiled again. "Yes, I suppose so. Eight-thirty, wasn't it?"

"Mm," I nodded.

"See you then." She turned rather abruptly and left.

I grinned vacantly at the screen for a moment—Tom, the big bad wolf.

Sighed and absently tapped in another number. The same.

I felt blind, having to accept information that the computer had been "told" by someone else.

There was another stir in the doorway. Trefor.

He grunted and sat at his desk, shuffled the papers as I turned back to the VDU. The shuffling grew frenzied and he swore under his breath.

My heart sank. "Trefor, is this what you're looking for?"

"What the hell are you doing with that?" He jumped up and snatched the list from my hand. "Have you been going through my desk?" he shouted.

"I have not. I needed a donation number and that was just lying—"

"I'll thank you to leave my desk alone in future," he stormed.

I stared at him in amazement. "Trefor. I'm sorry. I had no idea that those numbers were so important."

"They're not. Not particularly." His tongue darted out and touched his lips. "I just don't want my desk interfered with, that's all."

"Well, I'm sorry—"

"No. No! I'm sorry, I shouldn't have shouted like that—"

"I'd better leave you in peace." I started for the door.

"No! I had no right to fly off the handle like that, it—it was uncalled for, please carry on with what you were doing."

"All right. I'd nearly finished anyway."

Since I was morally obliged to stay for a few minutes, I took down the last number I had been working with from the screen, together with the information and dates.

Then I made my excuses and left, intending to go back to the hotel early and have a talk with Marcus.

"Mr. Jones!" The hoarse gravelly voice reached from the other end of the corridor. Falkenham. He beckoned with his finger, then turned and walked back to his office.

I hesitated for a moment, wondering whether to ignore him and pretend I hadn't understood, then reluctantly followed him. Enough enemies for one day.

"Ah, Mr. Jones," he said as I entered his office, "do please sit down."

I sat. The level of the soft armchair was well below that of his, so that I was forced to look up at his silhouette against the window.

"Mr. Jones," he said for the third time, "I thought we had agreed to meet daily to discuss your progress. You didn't come yesterday."

"I'm sorry, I had a very busy day."

"Really?" I said nothing. "What have you done to your hand?"

I told him the same story.

He made appropriate noises, then said, "Well, have you made any progress?"

"I think so."

"Only think?"

"Suspect, rather."

"Whom do you suspect?"

I hesitated. "I'd rather tell you what I think has been going on."

"Very well, what has been going on?"

"As I said, I have only suspicions." He waited for me to continue. "I'm sure it hinges on the fact that when a computer tells you something, you accept it as gospel. You forget that it was put there by someone else in the first place."

He waved an impatient hand. "That much is obvious. Go on."

"For instance." I tried to continue as though he hadn't spoken. "I realized this morning that you know nothing of the fate of the blood once it's issued. You can key in a donation number, and the computer tells you it was issued on a certain date, and since it hasn't been returned, you assume it's been used. But how do you *know?*"

"Because—" he began and then paused for thought. "Because if you want to, you can trace the fate of any donation at the hospital of issue."

"But that isn't done with all donations, is it?"

He gave a short bark of laughter. "It would be impossible."

"So how do you know?" I leaned forward. "Suppose you have an accomplice at a hospital, he could over-order and put the blood to one side as soon as it arrived."

Falkenham groaned. "Accomplices at hospitals, I don't think so."

"All right then, no accomplice, you simply over-issue. You tell the computer that you've issued twenty units to St. Helen's Hospital when in fact you only send ten. You put the other ten aside somewhere, and when they don't come back—how can they when they never even went —the computer, and the rest of us, assume it's been used."

His thumbnail went up to his mouth. "Is this what you think's been happening?"

"It's a possibility."

"You realize that there are very few people in this Centre in a position to do that?"

I nodded.

"Are you accusing Adrian Hodges?"

I hesitated. "I suspect him."

He pursed his lips. "Adrian may have his unattractive side, but I can't believe him a thief. Have you any evidence?"

"Only circumstantial so far. I need more time."

"Is that the only way that blood products could be stolen from this Centre?"

"I can think of at least two others." He waited, so I continued. "If returned whole blood isn't light-penned back into the computer, it's assumed used. I'm told that the plasma from it is valuable."

"But that's what happened in London."

"No reason why it shouldn't happen here."

"And the other way?"

"This only occurred to me this afternoon." I closed my eyes for a moment and concentrated. "At this Centre, increasingly large amounts of fresh plasma are being squeezed off and sent to CPPL."

Suddenly, I had his whole attention. "Whoever does it notes each donation number on a sheet which is sent with the plasma to CPPL, then they stick a bar code label on to the pack to tell the computer."

"Well?"

"Well, after the night shift has finished, what's to stop someone squeezing off another twenty, thirty, fifty packs and keeping the plasma?"

He waved a dismissive hand. "Because the figures wouldn't tally, that's why."

"Why not? You don't add those figures to CPPL's list; you just stick on the bar-coded Plasma Reduced label for the computer."

"And as I said, the figures wouldn't tally."

"Are you telling me that the Plasma Reduced figures are totalled from the computer and compared with returns from CPPL?"

"Yes, that's exactly what I'm telling you."

I shrugged. "Just an idea." I didn't believe he knew.

He said, "Do you have any more ideas?"

"Not at the moment, no."

He stared out of the window for a moment, drumming his desk with his fingers, then back to me.

"I must tell you, Mr. Jones, that I'm not very impressed with your progress."

Strong stuff. "That's your prerogative."

"Indeed it is. I believe you intended to finish your work by the end of this week."

"I had hoped to."

"I'm going to suggest that if you've made no further progress by then, we drop the investigation."

"Why don't you wait till the end of the week and decide?"

"What I was trying to say politely, Mr. Jones, is that the investigation will cease at the end of the week, come what may."

"You'll have to discuss that with my Department," I said.

I telephoned Marcus from the hotel and told him what had happened and asked whether he could get CPPL's figures for the amount of plasma sent from Tamar.

He grunted and said, "I'll see what I can do. Ah!" he added deafeningly so that I jerked the earpiece away. "That reminds me; you were asking about black markets for whole blood. Well, it's not such a good proposition as plasma in this country, because the red bit tends to go off, but there most certainly is a market for it worldwide. I got on to the

World Transfusion League today, and they told me that there's an Import-Export firm in Switzerland who actually solicit the stuff, provided it's reasonably fresh—"

"Solicit from whom?"

"Anyone who'll sell. Apparently, they can easily re-sell it to their 'foreign customers.' Red Gold, it's called in the Trade. Any help?"

"It could be. Supposing someone here got in touch with them, and transport could be arranged; it would save messing about separating it, wouldn't it? I'll look into it."

"Well, don't go getting beaten up again. What are you doing tonight?"

"Gotta date."

"Really? What's she like?"

I told him and he said, "Well, don't do anything I wouldn't."

I said, "You're always so original, Marcus," and hung up.

CHAPTER 7

Indicator flashing, the silver Metro detached itself from the stream of traffic and swooped into the space in front of the lobby. The uniformed attendant just beat me to it.

"You can't park 'ere, miss."

"It's all right," I soothed. "We're just going."

"Hi," she called brightly as I eased in beside her. "Been waiting long?"

" 'Bout ten minutes."

"Where shall we go?"

"I'll leave that to you."

"OK," she said, sounding for a moment very American, and with a glance behind, took off into the traffic.

She concentrated on her driving without saying much, so I concentrated on her. She drove confidently without haste or fuss. She was wearing the sort of light summery dress that makes even the palest skin look tanned—not that she needed it: her arms and legs shone a nutty brown with health. Still, not really my type.

The suburbs straggled for about fifteen minutes and then we were in the country, really in it, as though the town didn't exist. She turned off into a car park.

The pub was all beams and horse-brasses, but pleasant for all that.

"Let's take them outside," she said when I bought the drinks.

The air was light and scented and swallows shrilled overhead as they hawked for insects. We sat in a small walled garden at the back, at a white-painted metal table made golden by the last of the sun. The light magnified the hills that hung over us, making them seem more like mountains.

"So that's Dartmoor," I said.

"Mmmm." She nodded.

"I've always wanted to explore it," I said, "ever since I saw it when I was seventeen."

"Well, now's your chance. Why don't you?"

"No car."

"Well, I—" She changed her mind. "When were you here before?"

No harm in telling her. "Army exercises."

"You were in the Army?"

"You needn't sound so surprised. Do I look that soft?"

"You don't look soft at all," she said slowly, "rather nuggetty and hard. And sometimes all tensed up, like a spring." Pause. "What made you join the Army?"

"To get away from home."

"Was it that bad?"

"Yes, it was," I said shortly, then: "Not an interesting subject. What about you? I'd have put you down as the University type."

"The dream of all bright young things! I could have; I just didn't want to."

"No regrets?"

"None. I like my job; I get a lot out of it."

"It shows." I smiled. "But don't you think you could do better in a bigger Centre?"

"Possibly." She took a mouthful of her drink. "But I like it here."

"You live at home, don't you?"

"Mmm. I get on very well with my parents."

"And I suppose you've got friends here," I said quickly, shying away from families.

"Some."

"How about the people at the Centre—d'you get on with them?"
Time to get to work again.

"Pretty well, yes."

"Do I detect a hint of reservation?"

"You might."

"I'd have thought you were ambitious; that's why I asked if you thought of moving." My turn to smile. "D'you think you'd have a chance of Trefor's job if he did retire?"

Her eyes gleamed for a moment, then faded. "Chance'd be a fine thing; they'd never appoint a woman."

"They appointed Trefor."

"Ooh, you bitch!" She laughed. "Trefor's not that bad, he does try."

"What about Falkenham?"

"He's a poppet, all bark and no bite."

"Doesn't he ever bite?"

"Only when people deserve it."

"Ouch."

She smiled, her face glowing in the sunset. "I'll say this; I think he's got a soft spot for women. I get on with him."

"But he won't be around by the time Trefor retires, will he?"

Her smile vanished. "You've got a dirty mind, Tom Jones."

"Sorry, not meant that way." I drank some beer. "But he's already well over retiring age, isn't he? I wonder what made him want to go on working."

"You've been listening to Steve, haven't you?" Her voice held an edge.

I shrugged. "He just mentioned that he thought it was odd for a man in his position to go on working."

"Perhaps he loves his work; what's odd about that?" She leaned forward. "I'll tell you this: he knows more about blood transfusion than anyone else at the Centre."

"Even Chalgrove?"

"That's Steve again, isn't it? Yes, even Dr. Chalgrove. He's a brilliant man, but not mature enough to be Director."

"How do you mean, not mature?"

"Well, it's hardly mature to hide yourself away and sulk just because you don't get a job, is it?"

"Perhaps not."

"And I suppose he passed on the rumour that the Director's short of money and has to go on working?"

"No, he didn't tell me that," I said quietly.

"Well, if it were true, I'd feel sorry for him. And now I think it's time we changed the subject." She stood up. "I'm going to buy you a drink, Tom Jones, and while I'm gone, you can think of something else to talk about."

The sun had gone, a blackbird stuttered its alarm somewhere in the shadows, and the black moor hovered. I was the only person in the garden.

"A pint of beer, Tom Jones." She set it beside me.

"Why do you call me that?"

"It's your name, isn't it?" She sat down. "It suits you."

"Tell me something," I said.

"No more shop."

"All right." I took a pull of beer. "Are you American?"

Silvery laughter broke the shadows for a moment. "Why do you ask?"

"You sometimes sound like one. Not always."

She swallowed half her drink and leaned forward. "Steve once said the same thing, just after he came. Didn't you do history? Don't you remember a ship called the *Mayflower* that sailed not a million miles from here?"

"I see what you mean," I said slowly. "So your accent's the prototype."

"By the same token, hadn't it ever occurred to you that you could be mistaken for an Australian?"

"Certainly not."

"Snob," she said, laughing. "The first Australians were convicts transported from London. Think about it."

"Do I sound that bad?"

"What's so bad about it?" She took another drink. "No, you don't, but you're so obviously a Londoner, looks, voice, manner, everything."

"Am I?"

"Yes, except for your name. Were your ancestors Welsh?"

"I don't know."

"I'll tell you something else." She finished her drink and leaned nearer. "You must be the first man I've met who doesn't want to talk about himself."

"I'm flattered."

"So you should be. D'you know what they used to call me at the Centre?" Her face glowed solemnly. "I'll tell you, Auntie Holly."

"I prefer just Holly. It's a nice name."

"People like to confide in me, tell me their guilty secrets." Her eyes twisted away to the nearly dead sunset. "Then they resent me for knowing. They don't realize that I don't want their secrets. Not usually, anyway. Let's go in—" she broke off abruptly. "I'm cold."

She moved like a wraith in the semi-darkness, the faintest rustlings telling of her body's warmth.

I bought more drinks; we found a table in a corner and for a while talked of more neutral things. She told me about her parents who owned a small-holding the other side of Tamar, about their small struggles and triumphs, and I wondered how she would get on with my photosynthetic friends. Not very well probably, she was too much the real thing.

"Another drink?" I said.

"Better not. I'm driving."

"An orange juice, then?"

"All right."

Back to work, I thought as I bought them.

"Holly, I am sorry about today; it must have been embarrassing for you. I am puzzled, though: why does Adrian dislike me so much?"

"Why do you dislike him? You did make a bit of a fool of yourself."

"I know, but it takes two."

"Yes." She hesitated. "He's jealous."

"What of?"

"Me. All men." Another pause while she looked down at her drink. "If you haven't already guessed, we had a brief fling."

"Perhaps that's why."

She looked up. "Why what?"

"I dislike him."

She smiled a tiny smile.

"Tom Jones," she said after a pause, looking for something to say, "d'you realize that you've still managed to say almost nothing about yourself?" Her eyes touched mine, slid away, returned. "D'you like your job? How long have you been doing it?"

"Yes. And about six months. In that order."

"What did you do before that?"

Damn! I'd have liked to tell her. "Worked with computers. Always have, for different firms."

"And before that, the Army?"

"Something like that."

She regarded me with open curiosity, no longer needing something to say.

"You've been very unhappy in your life, haven't you? Are you married?"

I coughed to clear my throat. "No. I was, but it didn't work."

She nodded slowly, her eyes fastened on me. I could understand people confiding in her—the mixture of innocence and sexuality drew like a poultice.

"Children?"

"No. Just as well. Not fair on them."

"Is that what happened to you?"

"Not quite." I was going to tell her. Perhaps I had always been going to tell her. "I have a problem—Auntie Holly."

She shut like a clam. "Please don't call me that."

"Sorry. I'll be quiet."

"No, Tom!" She squeezed my arm. A tingling remained after her hand withdrew.

It was so simple. "It's so simple," I said, and stopped.

She said nothing.

"The truth is—I'm scared stiff of blood."

She nodded again. "Haemophobia—so that's why you jumped out of your skin today. Why did you take this job?"

"Had to. It was that, or out. Boss said it would do me good."

"How very insensitive."

"Not really. I'm beginning to wonder if he was right. Got to come to terms with it."

"Perhaps. D'you know why? Why you're scared, that is. All phobias have a cause, you know."

Wise girl. "Yes. I know why."

Another hurdle.

"My brother's a haemophiliac."

She nodded slowly. Something inside me began to relax.

She said, "You know who you ought to speak to?" I watched her warily. "Dr. Chalgrove."

"I thought you didn't like him."

"Perhaps I don't, but he understands haemophilia better than anyone else I know. He gave a lecture once," she continued reflectively. "He used to work in a haemophilia unit, you know. He actually said that one of the greatest problems was handling the siblings of haemophiliac children. Talk to him, Tom."

I said, "I'll think about it."

She didn't press. "I'll tell you something else. You must have fantastic self-control. I'd never have guessed."

Suddenly I wanted the evening to end, and was glad when the barman rang the bell.

I looked down to drink my untouched beer, then saw that the glass was empty.

We didn't say much on the way back; I just gazed at the patterns made by the pool of the headlamps, not knowing whether I was glad or sorry.

Outside the hotel entrance, I found myself saying, "Holly, I'd like to see you again. Not to off-load my problems, just to go out with you."

"I'd like that," she said, "but you're leaving at the end of the week, aren't you?"

"There's tomorrow or Friday?"

"Tomorrow I can't. Friday's the hospital summer disco; you can be my escort if you like. It's that or nothing, I'm afraid, because I'm on call. I can use the bleep up there."

"Madam," I said solemnly, "you'd do me great honour allowing me to escort you."

"Thank you, kind sir." She tried to drop a curtsey, difficult while sitting in a car.

As we laughed, I leaned over to kiss her. I felt her respond just as I drew away.

"Thanks, Holly," I said, searching for the door handle, "for everything." I wasn't being fair to her.

"That's all right," I heard her say as I shut the door.

I watched the tail-lamps merge with the traffic.

CHAPTER 8

"That's blood." Pete placed a pack in front of me and I didn't flinch, not even inside.

"It's about sixty per cent liquid, mostly water, and forty per cent solid, mostly cells. Ninety-nine per cent of the cells are red cells, which give it its colour. They also carry oxygen around the body. The other one per cent are white cells, which go round gobbling up bacteria and making antibodies against them. Clear so far?"

"Fine." I'd been in his laboratory perhaps fifteen minutes, waiting while he showed his assistant how to put up some tests. He was different here, not so many wisecracks.

"Now, when an ambulance brings in someone from a road traffic accident who's bleeding to death, what we really mean is that he's losing oxygen-carrying capacity in the form of red cells—are you all right?"

"I'm a bit queasy about blood, that's all."

"Why didn't you say? I could have put it differently."

It was as easy as that.

"Do you want me to go on?" he asked.

"Yes."

He thought for a moment. "The main purpose of transfusion is to transfer this oxygen-carrying capacity. Think of it like that, the transfer of a function. OK?"

I nodded.

"So, I hear you asking, why all this?" He waved a hand round the laboratory. "Why me? Why not just transfer this function from anybody to anybody? Well, the answer is . . . antibodies.

"The original workers, back at the turn of the century, couldn't understand why only half the transfusion cases they tried, lived—the Jehovah's Witnesses would have loved it, Judgment of the Lord and all that. Anyway, enter the father of blood transfusion, one Karl Landsteiner, who found the answer."

"Which was antibodies?"

"Right. Now, I expect you had measles as a child?"

"I can still remember it."

"So can I; it's a rotten illness. But the point is, you won't have it again. You know why?"

"Antibodies?"

"Very good. Because your white cells made antibodies to it, your body is now the proverbial stony ground so far as the measles virus is concerned. In fact, you make antibodies to any foreign protein that gets into your bloodstream, which is terrific, except for one thing." He paused for dramatic effect. "You also make them against other people's blood cells."

I digested this for a moment. "What about the fifty per cent of transfusions that did work?"

"Aha! You've got it, that's where blood groups come in. Come over here."

He left his seat and crossed to a poster on the opposite wall. "That's a red cell." He pointed to a disc-shaped object. "They look like that in all of us, but the proteins on the surface are different. Do you know what your blood group is?"

I shook my head.

"OK. Mine's A, which means that I have a particular protein, A, on the surface of my red cells. Donna over there"—the pretty girl with the dark curls turned at the sound of her name—"she's group B, and ne'er the twain shall mix."

"I've always thought we could mix quite well," she said coquettishly.

Pete coughed self-consciously. "Maybe, but not as blood brother and sister."

She grinned and turned back to her work.

"Where was I? Oh, yes. A and B, the two groups that Landsteiner discovered that are still the basis of present-day transfusion."

"A and B?"

"That's right."

"My brother is group O." I said it without a tremor.

"Really? How come you don't know your own group?"

"Just one of those things."

"I see." His deep-set eyes held mine for a moment. "Well, O just means nought, nothing. Neither A nor B. Now, because I'm group A, I carry anti-B antibody in my plasma—"

"Why?"

"Don't complicate matters, just accept that I do, all A people do."

"Do B people have anti-A?"

"Very good, so what does that tell you?"

"They don't get on?"

"Excellent! In fact they have an almighty punch-up, or at least their blood does. Which is why you don't transfuse A blood into a B person."

"So where does O come in?"

"Hold on, you keep jumping ahead. Or perhaps you don't. You can transfuse O blood into anyone. Follow?"

I concentrated for a moment. "Because O people don't have A or B protein, the anti-A or anti-B can't hurt them."

"The boy's a genius!" he declared to a spot over my left shoulder. "He's in the wrong job."

"He'll be after yours if you're not careful," said a familiar voice. Holly! I looked around and grinned at her.

"I think we've found a strong anti-Kell," she said to Pete. "Interested?"

They conversed in gibberish for a few minutes while cheeky Donna gave me the sort of smile that makes you feel older and younger at the same time, if you see what I mean.

Then there was silence, and Donna's smile vanished like a flower closing.

I turned just in time to intercept a mean gleam from Holly before she turned quickly and walked to the door. I'd never seen her face like that before.

"Now where were we?" said Pete, unaware of all this. "Oh yes, the ABO system, comprising three blood groups, A, and B, and O, and a fourth, the joker in the pack, that fooled old Landsteiner for a while—AB."

I dragged my mind back. "That would be someone with both A and B proteins on their cells?"

"I only wish these two were as bright as you."

"That's not fair," protested Donna, who'd been listening in.

"And why not, my pretty?"

"Well, he's older than me. Anyway, everyone knows that women are cleverer than men."

"More cunning and artful perhaps, but cleverer, no."

Something in his tone made her know when to stop. She contented herself with a "Huh!" and returned to her work.

"Can I have a pencil?" I said.

He handed me one and I wrote:

Group	A	B	AB	O
Antibody	anti-B	anti-A	Neither	

He looked at the paper, took the pencil from my hand and wrote "Both" under O. "Think of it like this," he said. "O is the universal donor; you can put it into anyone. AB is the universal recipient; you can put anything into it."

I studied the piece of paper and worked it out. "I can see why some of the early random transfusions worked," I said, "but you can't tell how many unless you know the frequencies of these groups."

"The computer man speaks." He handed me the pencil. "Write

them down. In this country, about 47 per cent of people are group O, 43 per cent are A, 7 per cent are B and the lucky 3 per cent, AB."

"Why lucky?"

"Because you can put any of the other groups into them and not do any harm."

I looked back down at the paper. "About half of the random transfusions worked, I think you said."

"That's right."

I scribbled down some figures. "I'd have thought more like sixty per cent."

A flicker of respect crossed his face. "That's right, about sixty per cent."

"Where does the positive and negative come in?"

"I thought you said you didn't know anything about blood."

I shrugged. "One hears these terms." And sees them on forensic reports.

"Well, it stands for Rhesus positive and negative, after a protein in the monkey of the same name. About 80 per cent of people have this protein on their cells and are positive, the rest are negative. The system's superimposed on the ABO system."

"I'm lost," I said.

"That's nothing; there are literally dozens of other blood systems, although not so critically important as ABO and Rhesus. My job is sorting them all out."

We spent the next half-hour or so talking about whether the computer could help him, then he stood up and suggested coffee.

"Thanks for telling me about blood groups," I said. "You should have been a teacher."

He gave a wry chuckle. "Funny you should say that, I've wanted to lecture full-time at a college for ages."

"You should. You'd be good at it."

He shrugged. "I've left it too late, you need a Ph.D. these days."

"Couldn't you get one?"

He smiled mirthlessly. "I've been working on one for—oh, forget it, let's get some coffee." He made for the door as though he regretted saying even this much.

In the tea-room I smiled at Adrian to see whether it would disconcert him. It didn't. Muddy brown eyes touched mine for an instant, then he looked expressionlessly away.

Later, I walked slowly up to the canteen, glad to be alone, glad of the time to think. The only other point of interest I gleaned from Pete was that the qualified staff in the Centre were interchangeable, and could all do each other's job on-call, so I couldn't eliminate anyone that way. Pity.

My eyes fell on Steve and David at a table, and on impulse I joined them.

David, who had been talking animatedly, fell silent as I approached. Steve gave his usual grin.

"Enjoy yourself in Pete's lab this morning?" he asked as I sat down.

"More than I thought I would."

"Learn much?"

"More than I thought I would."

He laughed. "Pete talks well about his subject. I can't promise you such an interesting time this afternoon."

David said, "Steve, I have to get back now."

"Fine. See you later."

"Aren't you coming?"

"Not yet. See you later."

David gave him a reproachful look before walking disconsolately away.

I said, "I didn't know you two were buddies."

"We're not. David's one of those people who has to have a shoulder to cry on. I'm this week's choice."

"Sort of male Auntie Holly?"

"Who told you about that?"

"She did."

He looked faintly surprised, then said, "I don't have her patience, except where David's concerned. She can't bear him."

"Why's that?"

"Why d'you think? He's such a toss-pot."

"And yet she puts up with Adrian."

His teeth gleamed wolfishly. "Jealous?"

"Of Adrian? That's a contradiction in terms, surely?"

He chuckled briefly, then looked sober. "It's not funny actually; those two give the rest of us a bad name. Oh well!" He made as if to leave, so I said quickly, "I didn't know Pete was doing a Ph.D."

Steve sat down again. "Did he tell you that?"

"Yes. Why?"

He shrugged. "He doesn't usually talk about it."

"Why not? It's something to be proud of, surely?"

"Perhaps." He looked down for a moment. "He's had a very difficult time with it. People are jealous."

"Are you?"

"Not of all the hassle. I probably will be when he gets it."

I grinned at his disarming frankness. "Is that why he's had trouble, because people are jealous?"

"Sort of." He gave a twisted smile. "It's another Falkenham story, I'm afraid. You see"—he leaned forward—"when you do a doctorate, you have to have an external assessor. Pete managed to clear it with the local polytechnic, no mean feat in itself, but when he approached the Director to be external assessor, Falkenham not only refused, but wouldn't allow him any financial support or time off. Pete's had to do it all on his own. D'you know how much it costs to do a Ph.D. these days?"

I shook my head.

"You're talking about five grand. I've nothing but admiration for him."

There was a short silence, then I said, "Why should Falkenham be so against it?"

He shrugged again. "Didn't like the idea of calling Pete 'doctor,' perhaps."

"So who is the external—er . . . ?"

"Assessor. Don Chalgrove, who else?"

I smiled slowly. "Those two really are diametrically opposed, aren't they? How did Trefor react to all this?"

"As always, he supported the Director. Look, Tom." He stood up. "I'm sorry, but I must go. See you later."

I sat back and thought about what Steve had said. Was he a reliable witness, or was his evidence tainted by his dislike of Falkenham? Curious how Steve seemed to dislike him more than Pete did, who had greater cause.

I thought about the web of relationships throughout the Centre; were they the threads that held the mystery together?

Holly, who liked everyone except David—why David?

Adrian, who disliked everyone except Holly. And possibly Trefor.

Trefor, the compleat establishment man, who carried his support for the underdog to a ridiculous degree—it was no good, I'd have to draw a map of everyone's loves and hates.

I wandered back down to the Centre, wondering what to do, then it occurred to me that there'd never be a better chance of examining the Blood Bank unsupervised.

I glanced quickly into Blood Issue, just a filing clerk busy filing her nails.

Trefor's office—empty. I slipped through the narrow corridor and pulled open the heavy door.

Everything seems to lead back here, I thought, as my eyes instinctively sought the chalk mark on the floor. It was still there.

Whatever had been going on, and I thought I knew now, revolved around this room. My eyes ranged the blood-filled shelves—strange, only four days and its power over me was so diminished; on Monday it had taken all my will-power just to walk in.

Time-expired blood, where would I find it? Perhaps in that crate over there marked "Time-expired blood." Genius!

I walked over. The crate was overflowing; it must have held nearly fifty packs. Well, Trefor had said that there was still plenty of it, but I hadn't expected this much.

I had an idea, and quickly crossed the corridor into Plasma.

Looked around at the clipboards hung at intervals around the wall. Which would it be?

Found the one marked "Expired plasma" and flipped back through the worksheets—a month, two, three. Hardly any Time-expired plasma was being separated, perhaps half a dozen a week. Until a week ago, when there were nearly forty.

Why the sudden increase?

There was an obvious answer—whoever had been nicking it had stopped after Mike Leigh had been killed.

So who was it? I still wasn't quite sure.

I replaced the clipboard and walked thoughtfully back into the cool of the Bank. Expired blood came back daily; had it been stolen daily?

Nightly probably, and Hill was still the most likely candidate for that.

Standing next to the "Time-expired" crate was another, marked "Returned Blood." I walked over. Two packs nestled upside down in the bottom. Why returned?

Without thinking, I knelt and stretched out a hand to pick one up, then recoiled.

Go on, I said to myself, you nearly did it.

My heartbeat burned my throat. I swallowed, reached out my hand . . . no, it was no good . . .

The room around me shadowed imperceptibly. I looked round as a voice demanded, "What the bloody hell are you doing in here?" His bulk filled the door. Adrian.

I slowly stood up. "Seeing where things are kept. Why?"

"Because the Blood Bank's a restricted area, that's why." He approached me. "Because you're supposed to ask before you come in here." He was no taller than me, but his mass seemed to hold me in the corner. "But mostly because I say so, because I don't like you being in here."

"Then I'd better find someone to ask, hadn't I?"

He didn't move. "It's me you have to ask."

"Oh no. I'm going over your head, to your boss, so if you'll excuse me . . ."

Still he wouldn't move. "I haven't finished yet. You can keep away from Miss Jordan; she's not interested in you."

"That's for her—"

"She's not interested in you"—he stepped forward, placed a foot over mine—"because I say so—"

"Get off my—"

"Because I say so, see?" He turned, twisting his shoe heavily, then walked quickly away.

I stared after him, trembling, wanting to run and kick him, pull him round and sink a fist in his gut, knowing that if I did, Trefor would have me thrown out of the Centre.

Impotently, I limped back to the Plasma Lab and forced myself to relax; it was one of the few times since giving up smoking that I really wanted a cigarette.

I metaphorically counted to a hundred, then went to Steve's lab to wait for him.

Just after two, a young man wandered in, politely asked if he could help me, and then sat at a bench and began working. He was followed by two others, a boy and a girl.

Steve breezed in five minutes later, his face slightly flushed.

"Hello, Tom, prompt as ever, I see."

"Just trying to set a good example to the provincials."

"Ooh! A cut to the quick." He theatrically clutched his heart. "Come on over here and I'll tell you what we do." He led the way to his desk and pulled out a chair for me. As I sat down, one of the boys came over.

"Steve, I can't get this group to work."

"Oh gawd! Excuse me a minute, Tom."

They went over to the boy's bench and talked for a few minutes, then Steve came back grimacing in mock resignation.

"Sorry about that. These little things are sent to try us." He sat down heavily. "Now . . ."

He was right about one thing: his work wasn't as interesting as Pete's, or perhaps he just didn't have the same gift of putting it over.

His job was to make the reagents used for grouping blood, not only for the rest of the Centre, but for all the hospitals in the region, using donor blood as his raw material.

I asked him if he used any Time-expired blood.

"Yes, I use some. Why?"

I shrugged. "Trefor was going on about it yesterday, what useful stuff it is."

"Well, he's right, up to a point. We pool it and use it to dilute reagents. Dr. Chalgrove uses a fair bit."

"What for?"

"Research. Factor VIII survival studies, or trying to extract some of the other factors. That's what I help him with, I'd go mad with boredom if it wasn't for that. Have you seen his unit yet?"

I shook my head.

"I'll show you round now if you like."

Might be useful. "All right."

He jumped up. As I followed, I found that my foot had stiffened.

"Hurt your leg?" said Steve.

"Stubbed my toe."

He grunted and strode out. When we reached Chalgrove's lab, he tried the door.

"Good," he said, as it opened, "it's kept locked when no one's using it."

We were in a brightly lit office with no windows. The whine that had been barely perceptible outside became much louder—I asked Steve what it was.

"Ultra-centrifuge," he said, "which is just a smart way of saying a centrifuge that goes very fast. The whole unit's soundproofed so that you can't hear it outside."

He pushed open a glass-panelled door and the whine increased. I followed him into a narrow room with a wash-basin and shelves filled with boxes.

"Gowning room." He had to raise his voice to make himself heard. "The lab through there is supposed to be sterile, so you have to gown up. Come and have a look."

He stepped over to another glass-panelled door, in line with the first.

Even in a shapeless gown and wearing mask and gloves, there was no mistaking the figure of Chalgrove. He raised a laconic hand in greeting as he saw us. The laboratory was surprisingly large and filled with shining stainless steel equipment.

"What's he doing?" I asked.

"At this precise moment, attempting to scratch his nose without dislodging his glasses."

"Very droll."

"He's spinning cryo precipitate. To get at the useful factors in plasma, you have to literally just melt it from freezing without letting the temperature rise above 0°C." He coughed, then continued. "If you get it dead right, a slimy crud forms at the bottom which contains the factors we're looking for. You have to spin that crud, which is what he's doing now, then treat it chemically to get the pure Factor VIII."

"Is that an infra-red oven over there?"

"It is. He tried using it experimentally to melt the plasma more slowly."

"Didn't it work?"

"Not very well. My throat's getting hoarse with all this shouting, let's go and have some coffee."

As he turned and pushed the door, a sharp click from behind made me look round.

"What's that?"

"It's a dead bolt. When I open this door, the other one locks automatically. Watch."

He let his door close, then pushed it open again. Chalgrove's door trembled slightly as the bolt shot out and held it.

"What's the point?"

"So that both doors can't be open at once—it's supposed to stop contaminated air getting through. Frankly, it's a waste of time."

Having thus dismissed the subject, he strode out through the office to the empty corridor. As the door shut, the sudden silence was eerie and disorientating.

Just before we reached the tea-room, I decided to take a calculated risk.

"Steve, how well do you know Adrian?"

"As well as anyone, I suppose, except perhaps Holly. He's not an easy character to know."

"Would you say he was violent?"

He stopped. "What makes you ask that?"

"This." I indicated my foot. "I didn't stub my toe."

"Adrian?"

I nodded, and Steve looked round.

"Look, he'll probably be in here. Let's go upstairs for a coffee."

As we climbed the hollow stairwell, he said, "He's got a nasty temper, but so have most people who are frustrated and inadequate. Then of course, he's got this ridiculous thing about Holly—very embarrassing for her, but she should have known better—" He stopped and stared at me. "You haven't been playing around with her, have you?"

"Well, I took her out last night."

His laughter rang round the concrete stairs. "Good for you—" he punched my shoulder—"and her—do her good. The thing is, does he know?"

"I think so."

"Well, that explains it. Come on, I want some coffee; tell me about it then."

I confined myself to the facts that concerned Adrian, but included Trefor's ticking-off of the previous afternoon.

Steve's face darkened as he stirred his coffee.

"That stupid burke Wickham. First he has to promote David, the biggest wanker in the place, because he feels sorry for him—'We must give him a chance, think of the wife and kiddies.'" His mimicry of Trefor's accent was devastating. "And now he encourages that slob Adrian. I keep telling him we can't afford any more weak links, and d'you know what he says? 'But Steve, somebody's got to look after the underdogs.' Underdogs, I ask you! Makes you wonder what he was like when he was younger. A cross between the two of them, I expect."

CHAPTER 9

Marcus sounded more subdued than usual when I phoned him that night, and I didn't have to wait long to find out why.

"What have you been doing to annoy Falkenham?"

"Oh no!"

"Oh yes. Says you've been upsetting his staff and haven't made any real progress, so he wants the investigation dropped. He's going to 'Make the strongest representations to the appropriate authorities'; those were his words."

"Marcus, I *am* making progress, I'm sure of it."

"Tell me."

I told him about Adrian and the loopholes in the computer system. "I want to do some checking on the computer records tomorrow, but I need those figures from CPPL you were going to send me."

"They're on their way, should be with you in the morning. Tom?"

"Yes?" Guardedly.

"These loopholes you've found—can they be easily blocked?"

"Oh yeah—until someone finds new—"

"Tom, it might not be a bad idea if we let Falkenham cool off for a week or two. You could come back here and write a report on the system we could show him—"

"I need more time here—there's something I can't quite put my finger on—"

"Falkenham wasn't kidding, Tom. He could make a lot of trouble."

"What's the matter with him?"

Marcus chuckled. "I bet I know what's the matter with you—it's that girl you can't put a finger on, isn't it?"

"Oh gawd . . ."

We eventually agreed to wait and see what I could find tomorrow before making a decision.

I spent the rest of the evening at the bar lubricating my mind, trying to find the answer. It didn't come.

The next morning, Friday, I went straight to the computer unit, from where I phoned Trefor, telling him I would be in later in the day. John Swift, the manager, was as helpful as he had been before, finding me a room on my own with a VDU and a password that would get into the record storage programs of the computer.

"How many people at the Centre have a password like this?" I asked.

"Falkenham, Chalgrove and Trefor Wickham"—he counted them off on his fingers—"although they don't use them much. I don't think Trefor would know how." We both laughed. "The others have access only to the programs that concern them."

"What's to stop them using each other's password?"

"I hope they don't," he said irritably, "it would make that part of the system pointless."

When he'd gone, I settled down and wondered where to start.

Time-expired plasma, I supposed. It was where everything seemed to begin.

I logged on, selected the program and went back to the date when records began, nine months before.

Not much expired blood was being returned, perhaps a dozen or so a day. Come forward a month, about the same, then another month, and another. The figure decreased to barely a dozen being returned a week.

Until two weeks ago. Then, as the sheets in the Plasma Lab had indicated, they suddenly shot up to forty or fifty being returned a day. Strong circumstantial evidence, to say the least, that expired plasma had been systematically stolen for the past nine months.

But wouldn't Adrian, assuming that it was Adrian, realize that this would be noticed? Then again, who else was there to notice it? Trefor certainly hadn't.

And wouldn't this push up the apparent blood usage per unit population, as Marcus's analysis had shown? Yes, but not by all that much.

Which brought me to my second hypothesis: that Adrian (or whosoever) had been over-issuing to hospitals, but in fact keeping back the surplus for Hill to separate (or perhaps dispatch whole) at night. Without getting at individual hospital records, I couldn't demonstrate this. Pity.

But if Hill had separated them, how would he have disposed of all the surplus packs of red cells? In fact, how were they disposed of anyway? I made a note to ask Trefor.

And so with a sigh to Jones's third hypothesis. A sigh, because it meant adding the totals of units of fresh blood separated each day for the last nine months.

For a moment I considered asking John Swift whether the computer could do this for me, then reluctantly dragged out my pocket calculator. It would have aroused his curiosity.

I went back to where records began and laboriously added the totals, day following day following day . . . It took me over an hour, by which time my fingers were sore and my eyes aching. Only then did I take out the envelope that had arrived that morning with the figures Marcus had gleaned from CPPL.

They were in monthly columns. I added them and then compared the two totals.

Well, there was a difference, and a difference on the right side, more blood packs had been separated in the Centre than plasma packs had arrived in CPPL, but it wasn't as large as I would have thought.

I stared at the figures for a moment, then worked out a statistical error rate on them. The difference between them was not significant; it could be explained by random error.

Statistics don't lie, not in the right hands. I scratched my head, then realized what I had to do.

Groaned aloud—it meant going back to the beginning, adding all the figures again, but this time into monthly totals.

Another hour passed.

I scribbled the totals down in the appropriate CPPL columns, then studied them.

For the first five months they were virtually identical, but for the past four, *they showed an increasing difference!*

With shaking fingers, I worked out a Standard Deviation on the sets of totals. There was no doubt: the differences between the Centre's and CPPL's totals were significant.

Statistics don't lie . . .

Which meant that my villains had turned their talents to fresh plasma as well as expired.

"Got you, you bastard," I whispered. Even Falkenham couldn't ignore this.

I leaned back for a moment, exultant.

Was it worth chasing up the hospital records to see whether hypothesis number two was right as well?

It might be, just to tidy things up.

I made up a chart of my findings, to present the evidence in the clearest way possible.

Was there anything else? I carefully looked over the CPPL figures from Marcus again. There was one other odd little anomaly that I couldn't explain. It seemed that the fresh plasma that CPPL *did* receive from the Centre gave a lower yield of Factor VIII than that from any other centre in the country.

Curious, I worked out the Standard Deviation from the yields of the other centres. The figure from Tamar was outside this; the difference was significant.

Perhaps they weren't freezing the fresh plasma quickly enough. However, that was their problem, not mine.

I had completed the chart just as John stuck his head round the door.

"We're off for a pie and a pint, Tom—interested?"

Is a sailor interested in sex? Besides, I had something to celebrate.

Some time later I trailed back to the Centre, at peace with the world. Glanced into Blood Issue, no change, the same filing clerk filing the same nails and Adrian glowering at me. I smiled sweetly. He still wasn't disconcerted.

Trefor was actually friendly—perhaps he'd been drinking as well; it *was* Friday.

"Hello, Tom, we've missed you today, must be getting used to you . . . No, really, people have been asking where you were. Now, what can I do for you?"

I explained that I didn't know how unwanted packs of cells were disposed of.

His eyes narrowed. "Why d'you want to know that?"

I shrugged. "Just curious. Doesn't matter."

He relaxed. "Well, in the old days we used to take them to the garden, marvellous fertilizer you know, but these days, since the scares over hepatitis and now AIDS, we have to destroy them. I'll show you if you like," he added, his eyes lighting up at the prospect of another Trefor-tour.

I followed him to the wash-up area, where I had been beaten up a few days before. It looked grubby and dirty in the daylight.

At the far end, in the shadows, stood a stainless steel machine with a crate of blood packs beside it.

He lifted the circular lid and I peered down into a sort of tapered well with rows of serrated edges at the bottom, arranged in circles.

"Watch," he said, and pulled a switch. The teeth became invisible as they spun and water flowed down the sides.

Trefor picked up some packs and dropped them in. Immediately they were chewed to a bloody pulp. My eyes clamped shut of their own volition.

Slowly I filled my lungs with air, lifted my head and opened my eyes. Trefor watched me intently.

I said, "Those teeth must be sharp."

"Have to be to cut through that tough plastic." He tossed in some more packs. "Wouldn't do to get your fingers caught in there."

"It certainly wouldn't." I swallowed. "What happens to the residue that's left?"

"It's ground up so finely that it can be sluiced into the drains." He picked up another handful of packs. "Might as well finish these off while we're here."

There was only one thing left I wanted to do that afternoon. I told Trefor I was returning to London, but that I might be back for a day or two next week. A foot in the door. Then I walked to Holly's laboratory. She was seated at her desk by the window, poring over some computer reports. She hadn't seen me, so with a wink at the girls, I walked quietly up behind her and ran a finger down her back. Reaction to the bag-crusher, I suppose.

She gave a shrill squeak and straightened up like a frightened animal.

"Tom, don't *do* that!" She meant it.

"Sorry, thought I'd surprise you."

"Well, I wish you wouldn't," she said, not mollified. "What do you want?"

"Just to check on the arrangements for tonight."

She shot a glance back at her staff and said in a lowered voice, "I thought all that had been settled. I'm picking you up at eight."

"Oh. Fine. Just wanted to be sure."

"Well, now you are sure, and I'm rather busy, so I'll see you at eight, okay?"

"Fine." I nodded, and turned back to the door.

They were all grinning, but the girl who had stuck her tongue out at her last Tuesday was grinning the most.

I walked self-consciously back along the corridor.

Well, naturally she had to keep discipline, and I could see some of the staff weren't the easiest, but . . .

But, I wondered, what other reasons were there for her nickname?

CHAPTER 10

Like most breaks, it fell into place from nowhere.

"Excuse me, please," I said to David Brown, wishing too late I'd picked some other point of entry through the crush around the bar. He and Adrian stared back at me.

Holly and I had arrived at the hall about half an hour earlier, had been spotted immediately by Trefor and his wife, and had sat at their table ever since.

David dropped his cigarette at my feet and trod on it before stepping back a pace. But as I moved forward, so did Adrian—I stumbled against David who spilled most of his beer down his front.

"You clumsy bastard," said Adrian deliberately.

I turned on him angrily, then saw the glint of triumph in his muddy eyes; he was dying for me to start something.

I turned back to David, who had pulled out a handkerchief and was dabbing at his front. "It was an accident; I apologize."

"Don't give me that crap," he muttered.

A weight shifted in my brain and I knew who had telephoned me last Tuesday.

My eyes hard on his face, I said, "I'll buy you another."

He slowly looked up. He read my eyes and was terrified.

"I'll buy you another," I repeated, then turned back to Adrian. "Your girlfriend was looking for you just now."

His face shadowed for an instant, he turned and looked to where she was sitting, then back at me.

"Get stuffed," he spat.

I shrugged. "Perhaps I will."

He hesitated, then incredibly started walking over to her.

"I didn't think he'd fall for that," I said conversationally. "You and I have got to talk. Same terms as before."

"I can't," he whispered.

I leaned towards him. "I promise you immunity from prosecution. Think about your wife."

"That's just it," he whimpered. "You don't understand."

"Think about it," I said, and made for the bar.

Pete had been watching me. He gave a solemn wink. "Bad company you keep," he observed, then moved away with a tray of drinks.

I was quickly served and turned back to David, who was lighting another cigarette with shaking hands.

"Take it." I proffered him a glass, then saw Adrian returning. "I'll see you later," I said, and walked away, making sure that I crossed Adrian on the open floor. But all he did was say, "Funny boy, I'll be seeing you later."

That makes two of you, I thought.

I was still trying to convince Holly that Adrian must have been mistaken, when a man in a crumpled suit clambered on to the stage and announced, "Grub's up."

We trooped out through the corridor to the waiting buffet, the usual collection of bits and pieces to be balanced on paper plates and consumed with plastic cutlery that snapped at the slightest pressure.

But I wasn't thinking about the food that we took back into the hall. I was wondering how to get David Brown on his own.

The door at the far end of the hall flew open and a huge Negro swaggered in. He wore an off-white cowboy suit with fringes, a cowboy hat and a shiny silver star. Spurs clicked faintly on his boots as he strode across the floor with a supreme arrogance, then leaped on to the stage.

The hall fell black, there was a roll of drums, a peal of guitars, and then lights of all colours boomed into the darkness in time with the music.

"C'mon, you people, move!" he shouted over the sound of the record.

Slowly, as the beat of the music deepened, he began, small movements at first, but graceful and in perfect sympathy, widening as his teeth glowed in an ecstatic smile.

Somebody cheered and there was a ripple of applause. From the corner of my eye I saw a girl in a loose white trouser suit tugging at her partner. With a reluctant smile, he rose and followed her jiggling figure into the centre of the floor. She faced him, and, grinning provocatively, moved from side to side in time with the music.

Another couple joined them, another, then more, all catching the fever.

I glanced at Adrian and David, wondering how to get them apart. There was only one way, and that was to make Adrian jealous.

I leaned across to Holly. "Come and dance with me," I said in her ear.

She looked up at the dancers and then back to me with a smile. "All right."

I made our excuses to the Wickhams and led her to the floor.

Her feet moved with the beat, but her body hardly at all—she wasn't infected yet.

The record finished and she smiled at me self-consciously as the black man bawled at us like a fairground hustler and the music grew louder.

We danced and laughed and gradually her body became more supple, revealing itself in the contours of her dress.

"I haven't done this for ages," she shouted.

"Neither have I."

"Liar!"

The music stopped.

"You dance really well," she said.

"I started young."

More records, more people, coloured lights like heartbeats, like fog lamps; savage guitar riffs, wailing saxophones and the unchecked laughter of people glad to be together.

She caught my arm. "I've had it, Tom, buy me a drink."

"In a minute."

People bumped into each other and laughed, trod on each other's toes and laughed; they even collided and fell on the floor and it didn't matter.

And then the music stopped.

I took Holly's arm. "Let's get that drink."

"I need it," she said feelingly.

As we walked towards the bar, I looked around, yes, there they were, Adrian glaring balefully. But when would he take the bait?

The press at the bar was two bodies deep by the time we got there, then the large body in front of us turned and revealed itself as Steve.

"Tom! What would you like to drink?"

I told him.

"OK, hang on and you can help me back with them."

Holly spotted Pete, who was sitting at a table nearby with two women, and went to join them.

Steve obviously had "Positive Bar Presence," because he was served almost immediately—or perhaps it was just the sheer size of him. He handed me two drinks and carried the others back on a small tray.

"Tom, this is my wife, Anita," he said when we had sat down. A striking-looking girl with bold eyes said hello and smiled. He turned to the other, who was older and had an air of permanent indignation about her. "And this is Eileen, who has the misfortune to be married to Pete."

The latter grimaced horribly and stuck out his tongue. Steve raised his glass to him and said, "Cheers"; Pete did likewise, and I suddenly perceived an affinity between them. They were so different, yet there was a bond, intangible but definite.

"How much respite do we have before that horrible noise starts again?" demanded Eileen.

Steve said, "It isn't that bad."

"No, it isn't," agreed Holly. "I haven't enjoyed myself so much for ages."

"Your partner may have something to do with that," said Pete. "Quite a groover, is that the right word?"

"About ten years out of date," I said. "Like me."

"You could have fooled me. Your enthusiasm was certainly apparent."

"Trying to recapture my lost youth, I expect."

"Pete was born in London, too," said Holly.

"Whereabouts?"

"Highgate."

"Shades of Karl Marx," said Steve. "Ugh!"

"Don't you knock old Karl," said Pete. "Not all his ideas were bad."

"Re-distribution of wealth, you mean?"

"Well, it's better than your filthy capitalist philosophy. One for one and all for one, eh?"

"Oh, do shut up," said his wife. "Whereabouts were you born, Tom?"

"Paddington."

"Always conjures up the image of bears, that word. Obviously really, I suppose. Does it make you think of bears, Holly?"

"N—no." She looked thoughtful. "To me it's a gateway . . ."

"That's because you're not a mother yet," said Pete, "unlike my old trouble and strife here. Talking of which"— he lowered his voice—"I think some may be on its way."

I glanced round as Adrian materialized beside Holly.

"Hello, Holly," he said with the clarity of a drink too many. "I was wondering whether you have the next dance or two free."

"Why, thank you, kind sir," she said with an attempt at lightness. "But there doesn't seem to be anything to dance to at the moment."

"It's starting again any minute now."

"God save us," muttered Eileen.

"All right," said Holly, "that would be nice. The next dance."

"Thank you." He turned and walked away. Good, I thought, sitting very still.

The short silence was broken by Steve. "I wonder how it feels to have so many admirers."

"Oh, shut up! It's not funny."

"Yes, shut up, Steve," said his wife.

"Sorry."

Pete said, "I wonder what's happened to his little mate?"

"Search me." David? I tried to look round casually.

"I thought I saw you counselling him earlier on," Pete continued.

"Oh, he was moaning about how unbearable life's become, nothing new. Gone away to sulk somewhere, I expect."

"He certainly has become a master-whinger, hasn't he? He was on to me yesterday about all the pressures—"

"Why do you two always end up talking about work?" demanded Eileen.

At this moment the hall darkened again and the black man reappeared, exhorting us to "Git to our feet."

"It's too much," she groaned.

Adrian re-materialized, and without a word Holly rose and they joined the other dancers. I looked round again. Where the hell was David?

"That's the last you'll see of her tonight," prophesied Pete gloomily.

"I hope not; she's supposed to be giving me a lift."

Steve raised his voice over the noise. "You know, I've always thought she still had a secret soft spot for old Adrian. Can't say I admire her taste."

"I can't stand any more of this!" shouted Eileen. "Come on, Pete, home! Nothing personal," she added to the rest of us, "the baby-sitter calleth."

Steve had put his hand on Pete's arm; there was a momentary lull in the noise and I caught the words ". . . see to it, will you?" I couldn't hear Pete's reply.

He stood up. "Love you an' leave you and all that," he shouted. "Enjoy yourselves." They wound their way to the exit.

I turned to Steve and Anita. "Would you two like a drink?"

"No, thanks, Tom, we've got to be going soon."

"I think I will, if you don't mind."

"Feel free."

I made for the bar, not because I particularly wanted a drink, but for a new vantage-point.

He wasn't there, so I scanned the hall. It was difficult with so many people; the writhing crowd on the dance floor swelled and lurched as though it were an animal in search of prey. A strobe light strayed over it at random picking out Holly and Adrian, and giving their movements a graceful togetherness. She smiled at him.

I turned abruptly to the bar and demanded a whisky. I wasn't jealous, just fed up.

I swallowed it, then wandered, apparently aimlessly round the perimeter of the hall.

No sign of him. Sulking in the corridor? More likely gone home, but
I checked anyway.

Hell, hell, hell! Why hadn't I watched him more closely? What now?
Find his address and pounce on him tomorrow? There was nothing
more to be done tonight.

As I re-entered the hall, I realized they had all gone: Trefor, Pete and
Steve, as well as David.

Where was Holly? Had she disappeared too? No, there she was by
our table with Adrian, looking around. I hurried over.

"There you are," she shouted above the noise. "I thought we'd lost
you."

Adrian obviously wished they had. "I was getting Holly a drink," he
said with difficulty. "D'you want one?"

"Thanks, I'll have a pint." As he made to turn away, I said, "D'you
know where David is?"

"Why?"

"Nothing. We were going to have a talk, that's all."

I sat down quickly next to Holly to let that one stew. He made for the
bar.

I grinned at Holly and said, "Enjoying yourself?"

"Mmm." She nodded reflectively.

"D'you have enough energy left for another turn with me?"

"I think so. But we'd better have this drink with Adrian first."

"OK."

A moment later he returned.

"What do you want to talk to David about?" he demanded as he
handed me a beer.

I said, "A personal matter."

He looked baffled. "Is it about work?"

"You could say that, yes."

He was dying to press me further, but didn't, and we sat in silence for
a few moments.

Holly finished her drink.

"Ready?" I said to her.

Her eyes flickered fractionally to Adrian, then she said, "All right."

As she stood up, he called out, "Don't forget the dance you promised me, I'll be along in a minute."

She appeared not to notice. As we walked away, I said in her ear,

"Holly, what is it with him? He's like the Old Man of the Sea, he never lets up."

"He's got a problem. Tell you some other time."

She moved to the music in a constrained, almost lethargic way, her face abstracted.

I followed her movements and waited, made no attempt to speak or smile.

Then a record was played that must have taken her back to the past. Her face softened into a smile that was completely for herself and her bittersweet memories. Her body became more fluid, her face animated; she caught my gaze and we both laughed.

More records, then, like an insect in a dream, another noise, discordant, insistent. On impulse, I caught Holly's wrist and drew her to the tall window overlooking the main entrance to the hospital.

Someone pulled the curtains aside as, like a bird of prey, an ambulance swooped from the curling road, its tom-tom horns breaking up the music, deep blue lamps breaking up the disco lights as people gathered round to watch.

The doors flew open and a stretcher was rushed inside.

"A hospital never lets you forget," said Holly in my ear.

The evening entered its final stage in slow crooning ballads. Some couples wandered away; others slipped into each other's arms.

"Come here," I called softly, and with a low chuckle she accepted my loose embrace. She settled into me, her dress as smooth as the skin beneath, as the room began to slowly rotate around us.

We remained moving even as the records were changed. She settled deeper, her hair smelt of the hay in the fields, her body of flowers, and as I melted into her I wanted her; my body wanted and hardened and began transmitting its urgent signals.

I breathed deeply, the room revolved and Adrian slid into view. He caught my gaze and his face sharpened with hate.

Then I did something stupid; I grinned at him. He started walking towards us.

Holly must have sensed me stiffen. She looked up as I felt a tap on my shoulder.

"I think it's my turn now, mate."

Hard desire hardened into anger.

"Oh you do, do you? Why don't you try next week if you want to dance with her?"

He smiled a friendly smile. "No need for that, mate. Share and share alike, eh?"

By this time I had released her and stood facing him.

She said, "Stop being silly, you two—"

"Tom doesn't mind, do you, Tom?"

He put a friendly hand on my chest and gave me a friendly shove. Or it might have been if he hadn't somehow slipped a toe behind my ankles.

I crashed to the floor with a bone-jarring thud that knocked the wind from me.

"I'm sorry, Tom, let me give you a hand." His face was all concern as he stretched out an arm. "You'd better come and sit down."

"Thanks," I said groggily and reached for his hand.

Steady now—I allowed my body to come up about a foot—God, he was strong—before snapping my bicep.

I fell back with a crash as he loomed over me—steady now—gave a cry of pain and brought up my knee as hard as I could.

His scream was so shrill as to be almost silent, like a finger on a windowpane.

I wriggled out from beneath him and unsteadily gained my feet.

"What happened?" cried Holly as a small crowd gathered.

"I don't know," I said helplessly. "I think he's winded himself."

"He ain't winded," said a gruff male voice in my ear. Adrian writhed and clutched his groin.

"Give me a hand, will you?" I said, and together we helped him over to a chair.

"Tom, what happened?" demanded Holly.

Before I could reply, the bleep attached to her pocket gave off its shrill intermittent alarm.

She snatched it up and switched it off. "Must be that ambulance," she muttered. "Tom, this could take a while; look after Adrian, will you? You'd better find a taxi home."

She sped for the door.

"It's all right. I'll take care of him," I said to the gruff voice. He grunted and drifted away.

I leaned over. "Adrian, can you hear me? I know all about you, and believe me, that was just for starters. Do you understand that?"

"Get stuffed," he wheezed.

I don't know why, perhaps because his fund of profanities was so limited, perhaps just because he was so pathetic, but suddenly I felt sorry for him.

"Listen," I said, "after I've spoken to David, why don't you talk to me about it? I can fix up the same deal for you as for him."

His face went completely blank.

CHAPTER 11

I took a last look round the hall for David, in case he'd come back, but he hadn't.

Another drink? No—had enough already; in fact I needed to shed some.

I walked into the corridor and found what I wanted, then stood and stared for a moment out of a window at the main entrance of the hospital as it lay bathed in its own floodlight. The noise of the disco had faded like a memory, been replaced by the heels of nurses and stethoscoped doctors criss-crossing each other's paths.

What a way for a job to end.

Glanced at my watch—11:30—couldn't face the thought of going back to the hotel. No, I'd find Holly.

But what if she didn't want to be found? I wondered as I hurried through the space walkway. A three-quarter moon hung over the distant moor and shed a dappled green light. Worry about that when it happened.

Clattered down the hollow concrete stairs to the next landing and pulled at the door. It was locked and I couldn't remember the way round to the other staircase. Anyway, that was probably locked as well.

The tiny notice above the key in its glass-fronted case read: BREAK ONLY IN EMERGENCY.

Not really an emergency, wanting to find Holly. Important, though.

I found an old shilling, which fitted quite nicely under the head of the plastic rivet holding the glass. A twist, and it was in my hand.

The door opened easily and I held it with a toe while replacing key and glass. They'd have to wonder about the rivet.

It was deathly quiet and the shadows in the corridor became the images of my last nocturnal visit, then I heard the whine of a centrifuge and saw the light coming from Pete's laboratory.

She was just as I remembered first seeing her, a white coat brought to life by the body inside.

She turned suddenly as she sensed me.

"Tom! What are you doing here?"

"I came to find you."

"You came . . . Oh Tom, not now," she wailed, "a man's bleeding to death and I'm trying to find the right blood for him."

"I'm sorry," I said humbly. "If you want me to go, I'll find a taxi . . ."

"Surely you don't want to stay!"

"I do, actually."

She was still staring at me when a timer went off, making us both jump.

"Oh, all right." She pointed a long-suffering finger. "But you sit down there, and don't say a word unless I speak first."

I thought I could detect a softening of tone and wondered about making a mock salute, but thought better of it.

She twisted a knob and gazed thoughtfully for a moment at the top of the centrifuge as the note of its whine fell, then turned and grinned at me.

"Actually, I wouldn't mind some company tonight, so long as you promise not to interrupt while I'm in the middle of something."

"Scout's Honour. Am I allowed to speak now?"

"Yes, for about half a minute."

"What are you doing?"

"Finding the patient's blood group."

"Then what?"

"I cross-match blood of the right group with his blood." The whine died away. "No more talking while I do this group."

She opened the lid of the centrifuge and carefully took out several tiny glass tubes that sparkled like jewels beneath the Anglepoise lamp. Then she extracted some of the contents of each on to glass slides, which she examined one by one under a microscope.

"A-Positive," she declared at last, making a note on a pad, "Good." She hurried out of the room.

My eyes wandered over the laboratory—how it reflect's Pete's mind, I thought, neat and efficient.

Holly's rapid footsteps approached, then she was back with a crate of blood packs which she lined up on the bench like soldiers. She sat down and started to work, her hands moving like birds among the equipment as ranks of tubes fell into racks, beads of serum glistened like oil as they dropped into them, to be joined by falling rubies of blood as the whine of the centrifuge rose and fell.

Then with a plop she submerged one of the racks in a waterbath, reset the timer and turned to me, leaning back against the bench with an exhilarated smile.

"Can I speak now?" I asked.

"If you like."

"What were you doing?"

Her smile widened; she was enjoying herself.

"I've set up a cross-match between the patient's blood and these donations. Finding the right group is just the beginning; you have to make sure they won't react because of some peculiar antibody or other."

She launched into a highly technical explanation that I couldn't follow despite Pete's lecture, but enjoyed through the vitality of her movements and expressions.

"Come over here. I'll show you."

She thrust a slide under the microscope, pulled the seat under her and leaned forward to peer down the eyepiece. The fine hair fell away on either side of her neck, and my eyes were drawn to the tiny duck's tail of shorter hairs at the margin. I drew close and the smell of her made me want to touch it.

"Now look." Her head turned and our noses missed by a thread. "Look down there," she said uncertainly, leaning back to give me more room.

Dutifully I applied an eye to the lens, but her nearness made it impossible to take anything in.

"The focus might not be right," she murmured, and our fingers touched as she showed me the adjuster.

Then without warning she slid away from the seat. "You'd better sit down if you want to look at it properly." The slightly teacherish tone was back in her voice.

I sat on the warm seat and looked again; this time a field of tumbling red discs like the one on Pete's chart swam into view.

"That's blood as you'd expect to see it." She swapped slides. "Now look again."

This time the discs were matted together in bizarre configurations.

"That's what happens if you put the wrong blood into the wrong patient."

"And you're looking for this sort of reaction in these donations?"

"That's right."

"What happens if they all react?"

"Panic."

"No, really?"

"Well, I'd find the antibody in the patient's blood that causes the reaction, then use the computer to see what suitable blood we have, then re-cross-match."

"Computers do have their uses, then?"

"Who said they didn't?"

"Plenty of people. Holly?"

"Mmm."

"How long d'you think before you've finished?"

"Oh, about half an hour. Why?"

"Come and have a drink with me in the hotel."

Again the characteristic hesitation. "Let's see how we feel when we get there, shall we?" A pause. "Tom?"

I looked up.

"Did you hurt Adrian on purpose?"

To lie or not to lie? Compromise.

"I didn't come out this evening wanting to hurt him. Let's say that when it happened, I did nothing to prevent it. He tripped me on purpose, you know."

"I know." The grey eyes wouldn't let mine go. "But did you have to hurt him so much?"

"He's got a screw loose—"

"He's not that bad; you don't understand him."

"Oh, but I do, he's pathological—"

"So it was deliberate, which makes you just as bad."

"Rubbish. Steve told me there was still something between you—"

"It's none of his business," she flared. "Or yours."

The timer went off and she abruptly turned to her work.

I could feel her resentment, her regret at letting me stay. So *why* had she let me stay . . . what was there between her and Adrian?

One thing was certain: there would be no cosy drink at the hotel bar tonight, or even cosier nocturne.

"Oh, damn you, Tom Jones!"

"What's the matter?"

"You've put a curse on this blood; every single one's reacted."

"I'm sorry—"

"Be quiet, I'm thinking."

She carefully examined the slides again, then picked up the tubes from which they had been prepared, holding each one up to the light. Then she jumped up and did the same with the tubes from the other rack.

She stared at the inky window.

"What are you going to do?" I ventured.

"I said be quiet." She nibbled a thumbnail for a moment, then crossed to the telephone, snatched up the receiver, and dialled.

"Dr. Petrie? Cross-matching Laboratory. I'm afraid we have a problem: your patient has an antibody."

The earpiece crackled.

"Yes," agreed Holly, "you'd better speak to the MO on call; that's Dr. Chalgrove." She gave a number, said yes a few times and then replaced the receiver.

She looked at me. "This could take hours; perhaps you had better find a taxi."

"D'you mind if I stay?"

She shrugged impatiently. "It's up to you."

She pulled open the door of the refrigerator and searched until she found a rack of small bottles. Then she started work again, her hands moving faster than ever.

The telephone rang; she sprang up, submerging her latest rack of tubes in the waterbath en route.

". . . Dr. Chalgrove . . . yes, I've just done it . . . Oh, ten or fifteen minutes, then perhaps half an hour for the cross-match . . . Yes, I thought you might . . . Yes, I'll let you know." She replaced the receiver with a sigh.

After a moment I said, "Am I allowed to speak now?"

"Oh—yes."

"I take it Chalgrove's been talking with the doctor in charge."

"Yes, he's advised him to use haemocell, that's a plasma expander."

"Sounds revolting."

She looked up at me. "It could save his life. By expanding what little blood he has left, it prevents his veins collapsing."

"So what do you do next?" I asked in a perfectly level voice.

Still her eyes were on me. "Put a name to the rare antibody in the patient that's causing the problem."

"Does this often happen?"

"Rarely. That's why they're called rare antibodies."

"Ha, ha smartass. Er—did I hear right just now when you told

Chalgrove that it would take three-quarters-of-an-hour rather than the hours plural hitherto suggested?"

She stuck out her tongue at me. "All right. I was just so *mad* when that blood wouldn't match; it would have to happen when it was most needed. Besides"—she tilted her head slightly—"I wasn't feeling very pleased with you."

The silence was filled by the timer and she hurried over to the microscope.

Minutes passed.

"Little e," she announced at last.

"I beg your pardon?"

She stood up. "Little e, that's the name of the antibody."

"Not very imaginative, they might at least have called it Ernie—"

"Which means that we'll need R2R2 blood," she continued, crossing to the computer terminal.

"Ronald, Reginald," I muttered as her fingers rattled the keys and the screen came to life.

"It's OK," she said a moment later. "We've got six in stock, I'll go and find them."

"Can I give you a hand?" I said nonchalantly.

"No, thanks, Tom." She paused and her eyes searched my face. "You can come if you like."

The coolness of the Blood Bank seemed to carry its own quietness.

"They should be in here." She pulled a wire basket towards her. "Hell! There's only three."

"Have they been issued?"

"Can't have been; they wouldn't still be in the computer. No, they're in among that lot somewhere." She indicated the regiments of packs and drew a piece of paper from her pocket. "Look, here are the numbers. You take that side; I'll take this."

With the slightest of tremors, I began shuffling through the rows of packs; this faded as they began to assume a malignant will of their own beneath my increasingly cold and clumsy fingers.

"Ah!" She had found one. I glanced over and mentally crossed the number from my list.

My fingers were completely numb now and kept getting tangled in the tubing; it was useless—

"Here's another, Holly."

"Well done."

We searched for another minute, then she said, "We've wasted enough time. These five'll have to do."

Back in the laboratory, I blew on my hands and rubbed them together as she put up another series of tests.

At last she had finished.

"How long now?" I asked.

"Twenty minutes or so. Tom?"

I raised my head. "Mmm?"

"You realize what you've been doing, don't you?"

I looked down again. "Mmm."

"Well, go on, say it!"

"I can't," I said at last. "It'll break the spell."

"No, you won't, you'll—" she searched for words—"you'll seal it, confirm it."

Silence, while the tip of my tongue touched my lips and I felt her eyes on me.

"I've been handling packs of blood."

"As though they were oranges in a supermarket."

"Yes."

"And you weren't scared?"

"No."

The warmth of her smile should have made me feel—I don't know—grateful or something, but that wasn't what I felt.

"I'd better tidy up," she said unsteadily, and turned and busied herself while I watched and waited.

I felt triumphant and lustful, and not just for her body. I wanted to tear away and destroy the layers of schoolmarmish sexlessness, awake her, plant inside her a mark that would prevent Adrian from ever touching her again.

And as I watched her, I knew that despite my ignoble motives, I was going to do it, because she wanted me to.

The telephone again. "Hello, cross-matching . . . Yes, I have five units which will be ready in five minutes . . . Yes, that'll be fine." The single ding as she replaced the headpiece seemed unnaturally loud. "They're sending down a nurse," she said, refusing to meet my eyes.

The alarm shrilled for the last time and she gratefully turned to her racks and tubes.

She was still bent over the microscope when there was an apologetic cough at the door. I turned to see a very young nurse.

"I've come for the blood for David Brown," she said.

CHAPTER 12

"The blood for whom?" I demanded, taking a step towards her.

She backed away, startled. "David Brown."

"Where is he?"

"Intensive care, they're about to operate."

"Whatever's the matter?" cried Holly.

I turned and snatched up the form lying in front of her. "D. Brown" was scrawled in one corner.

"David Brown," I said, holding it in front of her. "It's David; didn't you realize?"

"Realize what? There must be a hundred David Browns in this region!"

"I'm coming with you," I said to the nurse.

"It's not the same one," said Holly. "It can't be. We saw him scarcely two hours—"

"It's him!" I turned to the nurse. "What happened to him?"

"Multiple fractures. They're about to operate. I must have the blood, so if you'll excuse me . . ."

"OK, it's ready now." Holly packed it into a plastic box which she handed to her. "I'll be back in a few minutes," I said to Holly.

"Tom, you can't—"

"Just a few minutes. Could you wait here?"

"I don't think you should—" began the nurse.

"It's all right, I work here. David Brown's a friend of mine." I walked out of the lab and she had little choice but to follow.

"I'll open the doors for you," I said.

We passed out of the lobby into the starry summer night.

"Can I carry that for you?" I asked.

She clutched the box tightly. "I mustn't let anyone else touch it."

We walked in a fast uneasy silence across the grass by the side of the Centre towards the entrance of the main building.

"I was with him only a couple of hours ago."

"Oh."

"I just can't understand what can have happened. Don't you have any idea?"

"I think he had a fall."

We reached the main entrance and the doors hissed open automatically. A porter looked up from the reception desk as our feet echoed in the hallway.

Down a wide, brightly lit corridor. "Here," she said, turning to where the lifts waited with doors open.

Silence as they slid shut and we ascended.

Level five. She stepped out and along a corridor, not waiting for me. A blue sign said OPERATING THEATRES—AUTHORIZED PERSONNEL ONLY. Beneath it sat Falkenham and Sergeant Bennett.

"Mr. Jones," said the former tonelessly, "what are you doing here?"

The nurse vanished between some swing doors.

"I've just heard," I said. "I was with Miss Jordan. I didn't realize until—"

"You had no business to be with Miss Jordan. You have no business here."

I sat down beside them. "I think when you hear what I have to say—"

"This intrusion is in the worst possible taste. David's wife and mother are over there."

He nodded imperceptibly towards two women I hadn't noticed before on the other side of the hall.

"I'm terribly sorry." I lowered my voice. "How is he?"

"Not good," Falkenham said in an undertone.

Bennett was twitching with impatience. "What was it you had to say?"

Falkenham shot him an irritated glance.

"It seems irrelevant now, but . . ." I hesitated.

"Well, come on."

"David Brown was part of the conspiracy."

They looked at each other for an instant, then Falkenham said, "You were right; it is an irrelevance. I think you'd better go."

"How do you know he was part of the conspiracy?" asked Bennett.

"He admitted it to me tonight at the dance. Said he would tell me about it later."

Bennett softly whistled. "Had he been drinking?"

"Quite a bit."

"Well, that might explain it."

"Explain what?"

"How he came to fall."

"Where did he fall from?" I asked innocently.

"Top of the building, just where all that scaffolding is. It broke his fall on the way down, which is why he's still—"

A sharp nudge from Falkenham stopped him.

"Accident?"

"Probably," Bennett said shortly.

"When did it happen?"

"I think that's enough questions," said Falkenham. "I can't see how it concerns you."

"Very well."

"I think you should go now."

I nodded and stood up.

Bennett said, "I'll be needing a statement from you. I'll send a car along tomorrow."

As I walked away, a stifled sob made me look up, and for an instant my eyes met those of the young woman, David's wife. Strange to think of David having a wife and mother who loved him, I thought as I hurried away; he can't have been that bad. I was already thinking of him in the past tense.

In the main corridor was a telephone booth with an internal directory.

"Cross-matching Lab," said Holly's voice.

"It's Tom. I was right; it *is* David. I'll be down in about ten minutes."

"How is he?"

"Bad. See you in ten minutes, Holly."

"Tom—"

I replaced the receiver and walked slowly down the corridor—how the hell do I find my way to the roof?

A lift opened invitingly and I stepped in. Pressed seven.

It stopped; I stepped out and looked around. Just another brightly lit corridor.

Next to the lift shaft was a door. I opened it. A narrow concrete stairway. I walked silently up. The door at the top was marked LEVEL EIGHT.

It opened into a passage, I turned left. Another door, which I opened.

I found myself in a comfortable living-room; a doctor looked up in surprise from a magazine.

"Can I help you?" A pause. "This is the on-call doctors' suite."

I thought quickly. "Is Dr. Oakes here?"

"No. I don't think I've even heard of Dr. Oakes."

"I'm sorry. Is there another suite at the end of the passage?"

"No, that leads to the roof."

"Damn," I said. "Sorry to have bothered you."

I walked quickly away before he could think of any awkward questions. Paused outside to make sure he wasn't following.

The other door bore a notice—DANGER. AUTHORIZED PERSONNEL ONLY—surely it would be locked?

I tried it. It opened and I stepped into the balmy starlit night. The moon stood over Tamar and the faint hum of traffic was carried on the light breeze.

I looked around. A builders' Portakabin gleamed in the moonlight; beside it lay some equipment and a pile of bricks.

Where would he (or they) have gone? I crossed over to the parapet and looked over. A fear of heights isn't among my repertoire, but the sheer fall made me draw quickly back. A car crawled like an insect up the winding road.

A scaffolding platform stood out from the side of the building about ten yards away. I walked towards it beside the parapet. Just before I reached it, something caught my eye. I knelt and picked it up—a filter tip.

I couldn't make out the brand name, but it was similar to the ones David smoked.

I stood up. Looked out at the wooden platform that stood like a high-diving board over a swimming pool. Something glinted in the moonlight on the boards.

I looked carefully around. Nothing, just the Portakabin. Reached the platform, looked round again. Just out and back, deep breath, now . . .

Feet knocked woodenly, space between the cracks, knelt . . .

It was a cigarette, unlit. And a box of matches. And something shining near the edge, a flask . . . ?

I didn't hear the footsteps until they reached the wooden planks and by then it was too late. I tried to rise, but a blow caught the side of my neck.

I fell semi-conscious, but was caught by two powerful arms and was bundled towards the edge. I tried desperately to dig my heels in, no good, too strong, and I toppled over the side into space.

I seemed to hang there for a moment watching the stars, then turned, fell across something that knocked the breath out of me.

Clutched at a rough edge, felt my legs falling into a hole, my feet clatter against something.

My hands clutched; my body dangled into nothingness.

Consciousness. Cling to every atom of it like you're clinging to the edge of the rubble-chute . . .

I scrabbled with my feet, no purchase, the edges of the segments were all on the outside.

My stretched fingers gave and I fell into blackness.

As I fell, I threw myself backwards, and my back crashed against the side of the tube as my legs thrust against the other side.

My body held, a credit to the army assault course I'd hated so much at the time.

Only one way to go.

Down.

I relaxed my thighs a fraction and promptly slithered three feet before my muscles succeeded in breaking the fall.

"Steady, Jones, take it steady." The voice of the instructor, my hated guardian angel.

Gently now. Another foot.

Another. I looked up. The starlit circle of sky was like a great eye watching me. Another foot.

How far down? Blackness, don't look.

I must have made ten feet before something knocked against the outside of the chute, making it shiver slightly.

Again . . . what the hell?

Another foot, then with a loud rattle, something bounced down the tube and struck me on the leg.

I fell a yard before my trembling feet bit the side again.

Another object, but this time I was ready and somehow managed to avoid it. It was a brick. He was throwing bricks down at me.

I started the descent again, my trembling thighs like jelly. Two more bricks hit the outside, and then there was silence. Had he given up?

I had just begun to hope when the ominous rattling started again. I shot up an arm, fended the brick away so that it merely glanced my knee.

Looked up, the telescoped hole was much smaller, but not small enough. More bricks hit the edge and bounced harmlessly away.

I took risks, slithering two or three feet at a time, my legs like stilts not belonging to me.

Another rattle. This time I felt the pain as it struck my outstretched hand before falling heavily against my thigh. Another one like that and I'd fall.

I thought I'd made it when, like a crackle of a distant storm, the rattling began again.

Reached up, missed, it struck my feet and I lost all purchase and fell to the skip below.

It was only ten feet and I felt no pain, only the whoosh of my breath as I landed, and then lay dreaming on a pile of rubble.

A silvery light gleamed about five feet above my head. I blinked. It was the moon, but why . . .

Gradually, it telescoped away until it hung in its rightful place among the stars.

I had no idea how long I'd been unconscious—perhaps only a minute. Better get up. My body seemed glued to the rubble . . . so easy just to lie there and watch the moon.

Got to move!

Didn't know why, just knew I had to. With an enormous effort, I slowly raised a hand and clutched the side of the skip. It hurt, but the sense of urgency was still there and I flexed my arm, my body, thrust with my legs and flipped over the side to the warm grass below.

Immediately, there was a tremendous crash. Not that heavy, am I?

Struggled to my feet to see a cloud of dust hanging over the skip. As it cleared I could make out something, something that hadn't been there before. A wheelbarrow, upside down.

I looked up but couldn't see him, only the grid-work of the scaffolding and the worm-like body of the chute.

I shook my head to clear it and started to make my way round the side of the hospital to the Centre. My body began to ache in patches at first, then as a concentrated whole. I walked more quickly to try to loosen it.

The lobby door was still open, I stepped inside and tried to brush the worst of the dust from my clothes.

Holly must have heard me; she was walking quickly towards me.

"Tom, where have you been? I tried to tell you, Adrian was down here looking for you." She came closer. "You're covered in dust—what happened to you?"

"Adrian found me," I said, without thinking.

She said something else, but I didn't hear it as the thunderclap hit me. Those strong arms—Adrian!

But I couldn't tell her the whole truth, not yet.

She was brushing my jacket.

"What happened?"

"Like I said, Adrian happened."

"He did this?"

"That's right."

"Where is he now?"

I shrugged. It hurt. "Can you give me a lift back to the hotel?"

"Of course, but I wish you'd tell me—"

"Later—all right?"

We were walking across the tarmac towards her car before she spoke again.

"So it was David. How is he?"

"I don't know. Falkenham was there; he said it was bad."

"Does his wife know?"

"She was there too." I had an image of the ravaged face again and felt a twinge of pity.

"How was she taking it?"

"As you'd expect. His mother was there too."

"Poor them. Poor David."

We reached the car. She drove silently through the almost deserted streets, locked inside her thoughts.

Something was threatening to break loose inside me; I needed her, yet couldn't tell her the truth. What was the truth?

We reached the hotel.

"Come in with me, please, just for a moment," I begged before she could say anything.

"All right."

We went in; the night porter stared at me curiously.

"Shouldn't you get cleaned up?" she whispered.

"Need a drink first." A wave of pain stroked my head. "Maybe not. Lift's over here."

As we ascended, she said quietly, "What happened, Tom?"

"Christ, my head!" It wasn't all bluff; a scalpel blade seemed to be criss-crossing my scalp.

I raised a hand, my left. The loosened bandage was soaked in blood from the re-opened cuts.

Blood. David had needed blood; what had he looked like?

A strangled cry came from somewhere; I realized it was me.

"God, Holly, I can't stand it!"

"Shh." She put an arm round me. "Try to hold on, just till we get to your room. What number is it?"

I groped for the key. The lift opened. I shuffled out and along the corridor, my mind frozen. She got me into the room, led me to the bed and then shut the door.

"What did he do to you, Tom? You weren't fighting over me, surely?"

"My head. I can't think."

She opened her handbag. "First," she said, "you take a couple of these."

"What are they?"

"Painkillers, strong ones."

"Why do you need painkillers?" I asked groggily.

"Why d'you think? I'm a woman, aren't I?"

"I couldn't forget."

"Very gallant, I'm sure. Open your mouth."

Two oblong shapes touched my tongue; she filled a glass with water and held it to my lips.

"Now we must do something about that hand."

She took it in hers and gently started peeling the loose bandage away. I watched her face. She was right; she was all woman.

"Holly, you must be wondering . . ." I began matter-of-factly.

"Shh. Can you come over to the basin?"

I looked down then. It was all clotted and matted and covered the skin, yet it was shiny too—

A sob rose inside me and splashed around us.

"It's not that bad," she said, leading me to the basin.

My brother, my poor brother, I thought, oblivious of her. Why didn't I suffer as he did; why didn't I just bleed and bleed until—

"Don't think about it," she said, bathing my hand, and I realized I'd been thinking aloud.

"Can't help it, not after tonight."

Several things suddenly became very clear to me.

"If I don't get it out tonight, Holly, I never will." Our eyes met in the mirror above the basin.

"Go on."

"I've managed to keep Frank out of my mind for years, but now, David's brought it all back—"

"Frank's your brother?"

"I know it's selfish after what's happened to David, but this is my one chance. Please."

"All right." She led me back to the bed. "I need something to bind this with."

"In films, women tear up their petticoats."

"I'm not wearing one."

"You'll have to use your knickers, then." Knowing I was going to tell made me light-headed.

"I'll use yours," she said, getting up and pulling open a drawer. "A shirt, better still. And a bottle of whisky. It'll do for disinfectant."

She brought it over, soaked her handkerchief and applied it to the cuts. It stung. While she tore my shirt into strips, I filled the toothglass and drained it.

"Not too much on top of those painkillers." She shook her head helplessly as I filled it again.

"Hold out your hand," she said, and began expertly to dress it.

Silence, while I searched for the words I wanted to say. I thought: How could I ever have desired her? She's like the sister I always wanted, the sister to whom I could tell everything.

"What is it you want to tell me?" she said telepathically.

"About my brother," I said tonelessly, and our lives together flashed by like a video, like a floppy disc with pictures.

"You love your parents, don't you?" I demanded.

"Naturally, I—"

"I hated mine. They're dead now."

"That's horrible."

"I ran away and joined the Army," I said as if in a dream. "The Social Services decided to let me stay when they found out . . ." I trailed off as the whisky fumes reached my head.

"Found out what?"

"I did love my brother," I said after a pause. "We both tried, but as we grew older, the resentment and jealousy grew faster."

"You were jealous because he got all the attention?"

"Yes. And he was jealous too. Oh, that's obvious." I looked up. "We kept sparking each other off—we somehow depended on each other, but the dependence grew more and more destructive." The flashing pictures coalesced and for an instant he stood there in front of me.

"We had to share a bedroom—small house—and I used to go up to study. I was doing A-levels. Anyway, I'd been up there for about an hour when he burst in. He had every right to come in, of course, but this was different—you could see the fire streaming from his nostrils. 'What are you doing?' he said.

" 'What does it look like?' Then more reasonably, 'Nothing on the telly, then?'

" 'Oh yeah, Duke of Edinburgh's Award, how to get it. If you're normal, that is.'

"I saw his eyes dart to my sheath-knife. I wasn't supposed to have it. I used it to sharpen my pencils while studying; it was a kind of talisman. 'You don't know how lucky you are,' he flared, and before I could stop him he grabbed it, waved it about. 'I'm not allowed to have one of these.' 'Makes two of us,' I said carefully. I could see the cogs turning over in his mind. 'I think I'll keep it,' he said. 'Oh no you don't!' I sprang up. 'Keep away from me or I'll cut myself—' He pulled up a sleeve and waved the knife at his wrist. I thought: If he gets away with this, life won't be worth living. 'I'll kill myself,' he yelled as I made a grab at him, 'I will, I *will*— I warned you'—and he sort of drew it across his skin.

"It was very sharp and he bled, just drops at first; then they joined up, and he screamed 'Get away from me' and made a sort of chop at his wrist and really bled. Footsteps crashing up the stairs, I lunged, got the knife; he screamed and started bashing my head; the door flew open.

"It was Dad, he pulled us apart, saw Frank covered in blood and the knife in my hand, and hit me. I went down and he put the boot in and I blacked out.

"They took Frankie to hospital. Next day I didn't go to school, went to the nearest recruitment office and signed on. If he'd just said sorry, but he didn't, so I signed on. Later, the Social said I'd better stay in the Army if I was happy there, so—"

"Please," she said, "please let go of my hand. You're hurting."

I became aware of her fingers crushed together and released them. I'd had no idea that I'd taken her hand.

"I don't know what to say," she said at last, "except that I understand."

Without warning I burst into tears, tears that welled like acid burning my cheeks, I buried my face in her breast and felt the material stick to my cheek as she caressed my neck.

"Poor Tom, let it come," she said.

At last, with shallow breaths, it subsided.

"Have you never told anyone else this?"

"No."

"Not even your wife?"

I shook my head.

"D'you feel better for telling me?"

I nodded.

"Is there more?"

For perhaps half an hour I told her everything I could remember. I drank more whisky, yet felt better all the time, as though each word was a grain of sand draining away from a sack on my shoulders.

At last I wound down like a tired gramophone; my eyes closed and I fell back on to the bed.

I was dimly aware that she was undressing me. I didn't mind. She'd seen my soul, why not my body?

"Go to sleep, Tom."

"Stay with me."

The last thing I remember was her kissing me.

But not quite the last thing, because I had a very strange dream.

I dreamt that I was wide awake and holding her very tight, kissing her over and over. She took off her clothes and slipped in beside me.

Her skin was like the smoothest satin I ever felt, and inside a thousand tiny movements made me feel that all of me was touching all of her at the same time . . . her face watched me serenely . . . Dreaming and waking, which is which?

CHAPTER 13

They didn't come for me until mid-afternoon, which was fine as I'd been nursing a vicious headache since waking just after one.

The silent policeman skilfully piloted the unmarked Metro through the Saturday traffic and about fifteen minutes later I found myself outside Bennett's office again. I could see his musteline features as he pointed an aggressive finger at someone just out of sight.

Then he saw me and beckoned. When I saw who he was talking to, I forgot my headache for a moment.

"Marcus!"

"Hello, Tom. Thought I'd come and give you a lift back."

"Thanks," I said, as in a dream. "Thanks very much."

"You're looking a bit peaky. Are you all right?"

"Vile headache, that's all." I became aware of Bennett, who was staring at us.

Marcus said, "Taken anything for it? I've got some paracetamol—"

Bennett found his voice. "When you've quite finished . . . No, sorry, but could we *please* come to the business in hand?"

David had died on the operating table, and Bennett had spent the morning taking statements from those who had last seen him. Mine was the last.

"Why didn't you report the attack made on you last Tuesday in the Centre earlier?" he demanded when I had finished.

"I'm sorry; it didn't seem to be important at the time."

"Wanted to sort it out on your own, I suppose."

I thought tiredly: Wait till he hears about last night.

"You mention Adrian Hodges in your statement; he doesn't seem to like you much either. Claims you assaulted him after intimidating David Brown. What makes you suspect him?"

Headache or no headache, now was the time I had to show my reasoning as lucidly as possible, for Marcus's sake as much as anything.

I took a breath and slowly let it out.

"I suspected him almost from the moment I arrived, because he is more or less in sole charge of the storage and issue of all blood. It *had* to be him. If he were innocent, nobody could steal blood *without* his knowing."

"Motive?"

"I don't know," I said slowly. "He seems to hold a grudge against most people, me particularly—"

"Are you sure you're not prejudiced?"

"No, I'm not sure," I said coldly, "which is why all the evidence I have gathered is based on statistical analyses . . . may I go on?"

He gave a short nod.

"The system for storage, issue and retrieval of blood here is computerized, and therefore assumed to be infallible, and yet Marcus has shown, statistically, that Tamar Centre uses more blood than it should. That's why I looked very hard at the system. It's riddled with loopholes. For instance . . ." I told them how the fate of a pack of blood was completely unknown once it was issued.

"My first idea was that Adrian was over-issuing blood to an accomplice in a hospital, who sent it back at night for Hill to sort out and dispatch. Then I thought: Why have an accomplice; why not just issue it to St. Dennis's or wherever, but in reality, keep it back for Hill?"

"Is this what you think happened?"

"I don't know, it would be very difficult to prove."

Bennett groaned.

"Wait a minute." I swallowed. "We've assumed from the beginning that *blood* was being stolen, especially after Marcus found out about the Swiss firm and 'Red Gold.' " I explained these to Bennett. "But there is still the difficulty of its limited life. *Plasma,* however, is a very different matter." I told them about returned blood and the Time-expired plasma that should be harvested from it.

Marcus sat up. "West London," he said.

"Exactly."

"I wonder if they know about each other."

"Unlikely, but we'll never know—"

"Just what are you talking about?" demanded Bennett.

Marcus explained the West London conspiracy to him.

"Why didn't we think of it before?" he said to me. "It's practically identical."

Bennett said, "Can you prove this one?"

"Yes, I can." I told him of my discoveries in the Centre and the computer unit.

I turned to Marcus. "You're wrong on two counts about these cases being identical." I ticked them off on my fingers. "So far, this operation is peanuts compared with West London. What was it you told me they made? £150,000? This one can't have made a tenth of that. A fiftieth, maybe. Except that they didn't stop there."

I had their full attention now.

"The amount of plasma they could take was always limited by the number of bags returned, which was decreasing anyway. So they found another source.

"More than half of the blood that comes to the Centre has the *fresh* plasma taken off, that's about two hundred donations a day. It's then quick-frozen and sent to CPPL. Yesterday I worked out from the computer records all the totals of Fresh Frozen Plasma sent to CPPL by Tamar, then I compared these with the figures you sent me, Marcus, CPPL's records of plasma *received* from Tamar. And guess what?"

"There's a discrepancy?"

"Right. It's another loophole. The Centre's computer knows how much plasma has been separated, and CPPL knows how much plasma they receive, but ne'er the twain shall meet. Although I expect they will after this."

"But what on earth did they want *fresh* plasma for?" demanded Marcus.

"That's what puzzled me at first. You see, the only use for fresh plasma is making Factor VIII for haemophiliacs . . ." I swallowed and continued. "The fact is, they didn't care whether it was fresh or not, so long as it was plasma. Perhaps the people they were supplying wanted more, perhaps they were just greedy—I don't know.

"Anyway, I've worked out some figures. They were probably taking about two hundred units of expired plasma a month. They're worth about a pound each on the black market, maybe one-fifty, that's not much between three, or even two, people. But once they got the idea of taking fresh plasma, it took them up to, say, two hundred or so a week. That's a bit more like it, but—"

"But still not that much," said Marcus, "even tax-free."

"That was the other thing I found so puzzling at first," I continued. "When we found out that Leigh had been killed, I was sure there was big money involved—must be if it was worth killing for—"

"That's right!" cried Bennett, who had been listening intently. "But don't you see, it all fits now."

"How?" said Marcus, frowning.

"All this time we've been assuming that Hill killed Leigh, and wondering why. Well, in David Brown we have a young man who by all accounts was neurotic, unstable, in debt and couldn't cope with his life or job. Those peanuts must have come in very handy for him, but then he's caught. And who by? His old boss, who could see immediately that he was up to no good." The weasel leaned forward, poised for the kill. "But he's neurotic, unbalanced, and this pushes him over the edge. Don't you see? *He* killed Mike Leigh!

"He can't run, so he stays and pretends that everything's normal. Then you turn up, Mr. Jones; he somehow guesses who you are, which makes him even more unstable."

"That's right!" cried Marcus. "One minute he wants to confess to you, the next, he belts you over the head."

"You were lucky it wasn't worse," said Bennett.

I touched the bruise on my scalp and wondered.

"And then," he continued, "he realizes you're going to get him anyway and he can't face it; he cracks up. Has a skinful of drink and goes up to the roof." He gave a Gallic shrug. "Who knows why? Perhaps he went there to think things out and fell by accident. Or realized it was the end, and jumped, who knows? Let's say the former, for the sake of his family."

After a short silence I said carefully, "That's good thinking, but where's Hill?"

"Perhaps Brown killed Hill as well," suggested Marcus.

"It would fit," said Bennett slowly. "If a person's missing for more than a week, they're usually dead. Perhaps he had time to get rid of one body but not the other."

Marcus was nodding in agreement; they had the case wrapped up between them and the moment I'd been dreading had arrived.

"There's something else," I said.

Bennett fumed like a pressure-cooker, as I told them about the previous night.

"You were told not to interfere," he said with the calmness of impotent fury.

"David's fall was just too damned convenient; that's why I went. So who pushed me, and more to the point, why?"

Another silence.

"Who do *you* think pushed you?" said Bennett.

"Adrian Hodges."

"Why? Oh, you still think he's part of the blood conspiracy?"

"That's right."

"Wait," said Marcus. "Isn't he the one who loathes you anyway, because of that girl?"

"What girl?" demanded Bennett.

I told him briefly about Holly.

"There's your answer," said Marcus.

I gazed at him blankly.

"Jealousy. He's so eaten up with it, especially after you tenderized his balls and walked off with his girl, that he followed you down from the disco. We know he was looking for you and that Holly told him where you were. What was to stop him following you up and shoving you off the roof on impulse?"

"Nothing, Marcus, nothing!" I cried impatiently. "He pushed me, but not because of Holly—"

"You think he pushed David?"

"Yes."

"When? From your account, you were both squabbling over Holly at the time David fell."

He had a point. I put my head in my hands and tried to think, but it hurt too much.

"I'll have Hodges back this evening and question him," said Bennett, "but it sounds like good reasoning to me."

I looked up and their faces told me they thought it was all over.

"There's got to be more to it than that," I said tiredly, more to myself than to them.

The pain in my head had eased by the time we started back for London in Marcus's Rover. Bennett hadn't attempted to chew up my neck, but this was probably because he thought he had seen the last of me. I'd had every intention of disappointing him until half an hour later, when I couldn't have cared less.

Marcus hadn't said much and I was watching the sun settle on the edge of the moor and thinking about Holly, when at last he spoke.

"Tom, I came down because I have something to tell you."

I stiffened. "What?"

He hesitated. "Your brother."

Something inside turned over. "What d'you know about my brother?"

"He's ill."

My tongue touched my lips. "How do you know?"

"The Social Services have been trying to find you. They eventually got on to me."

"What's the matter with him?"

"I'm not quite sure," he lied, "but I think it's pretty bad."

He hadn't so much as glanced at me, yet I knew he was lying.

"What's the matter with him?" I repeated.

"He's in St. Mary's, Paddington." A pause. "They say he has AIDS. You know what that is, don't you?"

"Who doesn't?" I shouted. "It's smeared over the bloody Press every day. Well, whatever else he is, he's not a bloody queer."

"I didn't say he was," Marcus said quietly. "He's a haemophiliac."

"How do you know that?" I demanded.

"I've known for some time. It's my business to—"

"So you've been playing games with me. 'Oh, I can't imagine why you're so scared of blood,'" I mimicked.

"If you don't shut up, I'll stop the car and chuck you out."

"You do that."

He braked so hard that I was flung forward against the safety strap of the seat-belt.

He turned and faced me. His lips were white. "Before you go," he said slowly, and my inner respect for him made me pause. "Before you go, I want you to know that it's not your contempt for me that makes me so angry; it's your contempt for your brother."

"You think I feel contempt for him?"

"You haven't said, 'How is he?' or 'Is he in pain' or 'Will he live?' None of them. Not once."

"You don't understand."

"No, I don't. Get out."

I might have gone then, gone out of his life forever, and maybe out of mine before the night was through. But I didn't. For some reason I wanted to make him understand.

But what could I say, other than sorry? And that would be backing down and Tom Jones don't back down, not for no one.

"Well, are you going?" His face was a white mask.

"I want to try and make you understand—"

"Not a hope!"

"I'm . . . I'm sorry." I pushed the door open and swung out a leg into the warm evening air. He caught my arm.

"I never thought I'd hear you say that."

I faced him. "Well, I mean it. You're right and I'm sorry, and if you'll excuse me I'll go now."

He released my arm.

"OK," he said, and then released his own seat-belt. "I'll come with you. It's a lovely evening and perhaps the air will bring some sense between us. I'm sorry, too, Tom."

We walked in silence up a small stony path towards some ponies grazing on the skyline. They looked up then, as one skittered away over the horizon.

"I always wanted to ride, as a boy," said Marcus.

"Is he in pain? Will he live?"

"I don't know; that's something you must find out. And you must do it, Tom," he added. "For your own sake."

The last chord of the sun vanished beneath the inky black skyline and a chill struck the air.

I turned to Marcus. "Why didn't he contact me himself?"

"Why haven't you contacted him all these years? He was afraid you wouldn't care."

"I do care."

"He didn't know that. Did you really hate your father that much?"

"Yes." I stopped, turned on him in something like desperation. "You *don't* understand; you don't know what it was like."

"Tell me."

"He—he—" I swallowed. "He blamed me for Frank. He somehow twisted things round so that it was my fault."

Marcus slowly resumed walking. "Sure you didn't blame him?"

"Well, it *was* his fault, both of them. They knew the risks—it could have been me that was the haemophiliac. It wasn't, but they bloody well had to go on and have one that was. And then he blamed me. *Me!*"

"How do you know that?"

"He kept hitting me, didn't he? Every time poor Frankie had a bleed he thought I'd done it. 'You've-got-to-bloody-well-learn,' " I grated between my teeth. "That's what he always said as he hit me. 'You've-got-to-bloody-well-learn' again and again and . . . at last I couldn't stand it, not after the last time. That's why I buggered off into the Army."

We walked in silence for a while.

Marcus said, "Did you resent him? Your brother?"

"Yes! Yes, of course I did. I knew he was sick, but everything had to revolve around him. All the time."

"And did you take it out on him?"

"No," I mumbled at the rugged pathway. "At least, I didn't mean to."

"I believe you."

Shoes crunching on stones.

Marcus said, "You will go and see him, won't you?"

"Yes," I muttered.

"Good man." There was real warmth in his voice as we topped the horizon; we saw the sun again, a last chord, a lost chord as we stood in silence and watched it disappear.

"It's not every day you see the sun set twice," said Marcus.

A few minutes later, we started back.

Getting out of a car at the end of a journey is like climbing out of a bath you should have left ten minutes ago. The unreality pressed against my eyes and scalp as the sodium-lit pavement pressed up against my feet.

"Would you like me to come up for a spell?" said Marcus.

"No, it's all right, thanks."

"OK then." He couldn't quite keep the relief out of his voice; he was very tired. "Oh, don't forget your case."

I hauled it from the back seat and stood for a moment, hand on the open door. "See you Monday, then." And then: "Thanks, Marcus."

He waved a hand dismissively. "Take a couple of days off, I'll see you Wednesday. Oh, and good luck tomorrow."

The air in the flat wasn't damp or musty, yet it held the staleness that comes from stillness. I dropped my case on the bed, turned the immersion heater to Full and then threw open some windows. The curtains billowed like parachutes and I shivered slightly in the night breeze as I unpacked my case. Then to the living-room where I poured a large whisky, sipping it as I skimmed through the mail. Bills, bank statement, and a letter from one of my nouveaux country-house friends inviting me to stay for a few days.

Closed all the windows and then bathed with some difficulty, trying to keep my bandaged hand dry. Then another whisky, this time with a rare cigar.

Thinking about him was unbearable, yet I couldn't stop. Every line of thought seemed to lead back to him, back to tomorrow.

Getting unfit, I thought, coughing slightly on the cigar, need some exercise. Can't go to the gym, not with this hand, I'll have a run in the park tomorrow, after . . . after . . .

After seeing my brother.

More whisky. Scared of not sleeping.

I didn't give Holly or the Centre a thought until I was lying in bed and the pain in my hand reminded me. Sod them, I thought, sod all of them if that's what they want to think. Except Holly. No, I didn't include Holly.

CHAPTER 14

There's something about trains, any train, that plays on your anxieties like piano-wires, perhaps because no matter how often it stops, it's going to get there.

It was at Baker Street I came nearest to running away, after that came a kind of dull acceptance . . . *Marylebone.*

I don't have to see him, even if I get as far as the hospital . . . *Edgware Road.*

But I am going to see him—do I still blame him for Dad, for me? . . . *Paddington.*

The escalator drew me into the half-world of Paddington Station . . . along platform eight . . . hurry, hurry! Up the stairs and across the gangway . . . under the motorway and through the trees and there it is . . .

The hospital where princesses have their babies . . . and my brother lay dying.

The yawning entrance bade me in . . . the ward, the smell of the infirm . . .

"Can I help you?"

"I've come to see my brother."

"It's not visiting time, you know." She was petite—heart-shaped face and black stockings. "It's rather awkward just now, you should have phoned . . ."

"I'm sorry," I said. "This is my only chance . . ." I swallowed. "The only chance . . . I'm sorry."

"What's his name?"

"Francis Jones."

"Oh." The syllable said all. "He's in a side room. All right, I'll go and see."

I followed her down the aisle between the beds, white headboards like gravestones, the glitter of an eye following us the only sign of life.

"Wait here a moment," she said, and disappeared inside a door.

Voices, scarcely audible above the hammering at my chest and temples.

"You can go in for ten minutes." She hesitated. "You'd better not touch him." Her heels clacked back along the ward.

He was lying propped against the pillows, eyes burning in a burnt-out face. He didn't speak. His pyjamas were blue and white striped and hung loosely around him. One side of his face was stained with a livid red mark and a crusted sore spread from a corner of his mouth. He used to look like me, but I wouldn't have known him now, except for the eyes.

"Hello, Tom." The voice was husky and he cleared his throat.

" 'Lo, Frank." His dark hair was greasy and speckled with dandruff. "How are you feeling?" I sat beside him.

"Well, at least you didn't ask me how I was. The answer to both is bloody awful."

"I'm sorry. And I'm sorry I haven't been earlier; been away on a job. Only heard about you last night."

"Where have you been?"

"Devon."

"Oh." He smiled. "Glorious Devon. Still, I won't be seeing it again. Why d'you think they call it Glorious?"

"I don't know."

"Neither do I. Have they told you what's wrong with me?"

I nodded.

There was a small silence while his lips twitched; then he burst out, "It's the bloody stigma that gets me. It's bad enough feeling so ill, but the looks some people give me, as though I somehow deserve it. D'you know" —he shifted slightly— "I asked one of the doctors the other day to get me a notice, big black and white letters that say, 'I'm a haemo, not a homo.' Pretty good, eh?"

We both laughed and the years fell away until his mirth turned into a fit of coughing. Without thinking, I put a hand on his arm and patted his back.

"Hey," he said between coughs, "you're not supposed to touch me, remember?"

"I don't care, Frankie." I gripped his arm and my forehead touched his shoulder. "I don't care."

I felt his hand on my shoulder, grip and gently push me away. "Hey," he said again, "I don't want you to catch this thing."

His eyes told me that he meant it and I wanted to touch him more than ever.

"Devon," he continued conversationally, "I don't think I've been there since that holiday we had. D'you remember?" He smiled inwardly.

"I remember you swimming like a fish."

"It was the only thing I could do without bloody well bleeding."

"Even then you managed to hit your nose on a rock."

"So I did." He looked up. "What have you been doing down there?"

I told him, and he smiled rather mirthlessly.

"Funny to think that blood could be worth pinching. Perhaps not, though." He reached down and fumbled in his bedside cabinet. "This is a shot of Factor VIII." He held up a little bottle with some freeze-dried powder in the bottom. "It costs anything between thirty and sixty pounds, or so I'm told." He sighed. "I suppose it gave me some years of freedom, even though it gave me this disease in the end." His eyes hardened. "You might ask your pals down there why they never get around to making more of it in this country."

"I won't be going back."

"We boast about being a caring nation," he continued, as though I hadn't spoken, "welfare and all that. So what do we do? Three million or so unemployed, yet we buy in two-thirds of our Factor VIII from America instead of making it ourselves." I fleetingly wondered whether to try to stop him, then thought it might be better to let him get it out of his system. "America, where the main force in medicine is profit and the main growth industry is homosexuality. Did you know that when I inject myself with Factor VIII, I'm injecting material from over a thousand people? It only takes one of them to have AIDS; it only takes one virus to give it to me—"

He broke off and stared at me, his mouth open.

"D'you realize that's the first time either of us has said it? AIDS, I mean. It's like cancer, isn't it? The evil eye, if you so much as mention it, tantamount to a death sentence—" He stopped again.

"There, I've said that too, the other taboo word."

"Don't talk about it as though it were a certainty."

"Well, it is, isn't it?"

"No."

He hesitated. Then: "It's all right for you; you can say that, can't you? I'm the one who's—"

"It's not all right for me."

A longer pause. "No. You've always felt guilty about me, haven't you?"

"Pretty resentful sometimes."

He shrugged. "One always resents feeling guilty."

"You've become a philosopher."

"You have to be, in my position—"

There was a tap at the door and the sister looked in. "I think that had better be all for today, Mr. Jones." She tactfully withdrew.

"Don't philosophize," I said, "hope."

"Oh, come on—"

"Hope," I said, standing up. "I'll be back tomorrow."

The sister sat in the office at the other end of the ward with a harassed-looking young man in a white coat. She looked up.

"Thanks for letting me see him," I said.

"That's all right."

I hesitated. "I was wondering whether I could speak to a doctor about him." I glanced meaningfully at the white-coated figure who was still scribbling busily at the desk.

"Well, Dr. Day is rather busy at the moment . . ."

"Yes," said the man, not looking up. "At the moment Dr. Day is even more overworked and underpaid than usual."

"This gentleman's the brother of Francis Jones, the AIDS patient, Doctor."

"Oh." I found myself looking into a pair of round blue eyes beneath tousled fair hair. "Oh, all right. Be with you in a sec. Sit down."

He scratched at a few more forms, then put his pen away.

"Right," he said briskly. "If you could take care of these, Sister, I'll take . . . uh . . . Mr. Jones over to the examining room."

I followed him across the corridor into a room with a bed and a glass-topped trolley covered with instruments.

He shut the door. "Forgive me for being cloak and dagger, but I'd rather the patients didn't hear us." He cleared his throat. "Well, now, your brother. I take it you know what's wrong with him?" The blue eyes met mine and I nodded.

"Is it true?" I said quickly. "That there's no cure for it, I mean?"

"At the moment, I'm afraid so. But there is treatment, and the longer he survives, the better his chances."

"How long will he survive?"

"There's no way of telling. Some die quite quickly, although I'm sure your brother won't. Two chaps in America have had the disease for some years, and actually seem to be getting better—"

"Could that happen with Frank?"

"As I said, there's no way of telling. There are so many factors . . . Do you know anything about the mechanism of the disease?"

"Only what's in the papers."

"Ah. Well, it might help . . ." He pondered for a moment. "AIDS is an acronym, and a bad one in my opinion, for Acquired Immune Deficiency Syndrome. What the patient actually acquires is a virus—your brother got it from a Factor VIII preparation—which specifically infects and destroys white blood cells called lymphocytes. Without these cells, the immune system stops working, and the patient becomes susceptible to the kind of trivial infection that wouldn't bother you or me. Can you follow that?"

"Like a cold, you mean? Is that what he's got?"

"That sort of thing, yes. He's actually recovering from a rare form of pneumonia that wouldn't begin to harm either of us. It's under control with antibiotics at the moment; he'd be dead but for that."

"So he could go on getting these infections?"

"I'm afraid so."

"What are the marks on his face?"

"The lesion on his mouth is Herpes, the other . . ." He hesitated. "The other is a type of skin cancer called Kaposi's Sarcoma that a lot of AIDS sufferers get."

"Cancer!" I swallowed. "Don't these . . . lymph things ever come back?"

He shrugged expressively. "Nobody knows. There are drugs which boost their growth and seem to help for a short while, but unfortunately it doesn't last."

I thought quickly. "Doctor, I'm a computer systems designer and my last job was in a Blood Transfusion Centre. If these lymph cells are in the blood, wouldn't a blood transfusion help?"

He smiled. "That's good thinking, Mr. Jones. Again, unfortunately, lymphocytes don't survive for very long in a pack of blood; although having said that, it can help for a short time. Another approach might be a bone-marrow transplant, if we could find a suitable donor."

"Would I be a suitable donor?" Another part of me heard this and looked on in amazement.

"You could be, yes. But your brother's condition isn't critical yet; it might be best to keep you in reserve, so to speak."

I started to say something, but he held up his hand.

"The best thing you can do for the present, Mr. Jones, is to visit him as often as you can. It's amazing how big a part the will to live can play; it seems to be the force behind the two men still alive in America. I'm told that one of them practises some kind of meditation in which he imagines that his lymphocytes are rabbits that are busily multiplying." He shrugged. "It seems that his lymphocytes *are* increasing, and I've got no explanation for it. Look, I hate to sound like Mr. Micawber, but if he can stay alive, something'll turn up." He began edging towards the door, anxious to get back to his forms.

I said, "I really want to do something to help him."

He paused, pursed his lips, then looked up. "I'll tell you what, I'll speak to the consultant immunologist and tell her about your offer. She's in a much better position that I am to know whether it could help." He glanced at his watch. "I'm sorry, but I really must be going now. I expect you'll be in again soon, won't you?"

"Tomorrow."

"I'll arrange for the sister to take a sample of your blood for tissue-typing. And now if you'll excuse me." He held the door open and followed me out.

As the Bakerloo train rattled south, little pieces started falling away from the mass clogging my brain.

I knew I could help Frank, and not just by being there giving him the will to live.

The stuff inside me, my blood—even thinking it made me quail—yes, that's what would save him; the very perversity of it made sense.

But I needed advice.

My own doctor? No—he hardly knew me. The answer was obvious—Chalgrove, who'd actually worked at St. Mary's.

What I needed was an excuse for going back to Tamar.

As soon as I got back to the flat, I sat down with a pencil.

David. He'd been stealing plasma and had phoned me, hoping a confession would get him some sort of immunity.

But David a killer?

Possible—just. An unstable neurotic might be pushed over the edge by being caught in the act by his old boss.

Suicide? But if David had killed Leigh and then himself, *where was Hill?* Also killed by David? Bodies aren't that easy to hide.

Suicide? Surely not. David had liked himself too much.

Perhaps Hill *had* killed Leigh. But in that case, who pushed David? *And who pushed me?*

Adrian? He had two motives—Holly and my silence. He was still the most likely.

Back to the only fact I knew, that David had been stealing plasma. Had he thought of it himself?

Unlikely—not clever enough. Master-mind behind the scenes?

Surely not for £5,000, which was about all the operation could have made.

And yet Leigh's killing made no sense unless big money was involved. Unless it was a crime of panic.

OK, assume panic, then it had to be either Hill or David.

If it was Hill, what happened to David?

If it was David, where was Hill?

Round in circles. Yes, back to the beginning—there was another fact I'd overlooked: David had phoned me, yet it hadn't been him in the washing-up room. No—I shivered as I remembered those powerful legs kicking me—no, that hadn't been David.

I went out for a walk, hoping the exercise would shake the facts into a pattern. It didn't.

I went back to the flat, and on impulse rang Holly.

"Tom! How are you?"

"Fine. I wanted to thank you for . . . for last Friday."

"Oh, that's all right. I only hope . . ." she trailed off.

I said, "How would you like to give me a guided tour of Dartmoor?"
She laughed. "That would take months."

"I'll settle for an afternoon."

"It would be lovely, but when? I mean . . . ?"

"I've got to come back to the Centre next week to finish off what I was doing." Silence. "Holly?"

"I don't think that's a very good idea, Tom," she said quietly.

"But you sounded pleased just now—"

"Not next week, not so soon after David."

"I see what you mean," I said slowly, "but there may be no choice."

"Tom, it would be lovely to see you again, but not this way, please."

"I'll see what I can do," I lied.

"At least leave it until after the funeral."

"When is that?"

"We don't know; there'll have to be an inquest."

The happiness that had been in her voice was gone now, and after a few more sentences we rang off.

I felt sad, then suddenly angry. What a stupid way to break a friendship, but I had no choice.

I dug out and played the only classical record I possess, Stravinsky's *Rite of Spring*, and played it over and over until its violence drained away a little of mine.

I knew I wouldn't sleep, so in the evening I ran in the park, round and round until it got dark and my thighs ached and my hand throbbed. Back to the flat. Whisky.

Bed, where perversely I slept immediately and wished I hadn't. The night was wretched with dreams in which Frank kept changing into an undead David who chased me around the endless corridors of the Centre. A door opened and Holly beckoned, but just as I reached it, she slammed it in my face.

CHAPTER 15

It might have been a year ago, or yesterday, or perhaps just a parsec away; whichever it was, the feeling of being trapped in a time-warp was overwhelming as I emerged from the station into the brilliant sunshine of Tamar. The same sunlight scattered over the same bleached buildings, the same taxi-driver taking me to the same hotel, and it was with a shock that I realized that they hadn't given me the same room.

From this point, however, resemblance ended. I found a friendly local and sat back with a pint and toasted sandwich amid the clink and chatter of the lunch-time drinkers.

Today was Thursday.

On Monday I'd written up a full report recommending further investigation, and dropped it into the office for typing on the way to the hospital.

Frank was difficult—inevitable perhaps after the high of our reunion. When he heard my plan, he accused me of being patronizing and of trying to give him false hope. Haltingly at first, I told him of my phobia and its cause, which was the best thing I could have done, since it somehow brought us back on a level.

He said, "I think it was Dad who should have seen the shrink."

On Tuesday Marcus read my report, patted me on the head and said no further action was necessary.

We argued, and he told me that Bennett had been in touch with him.

"He can't shake Adrian Hodge's story, and he's going to close the case whatever we think."

I grew stubborn and he lost his temper.

"Look, you've done your bit; it's over, *finito!* If you go back now, you'll rile Falkenham and Bennett so much they'll go over my head to Sir, who'll conclude that we're more trouble than we're worth and close us down. Let's quit while we're ahead, Tom."

"All right, Marcus! You've got my report and we both know that there's something going on down there that stinks. What if it comes out *after* you've given the place the all-clear?"

He groaned and put his head in his hands and I knew I'd won.

It was fascinating listening to him a few minutes later trying to persuade Falkenham to have me back. He should have been a lawyer.

It seemed that David's body had been released on Monday for burial, and the funeral was tomorrow, Wednesday, so Falkenham reluctantly agreed for me to return on Thursday for two days.

Which brought me to where I was now, sitting in the pub with my second pint, wondering what my reception would be like. With a sigh I finished it, resisted the temptation to a third and walked out to the bus stop.

Fifteen minutes later I was toiling up the hill towards the hospital. It shimmered in the heat like a palace, and the first bead of honest sweat had begun to trickle when a car pulled up beside me.

"Tom!" cried Holly, throwing open the door. I climbed in beside her, leaned over and kissed the side of her mouth.

"Not here!" she giggled, drawing back. "Pooh! You've been drinking."

"Is it that bad?"

" 'Fraid so." She pushed the car into gear and let in the clutch. "I'd lend you a peppermint if I had any."

She smelt gorgeous and her body shone through her dress.

"Only lend, Holly?"

"Certainly. It's time you realized the value of things."

"You sound like a schoolteacher I once had."

"Oh, thanks."

"I use the word advisedly."

"I'll lend you a coffee when we get in if you like. What word?"

"Had."

"You *have* been drinking, haven't you? I think coffee's a must."

She parked the car and we walked in companionable silence across the tarmac to the darkened lobby of the Centre. As we were swallowed by its shadows, its sombreness seemed to reach into her. She stopped and put a hand on my arm.

"Tom, why have you come back?"

"To see you, gorgeous."

"No, really."

"Come and have a drink with me tonight and I'll tell you."

She smiled wanly. "I seem to have been here before."

"Let's say about eight. Same hotel."

"Oh, all right." She pushed the dark glass of the door and stepped inside.

As we rounded the corner into the main corridor, a figure emerged from the Blood Bank, nearly bumping into me. It was Trefor. As he recognized me, he face registered three, maybe four, emotions within the space of a second.

"Tom," he said colourlessly. "So you've come back."

"Hello, Trefor."

He forced a smile. "We'd better go to my office."

"See you later," I called to Holly.

As I followed his white-coated back, my mind followed the cascade of his expressions—surprise, anger, and then a resigned acceptance.

But between the last two, there had been something else. In the flicker of an eyelid, I had caught . . . fear.

So what was he afraid of?

He pulled his office door shut, in control of himself now.

"Why have you come back?" he demanded.

"To finish the job I started."

"You had finished."

"No, I—"

"You *had* finished, by God! The Director told me what your real job was. You've driven poor David to killing himself, isn't that enough?"

"That's hardly fair, Trefor, I—"

"Tell his wife that. It's *finished*, I tell you." With a crash he brought his fist down on the metal filing cabinet. "You're nothing but a ruthless, callous opportunist, Jones, and by God you'll get no help from me."

He was about to say more, but I cut in coldly.

"With or without your help, Trefor, I'm going to finish this job, so you'd better get used to it."

He stared at me open-mouthed, and something seemed to fall away from him.

"Sorry, I didn't mean that," he mumbled, "I suppose you're only—"

"I'll speak to you later, Trefor," I said, and left him before he could argue. Perhaps I should have put him under pressure then, but I wanted to see Chalgrove.

I knocked on his door and pushed it open without waiting for a reply.

He looked up from his writing, an eyebrow characteristically raised.

"Oh. What can I do for you?"

"Can you spare me a few moments?"

He looked at his watch. "A few."

His voice was no different, but I could feel the temperature drop. "It's difficult to know where to begin," I said.

Your problem, the deep-set eyes seemed to say.

"Can I sit down?"

He waved me to a chair.

I touched my lips with my tongue, then plunged.

"Holly tells me that you're an expert on haemophilia?"

"Well?" The eyes studied me intently.

"My brother's a haemophiliac."

"Is that why you've come back?"

"Partly."

"Go on."

Slowly at first, then more easily, I told him about Frank and my own problems.

He nodded slowly.

"Well, that explains one or two things. I'll give you any help I can, but—"

"It's not just that, he's got AIDS." I told him what had happened.

His expression didn't change, but he reached over and patted my hand.

"My dear fellow, I'm sorry."

"Do you know anything about AIDS?"

"A bit."

"Is it really incurable?"

He leaned back and thought for a moment.

"Nobody has actually recovered from AIDS," he said slowly, "*yet.* New drugs and new forms of treatment are being described every week. One day, one of them is going to work. Your brother's best chance is just to hang on as long as he can until that happens. Tell me about his condition."

I did so, helped by numerous promptings.

"Hmm," he said at last, "he'll survive six months, perhaps even a year or two." He looked up quickly. "I don't mean to be callous, but you do want the truth, don't you?"

I nodded.

"The patients who survive longest," he continued, "are those with something to live for. That's how you can help him."

"I've been wondering whether a transfusion of lymphocytes from me would help."

He smiled fleetingly. "Well, you've obviously learned something

from us. Unfortunately, it's been tried and it doesn't work. You see"—
he leaned forward—"even if your lymphocytes matched his, which is
far from certain, the virus would infect them as soon as they entered his
system. I'm sorry . . ." His voice trailed off.

"How about a marrow transplant? From me."

"You're serious about that, aren't you?"

I nodded. "That's why I came back. To see if you could help me.
He's in St. Mary's, Paddington," I added.

He studied me for a few moments. "I know what you're asking," he
said at last, "and I . . . it wouldn't be ethical for me . . ." He broke
off. "All right. I do know the immunologist at St. Mary's. I'll speak to
her, but I can't promise anything."

I thanked him somehow and found my way to the main corridor. I
felt absurdly happy, and suddenly wanted to finish the job I'd been
sent here for.

I glanced up at the clock. A quarter past three. The others would be
guzzling tea by now, wondering where I was, perhaps. I'd enlighten
them.

The talk stopped as I pushed the door open, but nobody gave me
more than a glance. Except Adrian, who shot up and barged past me.

"Do you mind if I have some tea?" I asked.

"Help yourself," said Trefor.

I did so and sat down.

There were just the four of them—Trefor, Steve, Pete and Holly.
The page of a magazine crackled as Pete turned it over.

I cleared my throat. "I hope you can all understand why I've come
back. I need to ask just a few more questions, then I can finish my
report and go."

"Feel free," said Steve, without looking up. "Although what we can
tell you that you don't already know, I can't imagine."

Silence. It was as though we were playing a verbal equivalent of the
"You blinked first" game. I finished my tea and left.

I did go round the Centre and ask questions, for all the good it did
me. The staff weren't hostile; they just behaved as though I were a
complete irrelevance. They moved; they performed their tasks, even
replied when spoken to, but the carefree and happy spirit which had
remained somehow uncrushed by Mike Leigh's death was now so
completely dead itself that I wondered whether it could ever come
alive again.

"Oh, Tom, I'm so sorry!"

Yes, but why did her eyes light up?

"What did Dr. Chalgrove say?"

I told her.

Holly had picked me up at eight as promised, but hardly said a word until we arrived at the pub, a building so old it seemed to have grown out of the pebble beach on which it stood.

Then she had asked me again why I had come back, and I told her.

"If Dr. Chalgrove says he'll speak to the consultant, then he will," she said now.

After a pause I said, "Why did you think I'd come back, Holly?"

"It doesn't matter now."

"It does, tell me."

I cajoled her until eventually she gave in.

"Well, if you must know, there's a rumour going round that you're some sort of private detective."

I laughed, hoping it didn't sound too hollow. "Who on earth started that?"

"Adrian, among others." She found my eyes. "He really hates you, Tom. He's been saying that you uncovered some minor misdemeanour of David's and hounded him until he didn't know what he was doing."

So Adrian knew about David's "misdemeanours" now.

"Is there any truth in it?" she asked.

"Not really." I lied easily. "My brief was to inspect your computer system for loopholes following the blood thefts in London. All Centres in the country are being checked, but there's no point in broadcasting the fact."

She nodded slowly.

I said, "When Adrian came down that night looking for me, didn't you realize he was going to attack me?"

"No, that's the strange thing; he said he just wanted to talk to you."

"Huh!"

"Well, I've tackled him about it since, and he completely denies it. And if I hadn't seen what he did to you with my own eyes, I'd have believed him."

I thought about this for a moment.

"Let's not talk about it any more," she said.

She bought me a drink and for a while we talked about Frank and his chances. Like Chalgrove, she was convinced that a cure, or at least a treatment, was not far off and her optimism made me feel better.

As I got up to buy another round, she said, "Let's have them outside and watch the last of the light on the sea."

A few moments later I followed her out and found her sitting on a bench, her face lit by the sunset like the candleglow of an Old Master.

I sat opposite her, tasted the subtle flavours of her face. Her eyes brooded on the sea, which growled softly against the shingle beach twenty yards away. A zephyr touched her fine hair; she turned to me and smiled.

"I hope you meant it about wanting a guided tour of Dartmoor. I thought this Saturday?"

I smiled back. "Fine."

"It was a surprise when you phoned. A nice surprise, though."

I swallowed. "I'd been thinking about you. I suddenly needed to speak to you."

"Needed?"

"Yes."

The sun had vanished, but the top of its halo drove across the water, straight as a tramline. The breeze ruffled the bronze surface.

"Beautiful," murmured Holly. "Let's go nearer, Tom." She picked up her drink and walked towards the sea.

I followed. The pebbles gave a ghostly rattle.

She sat on a ridge of shingle just above the water. I sat beside her.

"D'you know," she continued dreamily, "sometimes I wish I could dissolve and become part of all this. But now at this moment, I want to distill it, take it inside me to keep forever." She turned to me. "Does that sound selfish?"

I put an arm around her, felt her warm skin through her dress.

"We come from there," she breathed.

I listened as wave after wave reached for my feet, a sound so confident in its beginning, but inevitably failing and falling back in a death rattle.

"It's life itself," I said suddenly. "It's no wonder we sometimes want to go back."

"No, Tom." Her face was very close. "There's no going back. There's never any going back."

I turned my head to kiss her. Her lips were cool and salty and very soft.

"Come on," she said, some time later. "Time we were going."

I didn't move as she got to her feet and stood beside me for a moment. Her legs glowed in the light.

"Tom." She held out a hand.

I took it, scrambled up, and we walked back over the pebbles.

The Metro buzzed through the night air and I opened the window against my burning skin.

"Oh, lovely air!" Her eyes never left the road. "Lovely trees, lovely life!"

I silently agreed, wanting more.

"Thank you for a lovely evening, Tom," she said, as we stopped outside the hotel.

"Thank you." I leaned over and kissed her cheek. "It doesn't have to end now, come in for a while."

"Not tonight, Tom," she said matter-of-factly. "I want to go home. I'm tired."

"Oh, for God's sake!" Without thinking, I seized her, pressed my mouth to hers. Her lips went dead under mine.

She pushed me gently away and I fell back, dazed.

"You just don't understand me, do you?" she said.

"No, I bloody don't," I muttered, reaching for the door handle.

"Think about it, Tom."

I pushed the door shut, stumbling on the kerb as I stepped back.

I did think about her, nearly all night, but came no nearer to understanding her.

The next day, I sat fuming in the library, in front of me a piece of paper covered in names. They were all crossed out except one. Adrian.

And yet I still hadn't got anything concrete against him; it was all circumstantial. I screwed the paper up in disgust and went to look for the hospital bar.

Two pints later, I didn't feel any better. The attitude of the staff that morning had developed into a sort of passive resistance and I got absolutely nowhere. When I told Trefor that I had to talk to Adrian whether he liked it or not, he replied primly that any such talk would have to be in his presence.

I had avoided Holly.

I heard the word "haemophiliac," and tuned into a group of medical students at the bar.

"I tell you, haemophiliacs are nothing but a drain on this country," one was saying. "They're costing the rest of us a fortune."

I fled away before I hit him.

Adrian.

I was going to find him, accuse him, and beat the truth out of him if

necessary. As I stalked down the main corridor of the Centre, people
seemed to jump out of my way.

A hand on my arm. "Tom." I shook it off. "Tom, what's the matter?"

"Nothing."

"Well, if you could stop in your nothing for a moment"—the cool
grey eyes tempered my fury— "I thought I'd pick you up at about ten
tomorrow. Is that all right?"

"You still want to go?" I said incredulously.

"Of course, if you do."

I looked away. "So you think you'll be safe with me all alone on a
lonely moor?"

"Apologize for that, or it *is* off."

I apologized.

"I've been kicking myself all night," I said.

"Painful."

"I'll show you the bruises if you like."

"Save that for tomorrow."

Adrian appeared from nowhere beside us.

"You were looking for me," he said tonelessly.

"Was I?"

"Trefor said you wanted to ask some questions."

"I'll leave you to it." Holly slipped away.

"See you tomorrow," I called after her.

"You won't, you know," he said.

"Won't what?"

"See her tomorrow."

"And what's to stop me?"

"I am." He pushed his face closer. "I'm not like David. I don't scare
easily."

The anger bunched up inside me again, then something made me
look up, over his shoulder. Trefor was watching us from his office.
Adrian followed my gaze, then with a sneer, turned and walked towards him.

I had failed; that was obvious now. Adrian was like a rock, Bennett
couldn't shift him and neither would I. But did it really matter?

I was helping Frank. Seeing Holly tomorrow.

I thought about it all the evening at the bar. Yes, it mattered, but I
could live with it.

CHAPTER 16

I had been here before, of course, but the eyes of a seventeen-year-old squaddie see things differently from those of a thirty-two-year-old headcase. The Moor, we had called it, in the same jocular shortening as the inmates of Princetown; a place against which you had to pit your strength and skills.

Oh yes, after a twenty-mile hike in full kit you loathed the place—the stones that tripped, the mud that gripped your boots that were full of icy stream water anyway, and the grey clouds that pressed you against the dull green earth, pouring their rain into your eyes and down your neck and plastering hair on your forehead.

Oh yes, I was glad to leave— Gimme Salisbury Plain any day, as I said to my mates.

But today it was different, and the memory added a sparkle to a place I would have loved anyway.

First there was the suddenness. One minute you were climbing through the bland suburbs of Tamar, then with the drumming of tyres against a cattle-grid you were there, amid the gorse and heather and rank green grass that stretched everywhere.

I glanced behind. Virtually all signs of the city had vanished beneath us.

"Takes you unawares, doesn't it?" said Holly happily.

"Mmm."

The engine buzzed furiously as she pressed her foot to the floor to climb a hill, then expanded with relief as we crested the top. Another hill, third gear this time, and then the moor lay before us like a carpet suspended at points by puppet strings that might pull it into a different shape at any moment. As we dropped, I could see the summit of each point, or tor, clutters of rocks grey and smooth as lava dribbled from an eruption.

"Princetown," said Holly as we came to a junction. "Do you want to see the prison?"

"Not particularly; let's carry on." I'd seen that before as well, from the inside while interrogating a convicted fraud.

She drove on for a few more miles until we were looking down into a shallow valley with a mercuric gleam at the bottom.

She stopped the car. "That's the River Dart. We'll follow it up to its source."

"Why don't we go down and start from the bridge?"

"Too boggy, even at this time of the year. We'll follow that ridge"— she pointed—"and meet the river about three miles up."

"Three miles! Just how long is this walk?"

"About ten miles," she said innocently, "or is that too much for you?"

"No. I was worried about you."

"Oh yeah? We'll see about that, Tom Jones."

She jumped out, went round to the back and opened the hatch.

"Try these on," she said as I joined her, and handed me a battered pair of walking boots. "They're my brother's." They fit reasonably well.

Holly meanwhile had taken out a binocular case and knapsack.

"Lunch," she said.

"I'd forgotten about food."

"Typical man—you can carry it, then." She shouldered the binoculars and locked the car.

The ground was springy and crisp and the occasional clump of heather tinkled drily as it was brushed by a boot. As we left the road, I became aware of other noises—fairy birdsong that seemed to hang from the sky, the humming of insects and the faraway bleat of sheep.

"What are those birds?" I pointed to a fluttering smudge high above.

"Larks."

As I looked, I saw more of them, their notes multiplying until they seemed like streamers dropping softly through the air.

Holly walked on. She was wearing jeans and a cotton blouse, the first time I had seen her in anything other than a dress, and the contours of her body seemed to belong with the bare contours around her.

As I drew level with her, a pimple-like summit grew out of the skyline ahead.

"Is that where you're heading?"

"Mmm."

The distance was deceptive, perhaps because of the heat-haze, and the slope began pulling at my thigh muscles.

Then the pimple resolved into a jumble of rocks, which as we drew nearer I could see was not a jumble at all, but like smooth-cornered dice placed on top of each other.

"They're so perfect," I said breathlessly, as we approached them. "It's hard to believe they weren't put here by men."

"Or the gods, perhaps," she mocked. "No, the wind and rain first uncovered them, and then the frosts cracked them." She caressed one of the fissures with her fingers. "And then the wind and the rain continued their work, until you see them as they are now. All quite natural, which is the same thing as saying God's work."

I said, "Are you religious?"

"Big R or little R?"

"Either."

"Big R no, little R yes. Come on, we've miles to go."

We walked on. The ground dipped gradually into a shallow depression where the wind faded and the sun homed in, and after a while, I could make out a steeper valley in front of us.

"There's the river." As she pointed her uplifted arm drew her blouse tight and I could picture her body shaped smooth by the same wind as the rocks behind us. "It's come round in a circle from where we saw it in the car."

We dropped into the valley and the sound of dashing water took over from the other noises. It was well named "Dart" as it burst and gurgled through the litter of boulders blackened by repeated drenching, and the reflections were so dazzling you couldn't look into them. We followed the river up and I couldn't remember when I was last so happy.

"Look!" she pointed as a large tawny bird lifted from the bank about fifty yards ahead, uttering a strange cat-like cry as it struggled for height on long ungainly wings. "A buzzard. Isn't he magnificent?"

As if by magic a pair of crows appeared over the horizon and with black oaths set about the unfortunate bird, harrying it until it rocked sideways in its efforts to escape. Then with a last pathetic mewl from the buzzard, the trio vanished over the hilltop.

"What was all that about?"

"Crows don't like buzzards."

"That much was evident."

"They always attack them; I don't know why."

"Bullies."

"Not really, the buzzard always escapes, and he's the master when he reaches the upper air."

We walked on and soon found where the buzzard had been. A sheep lay on the ground, de-personified by death. We hurried past.

"What happened to it?" I asked.

She shrugged. "Could be anything—their mortality rate's pretty high up here. It might explain the crows, though," she continued, "if the buzzard was raiding their personal larder."

"Charming."

She looked up and pointed. High above, the buzzard soared effortlessly in circles on outstretched wings.

As the valley grew narrow, we criss-crossed the rushing water by clambering over the rocks. At last it levelled away into a plain of peat through which the stream wound, quiet now.

Peaks and tors vanished away into the distance, melting in the blue sky so that you couldn't tell which was which.

The stream oozed round a huge boulder, which acted as a dam for the pool which circled slowly behind it, the water so peaty dark that you couldn't see the bottom.

"Let's stop here for lunch," she said.

I don't remember eating much. Sitting beside her, watching as her warm scents overpowered me, I began to ache for her in tiny shivers that spread from the centre of my body. Was she really unaware of what she was doing to me?

I picked up a white stone and threw it into the pool. It disappeared.

"How deep is it?" I asked.

"I don't know."

"I'm going to find out." I jumped up and began stripping off my clothes.

"You shouldn't swim so soon after a meal," she said lazily.

"That didn't count," I said. "No offence meant."

"None taken."

I turned my back on her, pulled off my jeans and sat with my feet in the water. It was icy cold. Too late to back down now, though. With a push, I fell clumsily forward and went under. The cold gripped me. With a cry I surfaced and began swimming in circles.

"What's it like?" she called.

"Lovely," I lied. "Come and join me."

She regarded me calmly as I trod water.

"All right." She rose in a single movement and deftly removed her clothes, save bra and pants.

I gazed in awe at her body as she stood poised on the bank for a moment, then with a shallow dive she was beside me.

"Ooh!" she gasped. "You liar, it's freezing."

We splashed round in circles for a few minutes, then she disappeared. An instant later, strong hands pulled me under.

She was laughing as I came up. I struck out, cornered her, and she squealed as I grabbed her shoulder.

Then her arms went around me and we were kissing fiercely as we slid beneath the water.

"God, I want you, Holly," I croaked as we surfaced.

We reached out again and slipped under again.

"We'll drown if we go on like this," she gasped, and struck out for the bank.

I overtook her and pulled myself out, then turned to help her.

We stood in each other's arms for a moment, then I held her back to look at her. Beads of water slid down her skin like oil. A shoulder strap of her bra had slipped, revealing a rose-pink edge.

I kissed her gently, urgently, running my fingers down her wet skin. She groaned, moved closer and our thighs touched.

I fell to my knees, pulling her with me, kissed her neck, her breasts.

"Oh God! I want you."

"I know, Tom, but please not here." She kissed me open-mouthed. "Soon, but not here, please."

I looked in her eyes and realized that it hadn't been a dream, but that she was her own mistress as much as mine, that there was everything to wait for.

We walked for perhaps another two hours, completely at ease with each other now. As we started the final leg, a pair of curlew (so Holly said) floated over, their throbbing notes dropping slowly through the air. It was the saddest sound I've ever heard and will always bring back Holly and that afternoon for me.

"Forestry Commission," she said in disgust. "Between them and the Army, they'll swallow this moor soon."

We had stopped by a pile of rocks and were looking down on a tract of conifers covering the land like a suburban carpet.

I said, "People want cheap furniture."

"Huh!"

"They must be of some use, cover for birds and animals."

"Not really, nothing grows under them. They're sterile, like deserts."

A bird rose from the canopy, and I asked her for the binoculars. It was only a crow, which flew off in that deliberate way, which probably gave rise to the saying "as the crow flies."

A movement caught my eye and I re-focused. It was a man at the edge of the forest. He looked furtively over his shoulder and sidled up to a tree. What was he doing?

Then I laughed as he began to relieve himself.

"What's the joke?" said Holly. "Can I share it?"

I handed her the glasses and pointed. "Life in the desert."

A moment later she gave a cry. "My God, it's John Hill!"

CHAPTER 17

I froze for a moment.

"D'you mean the night orderly who disappeared?"

She lowered the glasses. "How d'you know about that?" she demanded.

"Never mind. Is it?"

She nodded and I almost snatched the glasses from her. He had finished and was slowly walking along the edge of the trees.

"How do you know about John?" Holly persisted.

"I'm just going to see which way he's going and then I'm going to follow him," I said as Hill continued his leisurely walk.

"Tom, why?"

I handed the glasses back. "I want you to stay here, Holly, and if I'm not back in half an hour I want you to ring Sergeant Bennett of the Tamar Police. Can you remember that?"

"Sergeant Bennett, yes, but I don't—"

"Please, Holly, I'll explain later." I was poised on my feet, watching the retreating figure.

"Tom—"

"Later." I kissed her and started down the slope, catching a faint "Be careful" before the scratch of the dry grass on my boots and the wind in my ears were the only noises. He was about three hundred yards ahead.

I walked quickly rather than ran; that way, if he saw me, he might not realize I was following him.

Two hundred yards—my boot caught a stone and I stumbled noisily. He didn't look back, but now I had to watch both him and the ground just ahead of me.

One hundred yards, ninety—and then for no apparent reason he turned, saw me, and de-materialized into the fringe of trees.

I forced myself to slow down, stop for a moment and look around as though I were lost. Reached the edge of the forest and casually glanced at my watch. Not quite three. Glanced up, trying to penetrate the rows of tree-trunks in gloomy black and grey on an uneven bed of green moss that covered everything like a fungus. Nothing.

Wait—a flash of colour—gone, and not a sound.

To run or not run, no choice now. I leapt over the grassy margin and ran. The hard dark foliage closed around me.

A mistake, but what was the alternative? The moss hid layers of slippery twigs that crackled soggily under my boots, and scores of rotted stumps about six inches high. I snagged one, staggered and tried to watch where I put my feet. A wiry twig slashed at my face, another; I glanced up to avoid them and almost immediately pitched forward, tripped by a stump. Outstretched hands saved my face from smashing into another, but the soft pad at the base of my thumb was torn open by a sharp stone.

I've lost him, I thought, my cheek buried in the rank moss.

But not quite, there was faint crash from ahead. I looked up. Nothing —but the noise had been there and I knew its direction.

I struggled up, pulled out a handkerchief to wrap round my thumb and started running again.

Fifty yards into the muffled gloom, or it might have been a hundred, I stopped and listened.

Nothing, not a sound, not a sign, just the grey trunks pressing around me.

A few more paces, I've lost him, lost him . . .

I looked hopelessly round the uniform green carpet, undisturbed save for those few scars . . .

Footprints!

I followed where his feet had torn the moss away to reveal the black mud underneath, followed through the trees. It became lighter, then I burst out on to a gravelled forestry track. No more footprints.

Chest heaving, I looked left and right, nothing. Crossed to the other side, searched the forest bed for more tracks. None.

So he had kept to the track, but which way? And for how long? He could have faded back into the trees again at any point.

But I thought not, no, his route had been too deliberate; he'd known about the track.

To the left, I knew it must lead back out of the forest, and he wouldn't have gone that way. No, he was headed further in, to the right.

I cautiously began walking, on the edge of the track at first, but then in the middle as I realized he might be waiting for me behind some tree.

My eyes flickered, to the left, to the right, looking for signs, a leg, shoes, a chink of colour.

Nothing.

I walked faster, eyes still searching. Nothing, he'd gone straight ahead—unless I'd already passed him! Spun round—nothing.

I kept on.

A flash of white—I ducked into the trees, no sound.

Stealthily I crept forward. Ahead was a cottage in a tiny clearing.

I slipped back into the wood and advanced, trying to avoid giveaway twigs. Now I could see it clearly, a dirty white cottage stained with years of neglect and light starvation; it was a miracle it had survived at all, in the middle of this grim place.

But survive it had, and was inhabited too, if the curtains were anything to go by. The trees grew to within twenty yards of its walls; I stole round the perimeter, watching the windows.

A movement on the lower floor, a face, a woman's surely, but now the advantage was with me, it was I whom the trees hid from the watcher.

I looked at my watch. Ten past three. Only ten minutes since I had followed him into the forest.

I watched as another five crept by. Nothing. No movement, no sound. I shifted uneasily. If I didn't go back to Holly soon, she would go for Bennett. That might take hours, even if he did anything at all. But if I left, Hill could escape.

My heart bumped as I made my decision. I walked up to the door and knocked.

Not a sound. The paint hung in stiff flakes from the wood, but the iron latch was rubbed shiny with use.

I grasped it, pressed the thumb plate and pushed. Almost immediately, the door was blocked and a face appeared in the six-inch gap.

"What do 'ee want . . . this be private property." A woman's face, a gruff voice.

No use pretending I was an enterprising salesman. "I want to speak to John Hill. It's very important, for him that is. Can I come in, please?"

A second's hesitation. "Bain't no such person yurr. This be private property, leave me be." The accent became more pronounced as the voice grew furious and she tried to push the door shut. She couldn't, because I had my boot in it.

"I beg you, please let me in, for his sake."

"Geddaway from yurr!" She kicked furiously at my foot and pushed the harder.

I put a shoulder to the door and heaved, she fell back and I stepped inside.

He was standing, straddling the narrow staircase, and as my eyes adjusted to the dim light, I could see he had a gun pointed at my belly, a shotgun.

We stared for a second in silence.

"Git out," he rasped, "or I'll blow yur 'ead off."

I took a step forward and he raised the gun threateningly.

"I only want to talk to you, John, please listen to me, just for a moment."

"Git back." He waved the gun.

"Your life's in danger." In a flash of inspiration I knew this was true. "Put it down and let me talk to you, for your own sake."

"There be danger all right—fer you. Git *back!*"

"It's about that night, John, you remember, the night you ran away." Uncertainty crossed his eyes. "You're in trouble, John, but I can help you." Another pace forward.

The single barrel of the gun opened as he raised it again. "Git back or I'll shoot."

It was a very old gun. I knew because I know about guns. This one had been made before cartridges were invented; it used black powder and percussion caps.

"Back, or I'll shoot." A croak, almost a plea. You couldn't get black powder now, so it was a bluff, a pathetic bluff.

I lunged and seized the barrel, pushing it aside and up.

The roar filled the whole cottage and its hot breath licked my face. Reflex tore my hand from the hot metal and nothing could have prevented him from bringing it down on my head, then his clenched mouth fell open as he stared over my shoulder.

"Miss Holly." I could barely hear him. "God forgive me, I didn' mean . . ."

I turned to see her figure framed in the doorway. Her hands covered her face and she slowly slumped to the floor.

I was beside her in a flash, gently turned her over and pulled her fingers away. The face was unmarked and her lips moved slightly.

I looked up at Hill. "You stupid bastard, you're bloody lucky, you know that?"

"I wouldn't hurt her for anything," he said. My ears were still buzzing.

She groaned and we leaned forward. Then I became aware of the old woman standing behind us.

"Could you get her some water?" I said curtly and she hurried off.

Holly was stirring now, and between us we lifted and carried her to a filthy old sofa that lay under the window.

Her eyes opened and focused on me.

"Tom? Are you all right? I thought . . ."

"Are *you* all right?"

"I—think so."

The woman returned with a cup which I put to her lips. When she finished, I said, "Are you sure you're not hurt?"

She nodded uncertainly.

I turned to Hill. "What did you have in that thing?" He gazed at me blankly. "Come on, what kind of shot?"

"Birdshot."

"What's the spread pattern of the gun? Is it choked?"

Again the uncomprehending look, then his face cleared.

"Yessir, it's choked." He held up his hands to indicate the narrow shot pattern and I sighed with relief. It was unlikely she'd been hit.

I turned back and examined her face minutely, then her neck and shoulders.

"You're sure you can't feel any pain?"

"N-no. No pain, Tom." Her voice was faraway; she was still in shock.

I wanted to comfort her, get her away as quickly as possible, but my head told me that this was the best time to get the truth from Hill, while he was still vulnerable.

I held her hand and turned to the old woman.

"Could you find a blanket, please."

She returned quickly and I wrapped it round the still form and kissed her forehead.

"Could you look after her, please?" I said to the woman, and then turned to Hill.

"She gonna be all right?" he asked, still dazed.

I grabbed his collar and gave him a shove. "No bloody thanks to you."

"Weren't my fault—"

Another shove.

"Shut up and listen. Sit down there." I pointed to a chair. "I want to know what happened that night when Mike Leigh was killed."

"You the police or sumthin'?"

"Yeah." Well, near enough. "You're in enough trouble already, Hill, so tell. Did you kill him?"

"Me? Why should I kill 'un—"

"I know you and David Brown were stealing blood, so it has to be one of you. Which was it—you or Brown?"

"Dave? You mus' be jokin', why should me or Dave kill 'un?"

I leaned over him. "Because he caught you at it, stealing blood. He was on call that night, wasn't he, so which of you was it?"

He shook his head from side to side. "You've got it all wrong, mister—"

"I've got it right, Hill. Who was it?"

"Weren't neither of us," he shouted. "Ask Dave, he'll tell you."

"Brown's dead," I said brutally.

His mouth fell open. "Dead? How?"

"Fell off the roof of the hospital. Sergeant Bennett thinks he jumped because he killed Leigh, but I'm—"

"Dave couldn't, 'e wasn' even there."

"So it *was* you!"

"No!" he screeched. "I found 'un and scarpered. Don' you understand? Me and Dave wouldn' kill Mike; 'e was one of us; 'e thought the whole thing up in the first place."

In the silence, a huge piece of coloured jigsaw fell into place.

From the sofa, Holly wailed, "Tom, who *are* you?"

I quickly crossed over to her.

"Better now?"

"Who are you?" she whispered.

I knelt and kissed her forehead. "Tell you later. Promise."

Hill's story came quickly now. Leigh had approached him when he was ripe for plunder, after Falkenham had banished him to permanent night duty.

"I jus' wanted to pay that bastard back," he said with clenched fists. "Though I s'pose the money came in handy."

They got their system working before the computer was there, when it was ridiculously easy, taking a little to start with, then gradually working up. David had made sure that returned blood was hidden in a corner of the Bank, and Hill had squeezed off the plasma after the night shift had gone. Leigh looked after marketing and dispatch.

Then the computer had been installed, but this had been by-passed. I wondered how much Leigh's influence as a section-head had to do with the loopholes in the system.

Then he'd become greedier and started on the fresh plasma, about five months before.

"Why? Did he have debts or something?"

Hill shrugged. "Don' think so; he just 'ad it in for the bosses, like me. Dave needed the money, mind, what with wife 'n' kids to feed."

"What about Adrian Hodges—wasn't he involved?"

"Naow!" scoffed Hill. "That stupid bugger. Mike an' Dave used to fiddle what 'e'd told the computer, an' 'e never twigged."

They'd continued for four months, Leigh becoming confident and taking more and more fresh plasma, until he'd come to Hill one evening, looking troubled.

" 'John,' 'e says to me, 'I think we bin rumbled. Better stop for now, an' if anyone says anything, jus' look surprised and say you don't know nothin'.' "

"Did anyone say anything?"

"No." He shook his head. "So after a week or two I asks Mike what was goin' on. He jus' grinned all over 'is face an' says . . ." Hill's brow furrowed in concentration. "It was somethin' like, 'You jus' never know, do you? The holier they are, the dirtier they are!' Or somethin' like that. Then 'e claps me on the back an' says, 'We're gonna do all right out of this.' "

"What did he mean?"

"I dunno. A week later 'e tells me to forget all about it."

I thought for a moment. "And that's all he said? What about David—did he know anything?"

"I asked Dave a few nights later when 'e was on call. 'E looked at me a bit funny an' says that Mike 'ad bin really worried. Then 'e said . . ." The brow furrowed again. "I got it. 'E said Mike 'ad bin worried until about a week before, then Dave found 'im comin' out of the freezing-room, 'orrible place that, Mike was blue, Dave said, but grinnin' all over 'is face an' sayin' that there won't be no trouble. Dunno why I remembered that—I 'ate that place," he finished reminiscently.

"Are you sure Mike didn't say anything else? Think."

He shook his head. "Nope. Jus' that our troubles were over."

"But they weren't, were they?" I said harshly. "Mike got himself wasted. What happened that night?"

He shuddered. "I never wanna go through that again." He collected his thoughts. "Mike came an' found me in the Issue Room. Like a cat with the cream he was—"

"This was Sunday night, wasn't it? What time?"

" 'Bout eleven. He says he's gonna fix things an' I was to stay put an' say nothin'."

"Then what happened?"

"Nuthin'! I stayed put for an hour an' thought he'd gone home. Then the phone rings, someone asks about some blood so I says I'll go and check . . ." The fear slid back into his eyes.

"Go on."

"I went to the Bank to look, the door wasn't quite shut, funny I thinks . . ." He swallowed. "I pulls it open and there he was on the floor with his head bashed in an' blood all over the place an' a gurt big spanner beside him . . ." He stared at a space over my shoulder as he re-lived it. "I picks it up, dunno why, then I hears a door bang down the end of the corridor an' drops it with a gurt clang . . ." He swallowed again. "There was footsteps, I was shittin' meself; I ran through Plasma, through the Wash-up an' out the other side; I could hear the footsteps after me. I runs straight out the lobby, on me bike an' away."

His chest heaved. I leaned forward. "John, who was it? Didn't you look behind you?"

"Not ferkin' likely—would you?"

I suppressed a smile. "Perhaps not. So you've no idea who it was?"

He shook his head.

He had gone to his digs, and then on impulse stuffed a few things in his pockets and cycled all the way to his sister, for that was who the old woman was.

They'd both been born in this cottage; the Forestry Commission had allowed her to stay in it and she'd watched the trees grow up around her.

Hill's story guttered out like a spent match; there was nothing more I could get from him.

The silence was self-consciously broken by Holly.

"Tom, I don't feel well. Can we go, please?"

Guilt caught up with me and I knelt beside her.

"Of course. Do you feel up to walking?" I turned to Hill. "Is it possible to get a car up here?"

"It's all right," said Holly. "I can walk." She stood up, gripping my hand so fiercely that I winced.

Hill said, "It's only 'bout a mile to the road."

"Can you manage that?"

She nodded and walked to the door.

I caught Hill's arm and said quietly, "What you've told me will have to come out, but if you tell the truth, you'll get off lightly." I hoped this was true. "But you'd better stay here for now, OK?"

He nodded. There was no more fight in him.

"I'll come and see you in a couple of days. We'll forget about the gun, I'd hide it if I were you."

A minute later he pointed the way we should go and we left them on the doorstep of the sad little house.

As soon as we were out of earshot, Holly said, "Tom, what is your job?"

Briefly and unsensationally I told her. She didn't seem surprised; her voice still seemed to have a dreamlike quality.

"What will you do now?"

"I don't know. Have a good think—I think. Write a report and tell my boss."

"Are you going to the police?"

"How much did you understand of what Hill was saying?"

She hesitated, then shook her head. "Not very much. Something about stealing plasma."

"How do you feel now?"

"Pretty rotten." She slipped her hand into mine. "Tom, are you going to the police?"

"Not yet, there's something I've got to sort out first."

"You're not going back to the Centre, are you?"

"Don't worry about me, the important thing is to get you to bed. Yours, not mine."

She smiled wanly.

We emerged from the forest and saw that we still had a mile to go to the road. That mile was longer than the rest of the walk put together. She began to flag; her feet dragged and she seemed close to collapse by the time we got there. It was another three miles up the road to the Metro.

I waved down the first car that appeared, and the owner rather reluctantly took us there.

Holly was in no state to drive, so I did. Then the air from the window seemed to revive her, and by the time we reached Tamar, she sat up and gave me directions to her home.

She retired to bed immediately, and her father, a tall man whose white hair accentuated the seamy tan of his face, drove me home.

I was too late for dinner, of course, so I made do with some cheese sandwiches before going up to my room for a shower, where I bandaged my thumb, then down again to the bar for some lubricated thought.

If I were a computer, so went my thoughts over the first pint, then I could easily handle the mass, or rather mess, of data input by Hill. First delete his ramblings, then correlate what was left with what I already knew.

But I only had my poor brain, which had to do it the hard way and hope for the occasional flash, denied to computers, that we call inspiration. Not that my record was very impressive in that department.

So it was Leigh all the time, not only in it, but the instigator. It had been too easy for him with such ready-made accomplices at hand—the disgruntled Hill and the neurotic David for whom life wasn't doing enough.

But had David killed Leigh?

It was possible, if he'd found out that Leigh was moving up to better things and cutting him out.

Another pint.

No, it wouldn't do; hadn't Leigh told Hill that bigger fish were up to bigger games? ". . . the holier they are, the dirtier . . ." Perhaps one of these pike had killed Leigh for being too greedy, and later perhaps, also killed David.

But why?

Because David had found out what Leigh had found out and become a security risk.

Yet Bennett was convinced it was suicide.

No, no, it *had* to be murder. Leigh had gone in that Sunday night to boogie with a big fish, not to appease a minnow.

But how, how . . . ? Leave it, get another beer and go back to what you know.

". . . The holier they are the dirtier . . ." What was there in the Centre that was worth killing for?

Holier, that would have to mean Falkenham, Chalgrove or Trefor. I couldn't see any of them as murderers.

But what if Leigh had meant his own peer group? Pete, Steve, or maybe this was where Adrian fitted in.

Leigh and David had been killed as soon as they had become nuisances. A cool ruthless brain.

Who? Who?

I shook my head. Go back a space.

How had Leigh found out? I closed my eyes and tried to remember what Hill had said. Leigh, looking pleased with himself.

Yes, but when?

Coming out and grinning. David said that, but where?

Then I had it: coming out of the freezing-room.

Would what Leigh had seen still be there? Surely "they" would have moved it?

Why? "They" didn't know *how* Leigh had found out, only that he had.

It was still there and I was going to have to find it.

Now.

CHAPTER 18

The taxi slid silently through the city and deposited me at the bottom of the hill. The sun had set, but its afterlight glowed on the main block. I walked up past the young trees. Not a leaf trembled. I began to sweat and took off my jacket, wishing for a moment that the taxi had taken me to the top. No—the orderly might have seen me and asked questions.

I glanced at him through the Blood Issue window; he was smoking a cigarette, immersed in his TV. I replaced my jacket and slipped in by the glass door, tiptoeing past the thin crack of light through which the fulsome tones of *Dallas* or some such filtered. Into the main corridor, shadows stippled as before, they didn't bother me now; nobody knew I was here. Left, into the Blood Bank corridor which led to the freezing-room. It was pitch dark.

I closed the door softly and switched the light on for a moment to get my bearings. The door leading to the freezing-room lay about five yards ahead. I walked past the Bank, through the door and pressed the next switch before going back to turn off the first. Wouldn't do to excite the orderly's curiosity if he came in for blood.

Then back to the freezing-room corridor, where I stood for a moment in front of the massively insulated door before gently pulling the handle. With a snap, the catch was released and it swung open. Glacial air washed gratefully around me.

It was dark inside—where was the switch? Beside the door. I turned the knob and a red lamp on the panel glowed as the room lit up. I stepped inside, pulling the door almost closed behind me.

Where to begin? The slatted shelves were filled with crates of bottles, wire baskets filled with tiny containers, and cardboard boxes.

I pulled out a plastic tray filled with thin cardboard containers. Opened one. Inside was a pack of frozen plasma. Replaced it and walked slowly round the perimeter, looking for what Leigh must have seen.

The cold pulled at my face.

Past the light which hung over one of the huge refrigerator units, silent for the moment because the door wasn't closed. The hairs in my nostrils froze as I breathed in.

Think: Why had Leigh come in here in the first place? Obviously to get something, but what?

I pulled out a metal basket, picked up a glass container. Nothing, just chilled fingers that I had to blow on to thaw.

Why would he come in here? He worked in Plasma, so something to do with that.

I walked round again, trying to read the labels on the crates and cardboard boxes through the thin layers of frost. Nothing. My eyelids prickled and I blinked. God, it was cold! The icicles hanging from the fridge unit were like delicate coral.

The shelves in the centre of the room were stacked with aluminum boxes marked FFP followed by a number. I pulled one out and prised off the lid with my fingernails. Inside was a row of frozen packs of plasma, lined up like ice-creams in a grocery.

FFP—Fresh Frozen Plasma!

Hill had said that Leigh had recently started on the fresh plasma . . .

I picked out one of the packs and rubbed at the number on it.

Another. Odd, they're quite different—shouldn't they be consecutive? Tried some more, but my frozen fingers wouldn't grip properly.

Put down the box and rubbed my hands together. No good, they were too cold. As were my feet—the concrete floor had sucked the warmth from them through the thin soles.

Better go and thaw out; take the box with me.

I picked it up and hurried round to the door, the cold pinching through my jacket. As I reached to push it open, it shut before my eyes with a gentle click. The fans in the freezer units hummed to life and a wave of freezing air hit my face.

Unbelievingly I pushed at the door. It wouldn't budge. Pushed the knob that Trefor had shown me, the one that released the catch from outside. It slid uselessly in and out. I pulled; it came free and the hole at the end where the pin should have been emptily mocked me.

I threw it down and shouted. No response, not a sound other than the fans.

The alarm siren! I reached up for the cord, pulled and held it. No sound. But there wouldn't be, would there? The room was insulated.

I waited as the pain stroked my frozen knuckles; where was the orderly? Come on, come on!

Then I realized that whoever had shut me in would have first ensured that the siren wouldn't work.

The lights snuffed out, leaving me with utter darkness and the cold breath of the fans.

I shouted again, beat at the door with my fists, screamed, kicked, begged . . .

Pull yourself together, I told my body as it shook as much from fear as coldness.

Think: The words of my instructor came back to me, as he had lectured us on exposure: *A man can survive intense cold for longer than most people realize* . . . yes, but what else?

It's not so much the temperature of the air that kills, but its movements . . . *a body loses heat much more quickly in a cold wind* . . .

The fans. I must stop them . . . But how?

I rubbed my hands together, breathed on them. How?

Jam them; poke something in them, like a stick.

I felt my way slowly towards the noise of the unit, touched the slatted wooden shelves; yes, they would do. Gripped one and pulled. Crates and bottles tumbled past me on to the floor and smashed.

Bottles, with frozen plasma inside. I felt around until I found one, cleared a shelf, and holding it like a cudgel, brought it down as hard as I could.

There was a splintering crash.

I felt for the piece of wood and twisted it free. Then, feeling up for the bars of the grille, I thrust it through into the spinning blades. The fan stopped.

One down, one to go, I thought, reaching for the bottle and lashing at another shelf. It missed, flew from my hands and landed on my foot.

I clenched my teeth and gagged as the screaming pain climbed my leg.

A breath, kneel, search for the bottle. Found it, up again, careful now —got it!

I felt my way cautiously round the back of the room to the other unit. A moment later there was silence, save for an angry muted buzz from the electric motors.

What now?

I forced down the panic and the conviction that anything I did would be futile, forced myself to run on the spot on feet I could hardly feel. Rubbed my hands together—no difference—futile.

Think! The air had stopped moving now, but the coldness would still be pouring down from the units. How could I kill them?

It was then that the idea came to me and I felt a surge of real hope.

If I could somehow rip the wires away from the units, it would not only stop them: If the wires shorted, a fuse would blow somewhere.

Yes! Units of this size would need a heavy current. If I could blow a main fuse, an alarm would be set off and the hospital engineers would come running . . .

I felt for the bottom of the unit, fingers disrupting the delicate icicles which tinkled on to the floor at my feet. Felt around the side; yes, here was the cable; it was fastened to the wall by staples of some sort; there was a gap where it went into the side of the unit.

I reached up and pulled out the slat holding the fan, which promptly hummed into life again.

So what? I carefully fed the wood sideways into the space behind the cable, squared my feet and pulled.

It snapped in my hands.

I screamed my impotence into the freezing air.

Stop it! Think, man, think!

I ran on the spot again, feverishly willing my body reserves to create heat. But a ten-mile walk and a cheese sandwich doesn't make for that many reserves.

Defeatist talk—think!

I shook my head violently from side to side as though this would somehow force warm blood into my thought cells.

That cable would need a crowbar to force it, and there was nothing like that in here, nothing . . .

The emergency doorknob, the one I had flung to the floor in disgust. It might do it; it just might.

I felt my way forward around the perimeter until I found the door. Feet crunched on broken glass, I stepped quickly back; it would easily go through my thin shoes—not that my feet could feel anything now.

I crouched down, feeling for the glass, working my way slowly forward, fingers searching for the iron bar. My hand blundered into something, a smashed bottle. Oh God!

Swallowed, edged forward again, pain in knee, forget it. Felt feverishly around with hands that felt only dull pain.

Would they be able to recognize it? Rub them together again, forward, feel!

Perhaps it was under the shelves. More glass, try the central ones.

My fingers closed around it and I cried with joy. Stood up. Walked slowly back to the single humming fan. Felt for the cable and fed in the pathetically thin bar of iron.

This was my last chance, my last hope. I set my legs apart, braced my shoulders, and heaved.

The blue flash lit for an instant the walls and the needle-sharp icicles; a shock jolted my whole body, as with a clang, the iron bar fell to the floor.

Silence.

What now? Try to short the wires or deal with the other unit? The electric shock had for a moment cleared my brain, made me aware of the crushing pain in my hands and feet.

The other unit. I found my precious iron bar and felt round the back of the room again. Found the unit and the gap between wall and cable. Fed in the metal bar and heaved.

There was a dull snap, and I knew that the staple holding the wire had come free. There was now no purchase.

With a cry of anguish, I threw down the bar, seized the cable, and pulled.

It bit into my freezing hands.

Gripping it ferociously, I raised one foot over a shelf and on to the wall, then the other, and heaved with my whole body, my whole being.

The flash as it came free merged with the lights in my head as it struck a shelf and I collapsed on to the concrete floor.

Let's stay here, I thought; it's not so bad . . . Then the pain returned and I slowly dragged myself to my feet. Another bottle fell and shattered.

The wires, how do I short the wires without electrocuting myself?

I felt around until I found the cable and, holding it, poked it to where I thought the metal casing of the unit would be. Sparks. Try the grille, where it goes round the side of the unit. I reached up. More sparks, but it wouldn't hold.

I would have to bend them, separately, so as not to short them on myself.

The first shock temporarily cleared my mind again, and with clumsy-cold fingers I bent each wire into a hook and, reaching up, hitched them on to the grille.

A flash. I tentatively let go and it held.

Now, the other one. Again, I worked my way round and gingerly felt for it.

This one didn't have such a long free length; it was still stapled to the wall. Better find the iron bar again.

But I knew that I couldn't, not again. Confusion was flooding my brain in waves.

Whimpering vainly, I tugged at the cable; it wasn't going to come, but then it did—

Somehow, I managed to snag the ends on to the metal grille and leaned back.

Done. But what now?

My tired brain couldn't function any further, I stumbled round to the door, tried running on the spot again on feet that weren't there—it was as though I was jogging up and down on the stumps of my ankles.

The non-pain forced me to stop; my mind wandered timelessly and then a dreadful lassitude began stealing over me. I knew what it meant.

It meant that I was going to die, that there was no one coming to my aid; my plan had failed.

Futile. I sank to the floor and thin tears squeezed from my eyes. I didn't want to die. They froze on my cheeks; my whole life had been a failure, and now it was going to end like this.

I tried to think of Holly, but my dimming brain couldn't hold her image.

Then my mind clarified suddenly and beautifully. I could hear the instructor again: *If you were a bull, where would you rather die, in the slaughter-house or in the bull-ring?*

No one had answered, we had just started, and he continued softly, *War is a bull-ring, remember that.*

So this was my bull-ring. Well, at least I had tried.

A lovely warmth crept over me, I knew what was happening but simply didn't care. Sleep beckoned and I gratefully allowed it to take me.

I thought: I wish Holly could have met my brother.

CHAPTER 19

Hell was pretty much as I'd expected, but with one subtle refinement. The never-ending fires were there all right, but not waiting in layers to be stoked. They were on the inside, coursing through the tubes and tunnels of my body, always on the point of consuming me from within but never quite succeeding, keeping me finely balanced on the point of everlasting torment, punishment for a lifetime of sin—my pride, arrogance, bloody-mindedness . . .

Had they been so awful, my sins? I supposed so; otherwise I wouldn't be here, would I? I tried to think of some more—greed, lust, cowardice—and in doing so, suddenly realized that the pain had gone.

It promptly returned—the pain of coming alive.

"How are you feeling?" inquired a gentle voice.

A distorted face hung above me.

"Are you the Devil?"

A low chuckle. "Good Lord, no! Where did you think you were—Hades?"

"Yes," I said simply.

He was young and fair-haired, almost angelic in white coat and stethoscope.

"How are you feeling?" he asked again.

"Pretty rough."

"Not surprising in—"

"How did I get out of there?" I demanded, trying to sit up.

"That'll keep for tomorrow." As he soothed me down, I became aware of a tube sprouting obscenely from my arm, trailing through some apparatus to a blood-pack hanging above.

"You're still in shock," he continued. "I'm going to give you something to make you sleep."

"I don't want to sleep." My voice became shrill. "I've got to know, don't you understand . . ."

But he had already uncovered my arm. I felt the cold touch of a swab and a sharp prick.

"You see, I knew I was going to die, and I must know . . ." I lost the ability to speak and fell through layer after layer of bedding as he faded from sight, miles above me.

When I next awoke, it was to meet the eyes of a dark-haired nurse, sweet but somehow not as angelic as the young doctor had been.

She smiled. "How do you feel?" It was obviously the standard question.

"Fine," I mumbled.

"That's good." She fussed around me for a moment while I tried to take in the meaning of what had happened.

She turned to go.

"Don't leave me," I croaked and she came and sat beside me, held my hand. I felt the strength of her presence flow into me.

She said, "I'll go and fetch Dr. York now."

I nodded and waited. Was he the one I'd called the Devil? I hoped so.

I looked around the room. The tubes and scaffolding had been removed. I felt for my arm. A thick wad of sticking plaster was wrapped just below the elbow and I became aware of a dull ache beneath it.

The door opened and Dr. York came in. He was the same one.

"Feeling better?"

I grinned and nodded.

"Good." He lifted a clipboard from the bottom of the bed and studied it before sitting beside me.

"You're a lucky man."

"I . . . suppose I am."

"Can you sit up?"

I did so.

"Good. Any feeling of dizziness?"

I shook my head.

"Right. I'd like to examine you; d'you think you could slide your legs out and sit on the side of the bed? Tell me if you feel any nausea or faintness."

He took my pulse and blood pressure, peered into my eyes with a tiny beam, made me squeeze his hands and push them away and finally produced one of the little rubber hammers used for testing reflexes.

"Well, you seem to have completely recovered," he said at last. "I think we'll keep you here for tonight and discharge you tomorrow."

"Thanks, but d'you think you could tell me what day it is?"

He laughed. "It's Monday. I suppose you've rather lost track of things."

"You told me before you would tell me how I was found in time."

He regarded me soberly. "So I did, fancy remembering that. Well, Dr. Falkenham has been asking to see you. I think you're well enough now, and I think he's the best person to answer your questions."

I didn't believe for a moment that Falkenham would be interested in answering my questions, but didn't say so. Instead, I pointed to my arm.

"I presume this means I had a blood transfusion? Why? I didn't lose any blood, did I?"

"If you'll get back into bed, I'll tell you."

When I had done so, he said, "In cases of hypothermia, which means that a body has actually *become* cold rather than just feeling it, the patient has to be re-warmed slowly. If it's done too quickly, the periph-eral blood vessels dilate, and the inside of the body remains cold. Fibrillation can occur and stop the heart, and even if this doesn't happen, the body now tends to overheat.

"That's why we started warming you slowly and gently, but because you're young and obviously fit, we decided to speed things up a bit by transfusing warm blood into you and taking heat inside where it was wanted."

I felt myself grin slowly. "I was convinced I was on fire from inside, that it was a new kind of hell."

He chuckled. "I've never heard that one before; I must make a note of it."

I had been thinking over and over what to say to Falkenham, but when he eventually came that afternoon, it was an anticlimax. At first.

He was ushered in by a nurse, a po-faced Bennett in his wake.

"Good afternoon, Mr. Jones, how are you feeling?" he asked solici-tously. "D'you mind if I sit down?"

He took the chair by my bed, then realizing there wasn't another for

Bennett, politely asked the nurse whether she could find one. Bennett followed her out.

"How are you feeling?" he repeated.

"Er—pretty well, I think," I answered warily.

"Good, good." He nodded. "It was a shock for all of us, as I'm sure you can imagine."

"It must have been."

"Well now, as I'm sure you'll understand, the Sergeant would like to ask you a few questions."

As he spoke, Bennett came back into the room carrying a chair, which he set beside Falkenham's.

The nurse, who had been hovering in the door, said, "I hope you gentlemen won't want to keep Mr. Jones for too long; he—"

"Don't you worry, my dear," said Falkenham, "just a friendly chat. Ten minutes, fifteen at the most."

She withdrew gratefully.

"To business," he began briskly.

"Before we start," I said quickly, "I must know—how was I found in time?"

"A fair question." He nodded. "You did a pretty good job of demolition on the freezing-room in the short time you were there." Despite the lightness of the words, an edge had entered his voice. "After you stopped the refrigerator units, you collapsed under the heat-sensor by the door. The temperature had risen slightly anyway, and the heat rising from your body set the alarm off. The laboratory orderly came to investigate. You were very lucky."

"I know," I said feelingly. So much for all my planning.

"The question is—" Bennett, who had been fidgeting impatiently, leaned forward—"what were you doing in there?"

"I was in there because somebody locked me in."

"Really?" said Falkenham gently. "Why should anyone do that?"

"As far as I'm concerned, it was attempted murder, which makes it your province," I said to Bennett.

"Don't start telling me my job," he grated. Perhaps it wasn't the most tactful thing to say.

"I'm quite sure we'll discover that it was all an unfortunate accident," said Falkenham smoothly.

"Or carelessness," took up Bennett. "Your criminal stupidity—"

"Let's just try to find out what happened, shall we, before we make any accusations," said Falkenham.

He turned to me. "Perhaps you would like to tell us what makes you think you were locked in."

"I left the door ajar," I began, gathering my thoughts. "I'd been inside about—er—five minutes when it slammed shut—"

"*Slammed* shut, are you sure of that?"

"I was just about to come out; I reached for it and it shut in front of me—"

"You said slammed just now," interrupted Bennett.

"It clicked shut; I saw it."

"You must have pulled it shut by mistake," he said contemptuously.

"That's ridiculous!" I began, but Falkenham cut in quickly, "There is another possibility."

We looked at him.

"The lab orderly could have shut it. After all, it is part of his job, checking that doors are shut. He had no idea you were there—why should he? You had no right to be there, so if he'd discovered the door ajar as you say you left it, he would have just pushed it shut and walked away."

There was a moment's silence.

"Is this what he says?"

"He denied it—probably afraid to own up, since it nearly cost you your life."

There was another silence while I grappled with this. It was possible, just, but I didn't believe it.

"Why didn't the emergency release work?" I asked.

"We've looked into that. The split pin that holds the assembly together was found on the floor by the door. It had lost its tensile strength, and when the knob was turned, it simply fell out. Very unfortunate, but tell me, Mr. Jones, why didn't you use the siren?"

I gazed at him blankly. "I *did!* The bloody thing wouldn't work."

"Well, I can assure you that it's working perfectly well now. We had it thoroughly tested the morning after you were found."

"Well, let me assure you," I said thickly, "that it damned well wasn't working last night."

"How?" demanded Bennett. "What *assurance* can you give us that it wasn't working?"

"Listen, I just know. It bloody well wasn't working; I'd have heard it."

They glanced at each other. Sceptically.

"It needs quite a strong pull," said Falkenham. "Are you sure you pulled it hard enough?"

"Yes!" I had another thought. "Whoever shut me in switched the light off *after* I'd been yelling and beating at the door. How d'you explain that?"

Falkenham sounded almost bored.

"Naturally, the orderly would switch the light out after closing the door. He didn't hear you because the room is virtually soundproof."

"He must have heard me," I said angrily.

"I think that's enough from you," Bennett said peremptorily. "I think it's time you told us what you were doing there in the first place."

Ah yes, the difficult bit.

"I wanted to check out an idea I'd had earlier," I said.

"At eight o'clock on a Saturday evening?"

"It was the first chance I had."

Bennett snorted derisively.

Falkenham said, "What was this idea?"

I hedged. "I believe that there's another conspiracy taking place in the Centre."

"Such as?"

"I don't know—"

Bennett exhaled noisily. "Just tell us what it was at eight o'clock on a Saturday night that made it so important to break into the Centre and smash up its deep-freeze."

This was where I'd have to tell them about Hill.

Silence.

I couldn't, something deep inside wouldn't let me.

"Well?" said Bennett.

"I don't think David Brown's death was an accident or suicide," I said at last. "I'm certain he was killed to keep him quiet." I realized as I spoke how feeble it sounded, but the alarm was still ringing.

"Well, this is most interesting," purred Bennett. "It may interest *you* to know that we've had the forensic report on his body. It contains an incredible amount of alcohol, but shows no evidence of any other party—"

"What about the cigarettes and matches I found?"

"I couldn't find them. In fact I haven't been able to discover anything that backs up your story."

"What about—?"

"In fact, I don't think you can distinguish truth from fiction," he overrode me. "That's your problem, but in the meantime, I can't take anything you say seriously." He stood up. "Naturally, we'll be needing a statement, but if I were you, I'd think very carefully about what you put in it."

Falkenham said, "Sergeant Bennett thinks I should put the Centre—er—out of bounds to you, and I regret to say that I agree with him. The staff will be told that you are not allowed in the building." He stood up. "Stick to computers, Mr. Jones; you did a good job there."

Bennett obviously felt that he should have the last word.

"And if you know what's good for you, you'll keep out of police business in future."

A few seconds later they had both gone.

It was over an hour later when the door opened and Holly looked round.

"Hello, Tom," she said quietly. "Can I come in?"

I tried to say yes, but the lump in my throat wouldn't let me.

She slipped across the room. "The nurse said it would be all right to see you for a few minutes."

I said, "God, I'm so glad to see you."

She made a tiny noise, a warm arm slid round my neck and she kissed me untidily.

"I only heard an hour ago," she said breathlessly. "There's a memo going round that you're not allowed in the Centre. I can't understand it, nobody could. Then George told me how he found you. Tom, what were you doing in there?"

I looked away for a moment, wondering how much to tell her. Oh, to hell with it, if I couldn't trust her . . .

"You haven't told anyone about Hill, have you?"

She shook her head.

"Do you remember what he was saying?"

Her eyes slid away. "A bit. Something about him and Mike being in league."

I told her. Her eyes widened and narrowed again.

"So that's why you went back! Tom, you've done enough; you must leave it to the police."

"The police! They won't believe me."

"How do you know?"

"They just don't." I told her about Falkenham and Bennett.

"Did you tell them about Hill?"

"No."

"Why not?"

I shook my head. "I don't know."

She drew back. "Tom, did you find anything in the freezing-room?"

"No, the door shut . . ." Memory twitched, the aluminum boxes, the cold. "The door shut and I was locked in." Needed time to let the thought settle.

"Tom, let me go to the Director—"

"Listen, I've got it!" I caught her hand and held it. "Just before the door shut, I opened one of those boxes, you know, the aluminum ones marked Fresh Frozen Plasma for CPPL." She listened resignedly. "They've got a batch number on them, right? And a range of donation numbers?"

"Just a batch number. The range of donation numbers are on a list in the Plasma Lab."

I closed my eyes. "OK. The point is, the boxes are filled with plasma from a range of donations, a consecutive series of numbers."

I opened my eyes again and she nodded.

"Well, the numbers I saw on the satellite packs were all over the place; they bore absolutely no relationship to each other."

"Odd." Her face cleared. "You must have opened a box of Time-expired plasma; we send that away, too, you know."

"Then why was it marked Fresh Frozen Plasma?"

She shrugged. "Clerical error. It happens."

"D'you really believe that?"

"Why not? You only saw one box, didn't you?"

"Funny I should pick the one with such an outlandish error."

She swallowed. "But why should anyone want to do that?"

"I don't know." But an idea began to form, a ghost on the edge of my mind.

"All right, Tom, suppose you're right; let's tell someone. Please, please let me go to the Director so that we can check it out."

"Better if we check it out first and then tell him, Holly."

"No." She tried to pull her hand away, but I held it tight.

"Holly, you must help me. I need to get back in there, for just ten minutes—"

"You're mad!" She pulled again and this time succeeded in wrenching free.

"Are you on call tonight?"

"No, I—"

"Make some excuse; you can let me in through the library stairwell."

"No, no, no! We'll be caught and I'll be sacked."

"More'n me job's worf, eh?" I mimicked.

"That's unworthy, Tom; you just don't understand." She backed
away towards the door.

"If you're sacked, you can always come and live with me."

She stopped dead, then gave a wry smile.

"If you really meant that, then it might be different."

"I do," I said.

She moved slowly towards me, bent over me, gently touched my lips
with hers. Her hand found mine, caught it, folded it over her breast.
Her clear grey eyes promised everything.

"Tomorrow," she breathed, "when you're out of here . . ."

"You'll help me tonight?"

She closed her eyes and shook her head.

"It's the wrong way, Tom. Let's talk about it tomorrow."

"I've got to find out tonight."

"Tomorrow, Tom. I'll come and see you then." Her cheek brushed
mine and the smell of her filled my nostrils.

She stood up and went silently to the door.

"I'll do it alone," I said.

She shook her head again.

"Tomorrow," she said and was gone.

CHAPTER 20

Strange and exhilarating, to have been at one moment a patient safely
tucked in for the night, and now me, Tom Jones, on my way to finish
the job.

It was easy to dress and, covered with a dressing-gown, slip ghost-
like between the aisles of mostly sleeping patients, past the office
where a sister and houseman conferred in subdued tones. I left the
gown on a laundry basket, and stepped into the brightly lit corridors,
where I could pass for a late visitor or perhaps an especially workaholic
NHS employee.

I found the main lifts, and a few minutes later I was in the spacewalk,
stars and moon clearly visible through the perspex.

The heavy door to the stairwell boomed shut behind me, and as I clattered down I felt curiously light-headed, almost as though I'd been drinking.

The door leading to the Centre was locked as before, but nobody had missed the rivet in the emergency key-holder yet. I slid back the glass and reached for the key. Better keep it this time; the doors in the lobby would be locked now, and I didn't know whether they could be slipped from the inside.

The Centre enveloped me in silence and darkness that after a few moments were neither; shadows loomed and the air clicked and buzzed with the sounds of refrigerators and incubators, and in the distance, an anonymous whine.

I walked quickly and silently up the main corridor, checked the slit of light from the orderly's room, then with pounding heart pushed open the door of the smaller corridor leading to the Blood Bank and freezing-room.

God! I didn't want to go back in there again. The realization hit me as I stood trembling in front of the massive insulated door.

Then, abruptly, I twisted the freezing-room light and pulled the handle.

The door swung open. I pulled it as wide as it would go and, instinctively glancing behind, stepped through the veil of mist into the crystal-hard air beyond. Sensations of pinched earlobes and frozen nostrils. I looked around, the rows of aluminum boxes were still there. But were they the same ones?

I grabbed one and backed out. Put it on the floor, pulled off the lid and examined the contents.

Eighteen consecutively numbered satellite packs of plasma, just as there should be.

I swore under my breath and replaced the lid. Well, it was only to be expected; they'd had two days to remove the evidence.

I replaced the box and took three more. They were the same.

With a sinking heart, I took another three, this time from the back and bottom of the pile.

By now my fingers were becoming numb, and it was with difficulty that I got the lids off the first two. They were the same.

The third lid wouldn't come off at all, and I nearly put it back unexamined. Instead, I felt for a coin—but found the key. Prised off the lid and with aching fingers pulled out a pack and rubbed at the number. Again.

They were different. And another. And another.

They were all different; they bore no relationship to each other.

But perhaps it was Time-expired plasma . . . I snatched at the box, rubbed away the frost from the batch number.

No! FFP 5921! FFP, Fresh Frozen Plasma. These packs had no right to be here.

Quickly I replaced them and pushed on the lid—how could I check out what they should be?

The files in the Plasma Lab! I picked up the box, swung the freezing-room door shut and switched off the light before feeling my way to the connecting door.

Not locked; only the bleed ward, stores and offices were locked at night. I put the box down on a bench, and blowing on my frozen fingers looked round—where were the files? I needed more light than the moon could give.

I spotted an Anglepoise lamp—too bright—picked up a thick roll of tissues and wound some round the bell-shaped shade before switching it on.

The tissued light filled the walls with bizarre patterns, but it was enough to see by.

Now where were the files? I hunted round the benches; they couldn't be far away—Ah! A clipboard hanging on the wall, stuffed with sheets. I took it back to the lamp and brought the box over. FFP 5921. I shuffled through the sheets. Hell! The last one was FFP 6023—where were the others?

I went back to where I found the clipboard—no more files. In the cupboards below, perhaps—God, don't let them be in Blood Issue, I prayed.

I pulled at the cupboard, it was stiff. Yanked, and it gave with a snap that echoed round the eerily lit walls.

I waited. Nothing. I looked inside.

There they were, layers of sheets tied together with string. I took the top bundle and carried it across to the lamp.

FFP 5950. Found the next bundle.

FFP 5902. Flicked back through—here it was, FFP 5921!

Below the batch number was a list of eighteen donation numbers. Eighteen *consecutive* donation numbers.

I hunted round for a piece of paper and pencil, then tried to get the lid off the box. It needed the key again.

Carefully I took each satellite pack and recorded its number. They bore no relationship to the numbers on the sheet.

So what were they?

I tapped a finger impatiently on the bench as I looked around for inspiration.

A computer terminal.

I hurried across with the list, sat down and reached behind for the switch. The terminal hummed into life. I gave it a moment to warm up, then pressed Return. The screen flickered and invited me to log on.

I did so.

This is not a valid password, the screen informed me.

I stared in disbelief, then tried again. The same.

They'd taken away my password!

I drummed my temples—Holly, what was Holly's password?

It was made up of her initials and date of birth.

Holly Jordan, what was her middle name?

I closed my eyes—pictured myself leaning over her shoulder as she logged on.

"What's the "E" for, Holly?—" "Never you mind."

And the numbers—a six, a nine—sixteen-nine, 169!

I tapped in HEJ.169.

What program do you require?

M for Menu.

D for Donations.

I pulled the list closer, tapped in the first number and watched as the information shunted on to the screen.

Donation taken (Date).

Grouped (Date).

Issued as *Whole Blood* (Date).

And that was all—this blood was not supposed to be here.

The same loophole that Leigh had used!

Somebody had taken the outdated plasma from the returned blood and substituted it for the Fresh Frozen Plasma that was supposed to be in the box.

So what had happened to that Fresh Frozen Plasma?

I scrawled down the donation details next to the number and tapped in the next one.

The same. And the next.

The same. They were all the same.

I sat back, chewed the pencil and thought.

The substituted plasma would be sent to CPPL and processed as though it were Fresh Frozen. They'd be certain to notice, surely?

But why?

They'd have a batch number, and eighteen packs of frozen plasma.

And workers used to handling hundreds of frozen bone-chilling packs would scarcely pause to check each number against the list before dipping them into liquid nitrogen to shatter the plastic. So long as the batch numbers matched, why query what the various Centres had sent them?

I jerked as from an electric shock as another revelation hit me. Of course!

That day at the computer unit, when the records showed that Tamar had a lower Factor VIII output than the other Centres, a *statistically significant* lower output. Naturally, when some of the FFP sent from Tamar wasn't Fresh Frozen at all, but outdated. Nobody would notice until months of results had been put together, and even then it would be assumed that it was something to do with the way Tamar harvested the plasma.

Why Fresh Frozen Plasma?

Why not? Leigh had found a black market for it, so could someone else.

But who? My brain went round the familiar list of suspects. Wickham, Chalgrove, Falkenham.

Or Steve, or Pete. Adrian? Perhaps someone I hadn't thought of. Perhaps, perhaps . . .

Better hide the evidence. I folded the paper and stuffed it into a pocket, re-packed the aluminum box and hid it in the most inaccessible cupboard I could find.

As I clambered to my feet, a wave of giddiness swamped me. I'd done enough, time for bed. Think up some excuse for the sister, if she catches me.

I switched off the terminal and Anglepoise lamp and waited for my eyes to adjust before slipping through the door into the corridor with its stippled light, electrical clicks and the distant whine of machinery.

I was suddenly glad that it was nearly over, that I was leaving the Centre for the last time, glad to be going back to bed—

It hit me and the shock sent me reeling to the wall.

What do you make with Fresh Frozen Plasma? Factor VIII, of course. Machinery! The Fractionation Lab.

I could feel the vibration of the ultra-centrifuge as I leaned back against the wall and snatches of conversation came back to me like an edited tape-recording.

Frank, holding up the little bottle with the freeze-dried powder stuck to the bottom: "This is a shot of Factor VIII. It costs anything between thirty and sixty pounds . . ."

Trefor, speaking of CPPL: "They make over six million pounds' worth every year, you know, and it's still less than half of what we need . . ."

Valuable stuff, Factor VIII.

And it was being made now, just a few yards from where I stood, shaking.

Shaking not from tiredness or fear, but with rage, a purple fury as I realized that people were making money from my brother's misery . . .

Were they selling it to the Arabs?

Recycling it back to this country?

My brother.

If they'd been straight, maybe Frank wouldn't have needed the American muck, maybe he wouldn't have AIDS . . .

I wasn't thinking logically.

In a red haze I thrust myself from the wall, walked automation-like round the corner and grasped the handle of the door to the Fractionation Lab. It opened.

I didn't stop to ask myself why, just had to know *who* . . .

The whine grew louder as the door opened.

Across the office, I looked through the glass panels of the two dead-bolted doors—couldn't see anyone.

Drawn as though by a magnet, I pushed my way into the gowning lobby.

A gowned figure was loading tubes into a pack, it turned at the click of the dead-bolt . . . Steve!

I thought: He might be here legitimately, but then our eyes met, and as though by telepathy, we knew, and both knew that we knew. My rage evaporated. I was in no state to take on Steve.

The dead-bolt clicked free as the door behind me swung shut. He put down his rack of tubes before throwing himself at his door, and that's what saved me. I lunged for mine and the dead-bolt shot up again as he crashed into it. I snatched a chair from under a desk and thrust it into the gap, so long as it was there, the dead-bolt would hold Steve's door locked.

As I leapt across the office, there was a crash as he tried to break it down.

Once into the silent corridor, I sprinted for the stairwell, fumbling in my pocket for the key. Skidded to a halt beside it, reached deep into the linings. It wasn't there.

It was still in the Plasma Lab where I had left it after prising the lid off the box.

A shaft of light as the Fractionation door flung open and Steve burst into the corridor. I turned like a rabbit, through the firedoor to my left, ran, no use going for the lobby, locked, swerved left again into the Wash-up area.

A moment's silence and filtered moonlight on glass bottles. Steve's footsteps, and a hiss of steam as I dived between the twin black shapes of the sterilizers.

The door creaked and I shrank further into the shadows; my hand contacted metal, hot metal and I jerked away. No noise.

"Tom?" His voice was gentle, as though he was waking someone from sleep.

A glint caught my eye, a bottle on the floor, a weapon. I leaned sideways and picked it up as a switch clicked and one side of the room was lit.

"Tom, I know you're in here. It's not what it seems; I only want to talk to you."

Footsteps.

"Come on out, Tom; let's talk it over like friends." His voice was so persuasive that I felt hypnotized, like a rabbit cornered by a stoat. His shadow almost touched my feet.

"All right then, have it your own way!" he snarled suddenly. His footfall receded and the light clicked off—the door creaked shut.

I slowly released my breath, then checked it. Was it a trick; was he still there?

I waited for a minute. Steam hissed again; it was breathlessly hot. Sweat started pricking and I felt faint.

Silence. Why hadn't he searched for me? But he didn't know how weak I was; perhaps to him I was a cornered rat. Yes—there had been fear behind that snarl.

I edged forward. Nothing, just the moon and the bottles. He'd gone, but where? Back to the Fractionation Lab to hide the evidence? I didn't know, only knew that I had to retrieve the key.

I closed my eyes for a moment, thinking, trying to remember Trefor's guided tour. There was a door from the far side of Wash-up to the Plasma Lab.

Out into the moonlight, clutching my bottle, trying to watch every angle.

Nothing. I edged crabwise across the room, into the shadows again, found the door handle.

Would he be waiting on the other side? No. I opened it slowly.

More filtered moonlight, no movement. The Anglepoise lamp, still wrapped in tissues, like some strange moonflower. And the glint of the key beneath it.

I edged round, grasped and pocketed it.

What now?

Back the same way—he'd seen me pass the stairwell; it wouldn't occur to him that I'd go back that way.

Back. Back through the door into the silent glass-lit room. Round the edge.

More steam. I jumped and swallowed.

Which door? The same one. Would he be waiting? No point in being coy.

Bottle in hand, teeth clenched, I yanked it open and jumped out.

Nothing.

Walked back up the corridor, glancing nervously around before reaching for the door. It was stuck.

Pulled harder. It was locked.

Trapped!

But was I?

There was the lobby, locked on Falkenham's orders, but surely there would be some way of unlocking it from inside, given time.

There was the other stairwell; perhaps my key would fit . . .

But that was where Steve would be waiting.

Yes, he would have locked this door from the other side, passed up the corridor to the other firedoor, locked that, and now be waiting where I had to go, by Trefor's office. There, he could cover both corridors, the stairwell and the lobby. There was no other way out.

Fire escapes? Two were now locked off, and the third would be covered.

The Bleed Ward and stores? Locked, I knew, although I would try them in a moment, just in case . . .

Was it possible to get through a Wash-up window into the courtyard? Yes, but what was the point?

Telephones! The Plasma Lab had a phone—but they all went through the Centre's own switchboard. I could still phone internally, the Lab orderly, tell him to get the police—

Then I realized that he was in it too . . .

Was he? I just couldn't take the risk.

A sick shudder ran through me, triggering the sweat glands of fear; I was really trapped. I could only wait for them here at the end of my burrow.

So why didn't they come?

Action. I peeled myself away from the wall—might as well check the Bleed Ward and stores doors.

Action. The voice of my instructor again. *"Action may not get you anywhere, but it does keep the enemy guessing."*

And again: *"Do what the enemy wants you to do; approach the trap. Because you know that it's a trap."*

Find out where he is.

I walked silently down the corridor, eyes fast on the end. Tried the doors, locked. Approached the corner.

What if he's waiting just round the other side?

No, he's there, in the centre of his trap. I got down on all fours and peeped slowly round the edge at floor level, where I was covered by deep shadow.

He was there, just where I'd thought he'd be, leaning almost non-chalantly in Trefor's doorway.

Silence. No, the growl of television from Blood Issue.

He looked up, I remained dead still, and he didn't see me . . . He pushed himself upright and walked slowly towards me. Still I was sure he hadn't seen me. Dead still.

Then at the lobby, he paused, looked out for a moment, then turned and walked back. I quickly withdrew my head.

Somehow, I had to distract him, so that I could get to the stairwell or the lobby. But how?

The telephone in Blood Issue? But even if I asked to speak to him, he'd guess before I had time to get out.

An idea germinated, blossomed.

It wouldn't work. It was all I had.

I padded back to the Wash-up area. Pushed open the door and lifted the bottle in my hand to hurl it down the corridor.

No, one bottle might not bring him; it would need several to bring him here, while I dashed through Plasma to the stairwell.

Even then, he might turn back and catch me. Somehow, he had to be enticed after me.

Prop the door open; that would bring him through. I went in and searched until I found the door wedge. Held the door open just enough for me to squeeze through and pressed the wedge in at the end so that he wouldn't see it.

It still wasn't enough. If he came through fast, he would still catch me.

I looked at the door and it came to me—a booby-trap!

But was Steve enough of a booby?

I slipped in, found a wooden chair and set it by the door. Climbed up, yes, a crate could be propped between the door and the upper skirting-board!

Stepped down, walked quickly to the stacks of crates full of bottles, grasped one, took it gingerly back. Stood on the chair. Yes, it balanced. I fetched two more and placed them on top of the first.

Almost ready.

I stopped. Why not wait behind the door, attack him as he came through?

No, I was no match for Steve even if he'd been hit on the head by a crate.

I took three more bottles and squeezed back through the narrow opening. Looked up.

Too obvious—he'd look up as well and see them. How could I keep his eyes on the floor?

Tried to force my brain to think as time fled by—no good, have to chance it.

But if he saw those crates, he'd be straight back.

Then I knew what I had to do and trembled. Couldn't do it. Had to, because it would work . . .

I put the bottle down and slid back into the room. Found it by the washing-machines—a piece of broken glass.

Back to the corridor, to the end. Hands and knees. He was still there. Backed off and stood up.

Holding my breath, clenching my teeth, I pulled the glass across the ball of my thumb. Blood welled and dripped.

Blood.

I walked slowly back. The red drops splashed starkly on to the light cream floor. At the door, I squeezed my hand, to force more out on to the paintwork; made a pool on the ground.

I was ready. If that didn't keep his eyes to the ground, nothing would.

Deep breath.

I picked up a bottle and smashed it on the floor. He must have heard. Another, half way down the corridor; another, lobbed further. And the last I threw with all my might.

Through the gap and sprinted.

Would it work? Had to—hurry!

The Plasma door. Couldn't hear him yet. Reached the far end. Stopped.

Where was he? I could hear the murmur of the TV through the door.

Had to risk it . . . then there was a crash somewhere behind me, a cry of surprise and pain.

No time to gloat—I was through—dashed to the stairwell, fumbled for the key, thrust it in.

Wouldn't turn, different lock.

Try the fire escape—locked, locked! Precious seconds wasted.

The lobby—I ran.

Light through the heavy glass from the road lamp beyond.

Where was the catch? Fumbled for it—stiff—gripped with both hands—it clicked back. Door still wouldn't open—bolts.

Reached, pulled them back and out into the blessed free air.

"Hell, Tom." A tired voice that I knew so well. He stepped from the shadows. "I think we'd better go back inside, don't you?"

The light glinted from a small automatic in his hand.

Even then I thought of rushing him, risking it, but as I tensed for the spring, the door burst open behind me.

"You little bastard!" Tousled fair hair and white wolfish teeth.

"No, Steve!" Chalgrove's warning rang out, but too late.

I saw his hand chop from sideways, a bright flash as I collapsed on to the tarmac.

CHAPTER 21

I was aware of being carried back along the corridors, of grunts and muttered curses, but it was all irrelevance. I was somewhere else, somewhere much better and had no intention of leaving.

But inexorably I was dragged back to the Planet Earth and the present, the square shapes of a room twisted into focus, and then the faces of Chalgrove and Steve.

"Sorry to be so melodramatic," the latter's voice loomed, "but I do feel more relaxed with you tied up."

We were in the office of the Fractionation Suite and I was tied to an old wooden chair, the same one that I had used to prop the door open, I think.

"The question is," continued Chalgrove, "what are we going to do with you?"

"I've already told you; there's only one thing we can do." Steve's hard eyes met mine without a trace of embarrassment or pity.

"I'm sure you realise what Steve means," Chalgrove said to me, "and I must say he has a point. However"—the word hung in the air for a moment—"I'm rather reluctant to kill you, if it can be avoided."

I tried to speak, but only a wheeze came out. Cleared my throat and started again.

"I don't see how you can avoid it, not if you want to keep going as you are. But you'll be caught sooner or later; you must know that."

He nodded slowly as Steve said, "Don't you believe it, mate."

Chalgrove said, "You're right, of course. Except for the fact that I have no intention of going on in the way I am now."

"You're going to make a run for it? They'll catch you."

"I wasn't thinking of that either. You see, I'd have stopped before now if I didn't have a contract to fulfill with some . . . er . . . gentlemen in America. These gentlemen belong to an organization that takes a dim view of uncompleted contracts."

"I see. More fool you for getting mixed up with them."

"Do you see? I doubt it. The point is that the contract *is* very nearly complete, so I can and will stop. The interesting piece of paper we found in your pocket"—it rustled as he held it up—"leads me to believe you know what we've been doing."

I cleared my throat again. "You've been stealing fresh plasma and making Factor VIII from it."

"Very good. When did you work that out?"

"Tonight."

"Bad luck. Your bad luck. If you could only have curbed your thirst for knowledge just a little longer, we would have finished and could have all lived happily ever after. As it is . . ."

"We're wasting time," said Steve impatiently. "Let's get it over with."

"Another body?" I said to him. "Really, the staff'll be tripping over them soon."

He grinned at me. "No body. It won't be too difficult to feed you into the bag mincer and flush you away."

He meant it. I realized that he was one of those rare things, a genuine psychopath, and began to understand what had happened to David.

"It may not be necessary," said Chalgrove.

Steve snorted. "Come off it, Don—"

"Just be quiet and listen." The quiet voice was shot with iron, and I perceived that their relationship was more strained than was apparent on the surface.

"I don't want to kill you," he said to me. "There's been enough killing. Besides, I think you might be more use to us alive. Basically, I'm offering you your life in return for your silence."

"You're mad," I said. "What possible guarantee could I give? You know I'll shop you the first opportunity I get."

I had realized that he was telling the truth; he really didn't want to kill me. But my only chance was to play hard to get; he had some arrangement in mind, I was sure, but it would have to come from him.

He nodded slowly. "You'd like to shop me, wouldn't you—hand me over to justice? At this moment, you hate me; you blame me for your brother, don't you?"

"Dead right," I croaked.

"Mmm. Well, remember that. Now, I'm going to tell you a story, the story of how we three came to be here." He smiled faintly. "And I'm not worried about boring you, since in you I have a truly captive audience." He grinned at his own joke.

"Don," Steve's pained voice cut in, "what's the point of all this?"

Chalgrove ignored him, kept his eyes on me. "I should have been Director of this Centre. I was to have been. The last Director retired not long after we moved into this building some three years ago, and I was—er—tipped the wink. And I had plans, progressive plans for the whole Centre, and for anyone with initiative—" He stopped himself and swallowed before continuing.

"Well, it wasn't to be. Dr. Falkenham, who had recently retired from his Directorship elsewhere, suddenly decided he wanted to serve five more years. It's a lovely word, isn't it—serve? Nearly always a misnomer, and this time was no exception. The truth is, he couldn't bear the idea of relinquishing power.

"The administrators at the Regional Health Authority were very apologetic and assured me that my name would be among those considered next time round—well, thanks very much. I was on the point of walking out in high dudgeon when I realized that there was nowhere else available with a unit quite like this. I designed it, you see. Also I'd been working on the novel idea of using infra-red heat to melt Fresh Frozen Plasma prior to extraction of Factor VIII—it's the melting that causes so much loss of the factor. I didn't want to give this work up, so I stayed.

"However, if I thought for a moment that I was to be left alone in my deputy-ship, Falkenham soon showed me that I had another think coming. He was always sceptical about my infra-red idea, the first thing he said to me on Day One was that the equipment I'd brought in was a waste of money—talk about the pot calling the kettle black!

"Well, when my first series of experiments went wrong, his gloating was positively obscene. He ordered me to drop that line of research and concentrate on looking for improvements to his own methods, which had been out of date for years. That's when I first started staying in the evenings and nights; it was the only time I could work in peace.

"The problem was, how to distribute the heat generated by the rays evenly throughout the plasma—ah, I see I'm beginning to bore you, but bear with me a little longer. I tried putting a turntable inside the oven, then a revolving drum, then I tried turning the drum through three axes—no good.

"It was Steve who found the answer—a simple sphere with completely random movement. We set up some experiments, and on our first run more than doubled the yield of Factor VIII from a given volume of plasma. At this point, I realized I had to tell Falkenham what we were doing. I knew he wouldn't like it, but to tell you the truth, I was rather looking forward to rubbing his nose in it.

"Well, it was he who did the rubbing, and my nose that was rubbed. He simply refused to believe me and forbade me to do any more work on it. When I told him that I was going to publish what I had found so far, he reminded me that he was on the Editorial Board of virtually all the respected journals.

"I probably could have published eventually, maybe even won Falkenham round, if I'd given him some of the credit—"

"It would have been published under Falkenham's name," cut in Steve.

Chalgrove shrugged. "Perhaps. Anyway, it was Steve once again who came up with this idea. Just a joke at first, wasn't it, Steve?"

I'll bet, I thought.

"We'd stayed behind one night and made a batch, to prove it could be done. It was easy. I showed Falkenham, but he simply wouldn't listen, and threatened disciplinary action if I disobeyed him again.

"Shortly after this, I went to the States to give some lectures. To cut a long story short, I was actually approached one evening by one of the 'gentlemen.' I said no at first."

"What was wrong with their own Factor VIII?" I asked, intrigued despite myself.

He regarded me quizzically. "I'd have thought you would be the first to know that. Something like a thousand donations of blood go into a single batch. If any one of the donors has hepatitis, or as we now know, AIDS, then the whole lot is infectious. And I don't need to remind you that American donors have a much higher prevalence of these things than we do—certain people in the States are prepared to pay an awful lot for British Factor VIII.

"Anyway, when I thought about Falkenham, I changed my mind. We began production very slowly about two years ago and gradually worked it up, substituting Time-expired plasma for fresh. I don't think CPPL have noticed once, have they, Steve?"

Steve shook his head; he was looking bored and sulky again.

I said, "How much have you actually made?"

"Factor VIII or loot?"

"Both."

"We can make a hundred vials of freeze-dried concentrate in a night. We've been doing this on average once a week, so I suppose about ten thousand vials."

"That must be worth a quarter of a million."

"He's fast, isn't he?" Chalgrove said to Steve. "However, you're forgetting that our preparation contains more than double the factor—"

"You made half a million?" I said incredulously.

"No, you were right the first time, a quarter. It was the best price we could get. But we digress. Our operation went very smoothly, until a few months ago, when we ran into a problem. A shortage of Time-expired plasma. We couldn't understand it. Steve investigated and unearthed the sordid little plot of Leigh, Hill and Brown. It was a severe problem, the last thing we wanted to do was to alert them to our operation, and yet they had to be stopped. It wasn't just the shortage of plasma; they were bound to be caught sooner or later. Then there would have been a real tightening up of the system, and *that* would have starved us of plasma. Then we discovered they were taking fresh plasma as well.

"We formed a plan. Steve befriended Brown, whom he quickly discovered was even more unstable and dangerous than we had realized, but he did find out all he needed to know about their conspiracy. We agreed that the best way to stop them was to frighten Leigh; the others didn't count.

"I tackled him, told him that we knew everything and that it would have to be reported. He positively gibbered with terror, said he'd do anything if I let him off. When I informed him that, provided he stopped what he was doing, I wouldn't report him, he was pathetically grateful. However, to reinforce the lesson, I concocted the letter from the indignant char and sent it to Hannibal House. Nothing like a visit from a department inspector to put the fear of God into him."

Chalgrove spread his palms. "I was wrong. A week later, he told me he had something to show me that evening. He was so sure of himself that I guessed we were in for trouble, but thought I could bluff my way out of it, scare him with the letter. Again, I was wrong. He'd worked out exactly what we were doing and he wasn't interested in blackmail, or even coming in with us. He intended to take the operation over, make it even more profitable, as he put it."

Chalgrove's voice began to shake slightly with emotion as he remembered.

"His arrogance was incredible. He said that I had more to lose and had better go along with him. When I told him that I'd rather give myself up than adopt his idea, he laughed as though it were a joke. He had no caution or scruples whatsoever.

"He was . . ." His eyes twisted away, searching for words. "He was like a fox in a henhouse who has eaten all he needs, yet goes on killing until every last hen is dead. And makes so much noise doing it that the farmer is waiting outside with his shotgun. That was Mike Leigh."

And not the only one, I thought, glancing at Steve.

"I explained patiently why we couldn't do as he asked. I offered him a share and d'you know what he did? D'you know?"

The question wasn't rhetorical. "No," I said.

"I'll never forget it." His eyes were faraway. "We were in the Plasma Lab, next to the nitrogen cylinder. He told me, quite pleasantly, to shut up and do as I was told. He reached out and tweaked the lobe of my ear, quite painfully. He said he would sleep on it and tell me what he had decided in the morning. Then he walked away, chuckling to himself.

"I suppose I knew what I was doing, I don't know. I just picked up the spanner and hit him. He died instantly. I don't know what made me do it, but I dragged him through into the Blood Bank, wiped the spanner clean and went to phone Steve."

"You panicked," said Steve.

"Yes, I suppose I did. Anyway, Steve wasn't in. I realized I couldn't leave Leigh where he was and went back. I heard Hill scream and drop the spanner and run. For a crazy moment I ran after him, then stopped. It was obvious he would get the police. There was only one thing I could do—go home, prepare my story and look surprised the next day. If I'd just kept my head . . ."

I shifted in my seat to ease the cramp and the noise broke the deep silence.

"What happened then?" I said.

He sighed deeply.

"Well, the next day there were police all over the place. Everyone was questioned, including me, by that police sergeant, the ferrety one—"

"Bennett," I said.

"That's right, Bennett. Well, later in the afternoon, the three of us, Bennett, myself and the Director were discussing how to handle the situation when there was a telephone call and the Director was told of the probability that blood had been stolen from the Centre. He immediately leapt to the conclusion that Hill had been doing the stealing and had killed Leigh. I pretended doubt, which convinced him more than ever of his own genius, and Bennett, needless to say, agreed with him.

"Steve and I left things as they were, thinking that by the time they caught Hill and sorted out the mess of his story, we could have finished the contract and cleared up. Unfortunately before this could happen, another problem came along." He looked at Steve, who took up the story for a moment.

"Yeah, two problems. You"—he pointed to me—"were one of them, but we thought we could head you off. David was the worse problem. He'd been wetting himself ever since Mike was killed, saying that Hill was dead too, and that he was next. He kept begging me to tell him what to do. I said do nothing, but he kept on about giving himself up to the police.

"Then you turned up. I told David who you were to keep him quiet, but instead, he arranged to meet you that night in the Centre. When he rang me up and told me, the only thing I could do was to make him stay at home and take his place."

Chalgrove said, "That was a mistake, Steve."

"So you keep saying."

"You should have let David tell his story. Tom might have been satisfied with that."

"Yes, I think I might," I said, not necessarily because I believed it, but to deepen the friction between them a little further.

"All right, all right!" Steve bit off the words. He looked at me. "I'll admit that we underestimated you. I thought that one good thumping would send you back to London, tail between legs. I was wrong, I admit it."

"I never did underestimate you," said Chalgrove. "I'd been hoping that you'd discover the mechanism of Leigh's conspiracy and be happy with that. But then, unfortunately, came David Brown's demise."

"We've been all over that, Don," Steve said sharply. "I did the only thing I could at the time."

"An unnecessary killing that put Tom on the track of us."

"It nearly sent him back home for good."

"It *was* you, then," I said to Steve.

"That's right. I don't know what you said to him at that dance, but he was terrified, said he'd get blamed for the killing unless he told you everything. *Did* you know it was him?"

"I'd recognized his voice from when he phoned me." Time to give the pot another stir. "What I couldn't understand was how someone of slight build like David could give me such a hiding."

Chalgrove looked disgustedly at Steve, whose lips tightened.

"Shut your trap, smart-ass."

"All right. But I don't understand how you killed David."

"It was easy. I said we had to find somewhere quiet to talk and he suggested the roof. I tried to persuade him not to talk to you, but he wouldn't have it. He was already pissed and kept taking swigs out of a hip-flask, but he was adamant about going to you; I couldn't shift him.

"Then it came to me. I walked out on to the platform and he followed. He wouldn't come very far, so as soon as he tried to light a cigarette, I grabbed him from behind and bundled him over the side. He—"

"I wish you'd stop sounding so pleased with yourself," snapped Chalgrove.

"Why shouldn't I?" Steve demanded belligerently. "It was quick thinking; it had them all fooled." He turned to me. "You got some comment?"

I shrugged. "As your boss said just now, it was all unnecessary. If you'd let David talk to me, that might have been the end of it."

"I told you to *shut up!*" The back of his hand slashed my face as he screamed the last two words.

"Stop that!" Chalgrove's voice was like a whip, and he backed off.

I swallowed the warm taste of blood. "I suppose it was you who pushed me off."

"That was my worst mistake," he said thickly, "not making sure of you."

Chalgrove's voice was filled with contempt. "It seems that in his haste, Steve forgot to remove the hip-flask which was covered with his fingerprints. He was trying to retrieve it when you arrived."

"Wasn't your lucky night, was it?" I said to Steve. He lunged at me again, but Chalgrove held him off.

But for how much longer? I wondered.

"I suppose it was you who locked me into the freezing-room."

White teeth flashed as he recovered himself. "Right every time. I'd just gone round to substitute the plasma for this batch and found you poking around in there. I removed the clip and pin from the bolt and left them on the floor, then opened the fuse-box and pulled the fuse for the siren out a centimetre before shutting the door." He shrugged. "It was just bad luck you were found in time—"

"That's enough," Chalgrove said coldly. "There's been too much killing as it is."

"Well, he's got to go—"

"Shut *up!*"

He turned to me. "You see, Tom, I really don't want to kill you if it can be helped. I believe there is an exchange we can make which will obviate that possibility."

For a moment I thought he must know about Hill. "What exchange?"

He said, "Your brother."

After a pause I said, "What about him?"

"He's got AIDS, and you know what that means."

"I know he might not have got it if you'd publicized your work rather than made money out of it."

He considered this for a moment. "It's unlikely. Even if I'd published two years ago, he'd still have used infected American Factor VIII." Somehow, I believed him.

"The fact is, he's got it now, and what you've been doing hasn't helped."

"But that's just it, Tom, I *can* help. That's what I'm offering."

The silence lasted probably only a few seconds, yet I felt as if I was floating on time itself.

"How?" I said at last. "How can you help him?"

He leaned forward. "So far as the media is concerned, there's no treatment for AIDS, and it's one hundred per cent fatal. Right?"

I nodded.

"There is a treatment. Treatments, plural."

"Why haven't I heard of them?"

"They're new. The Americans have found a drug called Suramin and tried it on a handful of volunteer patients. It's early days yet, but it looks as though it might work."

I swallowed. "Well, either it does or it doesn't."

"Not that easy. The drug kills the virus that's been killing the lymphocytes. That's fine, except that you still haven't got any lymphocytes. But"—he lifted a finger—"if you could give a marrow transplant after suramin treatment, it might have a chance of growing without the virus to kill it off. That's the deal, Tom. I arrange for your brother to have suramin, and then a marrow transplant from you."

I swallowed again, tried to sound sure of myself.

"How do I know you're telling the truth?"

He reached across the desk for a copy of the *Lancet*, flipped it open and held it in front of my face.

"Suramin," read the heading. "In vitro killing of HTLV-III."

"What does that mean?"

"Read on. Down there." He pointed to an abstract below the heading.

"HTLV-III, the putative agent of AIDS is selectively killed in vitro by the drug suramin . . ."

"All right, I believe you," I said, not looking up. "But how can you get this drug?"

"The 'gentlemen in America,' " he replied simply.

I thought: This is the time to accept. It's all he's got to offer; there's nothing more. All I have to do is to convince him that my acceptance is real.

Deeper inside, much deeper, I was thinking: Why not accept for real? It could save Frank. It would be easy; the police and Falkenham, even Marcus, *want* to believe that there are no more conspiracies. Chalgrove is going to stop, so why not?

"Well?" said Chalgrove.

"All right." I nodded.

"Wait a minute," said Steve, "what happens when his brother either gets better or dies? There's nothing to stop him shopping us then."

"Except that by that time he will have been our accomplice; he'll be in almost as much trouble as us. Besides, by then we will have completed the contract; we'll cover our tracks so that he won't be able to prove it."

Steve hesitated unwillingly, and looking at his face, I could see that he didn't want to stop and could see no obstacle to going on, except me . . .

"No," he said, "it's too risky. He may have convinced you, Don, but not me. It's safer to get rid of him."

Chalgrove was looking down at the floor by my feet with pursed lips.

He's going to give in, my brain screamed; do something, say something.

I cleared my throat and they looked at me. "There's something you've forgotten."

"Oh?" said Steve.

"Yes. Whether I have anything to offer you."

"And have you?"

"Yes."

"What?"

"Hill."

A short silence.

"What about him?"

"I know where he is."

"I don't believe you."

I described Hill and his version of events.

"He knows," said Chalgrove.

"Hill's no problem to us now. Who would believe him?"

"Tom did."

Steve snorted. "Tom'd believe anything, or at least that's what people think now. Hill's not important, Don."

"As your boss just said, it was Hill who led me to you."

"Fluke."

"I'm not so sure," said Chalgrove. He turned to me. "What do you propose doing about him? Kill him?"

I shook my head. "Not necessary, now that the police think that David killed Leigh. We'll let them go on thinking it. Hill trusts me; he'll say what I tell him to say. I can make sure he's no trouble to you."

"I believe you could," Chalgrove said softly.

"Well, I don't," said Steve impatiently.

"You don't believe I can talk him round, Steve?"

"That's right."

"You think that whatever I tell him, he's still a time-bomb so far as you're concerned?"

"I just said so, didn't I?" He turned to Chalgrove. "Don, he's just playing for time."

"Because in that case," I cut in, "you've just contradicted yourself. A minute ago you said he was no problem, not important. Now you think he's a time-bomb. You're right—he's ticking away at this moment. It's like the Sword of Damocles waiting to fall on you—"

"Shut up!" He hit me again, with clenched fist this time. "You really think you're it, don't you?"

"Cut it out." Chalgrove's quiet voice was like ice, and Steve slowly straightened up.

"Sorry, Don," he said with difficulty. "He really gets to me."

"It shows."

"I can talk Hill round," I said quickly. "You'd better believe it, Steve; it's your only chance of stopping him talking."

He stepped up to me, his face hollowed with hate.

"So you're not gonna tell us where he is?"

I smiled and shook my head.

"Don't be so sure." He turned back to Chalgrove. "I can make him talk, Don."

"How?"

"Just give me an hour with him," he said. "He'll talk."

"Why should I talk?" I said. "Hill's my insurance policy."

He stiffened and I was sure he was going to hit me again, but then he looked down at me almost softly, his head cocked to one side and his mouth slightly open. He reached out and stroked my cheek with the back of his hand, I flinched, and the side of my eye caught Chalgrove putting his hand into his jacket pocket. With a caress, Steve cupped my chin in his fingers, pulled my face to meet his eyes.

"I know all about you," he said gently. He knelt, drew closer so that I could see into his mouth, feel his breath on my face. "I know all about your brother and about your fears. With a little time, I swear I can make you talk."

"You're too late," I said between my teeth. "Blood doesn't bother me now."

I realized as I spoke that it was true, and he realized it too.

Silence.

Then the light grew in his eyes again.

"Bet I do know something that bothers you. The freezing-room, remember? The place you nearly died? Twenty minutes in there and you'll tell me, even if you know I'll kill both you and Hill afterwards."

"No difference, if you're going to kill me anyway," I said between my teeth again.

Actually there was a lot of difference, as the pricking pain in my bowel told me.

Chalgrove said easily, "OK, Steve, you've had your fun; now let's sit down and talk seriously about what we're going to do." He still had his hand in his pocket.

Steve's face became completely expressionless. Then, as he stood up and turned, he pulled my face down slightly, then hammered it up with his palm. Blood poured from my bitten tongue.

"All right, Don, just suppose we do as you say. That's two people. How many more are we going to have to take on trust?"

As though in answer to his question, the door opened and Holly's head appeared. Her eyes opened wide as they took in the three of us; then as if by magic, she disappeared and the door clicked shut.

For an instant, we were all frozen, then Steve leapt for the door.

"Stop!" yelled Chalgrove.

Steve turned and saw the automatic in his hand.

"Are you nuts—she'll get away—"

"You're really prepared to kill three more people?"

Steve lunged at him. There was a crack, and he stiffened and sank to the floor, his astonished eyes on Chalgrove's face.

Chalgrove looked down and deliberately shot him twice more in the head. He remained looking down for some time—I don't know how long—then slowly turned to me.

"You shouldn't have killed him," I said, my voice sounding miles away. "You've made it worse for yourself."

"I don't think so." He gave a twisted smile. "A doctor's supposed to serve mankind. That was the best I could think of in the limited time left to me."

I knew instantly what he meant.

"Don't do it, please," I begged. "There are still ways you can . . . serve people."

"Serving a life-sentence? But you're thinking of your brother, aren't you?" The smile again. "Were you really going to join us, Tom?"

"I don't know. Were you going to let Steve kill me?"

"I don't know either. Correction—no, I was not." He raised the gun.

"Please," I said, "I'll do my best for you."

He hesitated. "Your brother, Tom. My advice to you is make as much fuss of him as you can, give him the will to live. Show him the journal I showed you. Offer yourself for marrow transplant. Don't take no for an answer—if you make enough trouble, they'll listen." He smiled. "Believe me, I know the medical profession. I'm one of them."

He whipped the gun up to his head, and there was another crack. He sank slowly beside Steve, twitched once and then lay still.

I flexed my cramped body against the bonds and tried to take in the incredible fact that I was safe.

Holly. My brother. Both of them alive and waiting for me.

What a waste, I thought, looking at Chalgrove, what an imbecile waste.

The blood from the two bodies ran together and trickled slowly towards me.

ABOUT THE AUTHOR

Andrew Puckett was born in Dorset, England, and grew up on his father's farm. After several jobs, he was employed at a germ warfare research establishment, which was the start of a career in microbiology. He is now Chief Medical Laboratory Scientist in charge of the Microbiology Laboratory of the Regional Blood Transfusion Centre at Oxford, England. This is his first crime novel.